P9-BZZ-142

The companions really didn't have a choice

"Are we all agreed, then?" Ryan asked, looking from face to shadowy face. "We fight them?"

The answer was unanimous and in the affirmative.

"When we last met, the she-hes took us by surprise," Ryan said. "That's why we ended up at Ground Zero in laser manacles. We're going to make sure that doesn't happen again. They still have their tribarrels and EM armor, but from what Big Mike said, they don't have near as many wags as they did before. And mebbe only the single attack aircraft for backup.

"It's not going to be easy, no way around that, but we know where they are, and they don't know we're coming. We can't let any of them slip away. We've got to chill them all."

After a moment of silence, Mildred said, "They were gone from this universe for a long time. I can't help wondering where they went after they left."

"Wherever it was," Ryan assured her, "we're gonna make them wish they'd stayed there."

JAMES AXLER

DEATH LANDS®

Doom Helix

A GOLD EAGLE BOOK FROM

WORLDWIDE®

TORONTO • NEW YORK • LONDON
AMSTERDAM • PARIS • SYDNEY • HAMBURG
STOCKHOLM • ATHENS • TOKYO • MILAN
MADRID • WARSAW • BUDAPEST • AUCKLAND

If you purchased this book without a cover you should be aware that this book is stolen property. It was reported as "unsold and destroyed" to the publisher, and neither the author nor the publisher has received any payment for this "stripped book."

Recycling programs
for this product may
not exist in your area.

First edition September 2010

ISBN-13: 978-0-373-62604-5

DOOM HELIX

Copyright © 2010 by Worldwide Library.

All rights reserved. Except for use in any review, the reproduction or utilization of this work in whole or in part in any form by any electronic, mechanical or other means, now known or hereafter invented, including xerography, photocopying and recording, or in any information storage or retrieval system, is forbidden without the written permission of the publisher, Worldwide Library, 225 Duncan Mill Road, Don Mills, Ontario, Canada M3B 3K9.

This is a work of fiction. Names, characters, places and incidents are either the product of the author's imagination or are used fictitiously, and any resemblance to actual persons, living or dead, business establishments, events or locales is entirely coincidental.

® and TM are trademarks of the publisher. Trademarks indicated with ® are registered in the United States Patent and Trademark Office, the Canadian Trade Marks Office and in other countries.

Printed in U.S.A.

But I can tell you what your folly and injustice will compel us to do. It will compel us to be free from your domination, and more self-reliant than we have been.

—John H. Reagan
1881–1905

THE DEATHLANDS SAGA

This world is their legacy, a world born in the violent nuclear spasm of 2001 that was the bitter outcome of a struggle for global dominance.

There is no real escape from this shockscape where life always hangs in the balance, vulnerable to newly demonic nature, barbarism, lawlessness.

But they are the warrior survivalists, and they endure—in the way of the lion, the hawk and the tiger, true to nature's heart despite its ruination.

Ryan Cawdor: The privileged son of an East Coast baron. Acquainted with betrayal from a tender age, he is a master of the hard realities.

Krysty Wroth: Harmony ville's own Titian-haired beauty, a woman with the strength of tempered steel. Her premonitions and Gaia powers have been fostered by her Mother Sonja.

J. B. Dix, the Armorer: Weapons master and Ryan's close ally, he, too, honed his skills traversing the Deathlands with the legendary Trader.

Doctor Theophilus Tanner: Torn from his family and a gentler life in 1896, Doc has been thrown into a future he couldn't have imagined.

Dr. Mildred Wyeth: Her father was killed by the Ku Klux Klan, but her fate is not much lighter. Restored from predark cryogenic suspension, she brings twentieth-century healing skills to a nightmare.

Jak Lauren: A true child of the wastelands, reared on adversity, loss and danger, the albino teenager is a fierce fighter and loyal friend.

Dean Cawdor: Ryan's young son by Sharona accepts the only world he knows, and yet he is the seedling bearing the promise of tomorrow.

In a world where all was lost, they are humanity's last hope....

Prologue

Dr. Huth strained to see past the force-field barrier, which his helmet visor's infrared sensor had turned a ghastly, translucent lime green. Outside the shimmering containment dome, backdropped by the megalopolis's skyline, jumbled shadows dashed, darted and swooped. Discharging automatic weapons winked at him like strobe lights, grenades flashed a blinding chartreuse, but the only sound inside the battlesuit was the violent thudding of his own heart.

Dr. Huth had long since shut off the armored suit's external microphone. The force field didn't completely block the passage of sonic waves, and the sounds that filtered through—the screams, the wild volleys of gunshot, the explosions and the tearing, bursting, bone-snapping sounds—made it impossible for him to think.

From the frantic movement at or near ground level, slaughter continued apace, and in 360-degree-surround.

Blood and death.

On a scale that was almost incomprehensible.

Through the soles of his boots, Dr. Huth felt the rumble of the jump engine's power-up. The familiar vibration knotted his stomach with dread. A lifetime of intellectual effort, of unparalleled accomplishments, of sacrifice in the name of Science had all come down to this: there was either enough nuke energy left in the storage cells to leap universes one more time, or he was going to be stranded in hell's darkest pit. Stranded with less than two hours of force-field power supply remaining; after that, his only protection would be the battlesuit.

Whose power in turn would fail.

And when that happened, the armor would become his coffin.

A female voice crackled through the battlesuit-to-battlesuit com link. "Commander, the jump perimeter will be enabled in three minutes. Repeat, we'll be jump-ready in three minutes."

"There's no point holding anything back, Mero," said another voice, also female. "Divert the force-field batteries to the jump. Make sure you drain them dry."

Com link static hissed in Huth's ears as the consequences of the leader's order sank home.

All or nothing.

A split second before they leaped realities, the containment domes would collapse. If this universe wasn't slipped on the first attempt, there'd be no temporary respite; they would be left exposed, unshielded in the middle of the city's vast main square, in the middle of the mayhem.

Dr. Huth knew it was the logical decision, the only decision from a strategic point of view, but it made the knot in his guts cinch tighter.

After a pause Mero responded, "Roger that, Commander. We will be jump-ready in an estimated seven, repeat seven minutes."

Dr. Huth lowered his head and set off across the force-field enclosure in short, deliberate steps, beelining for the sterilization chamber. Moving quickly in the battlesuit was difficult for him. Nothing fit properly: his arms, legs, torso and head banged around inside it. The intelligent armor fit the others like a second skin, but they were Level Four, genetically enhanced females, the ultimate warriors of his native Earth. As a relatively uncoordinated Homo sapien male, Dr. Huth could only utilize a few of the battlesuit's basic functions. And it wasn't just a matter of body size and strength differential; his unmodified nerves and synapses couldn't fully interface with the suit's controls or handle the speed and volume of data transfer.

The sterilization unit was a ten-foot-long section of corrugated cylinder laying on its side, tall enough and wide enough to admit a single warrior dressed in full battle gear. Decontamination had been part of their pre-jump regimen ever since Shadow World, the first parallel Earth targeted for conquest.

Unlike their own exhausted and dying home, Shadow World had had bountiful, untapped natural resources on land and sea, and a relatively tiny, technologically stagnant human population that was easily subdued. But before the invaders could gain a foothold, infection by an indigenous lethal microbe forced them to make a hasty exit to another parallel Earth. Dr. Huth had solved the immediate crisis by killing the bacteria with bursts of X-ray radiation, but the replica Earth on which they had rematerialized was long dead and worthless to them. So, they had had no choice but to jump again.

And again.

And again.

And again.

World after human-occupied world they found either already destroyed and uninhabitable, or in the midst of annihilation. The Apocalyptic scenario that had driven Dr. Huth and the warriors from their home Earth replayed over and over in parallel dimensions—the same horrendous outcome, only with different chains of causation. For one reason or another, in every version of reality that they visited, humankind and its birth planet were doomed.

Then, finally, on the tenth replica of Earth had come a glint of hope.

Like their native world, it had a vast human population, but ninety per cent of it was well past reproductive age and rapidly approaching maximum lifespan, with accompanying mental and physical diminution. The machinery of its global society still functioned, extracting and transporting still-plentiful resources, but just barely. It was a wrinkled, limping planet. An overripe plum ready to pluck.

Dr. Huth had been confident that they would be the ones doing the plucking.

But he was wrong.

The scourge had appeared a few weeks after their arrival, after they had seized the reins of power, but long before their advanced genetic and weapons technologies could give them full control over a weakened and stunned populace. It was unlike anything the planet had ever endured, unlike anything the whitecoat Dr. Huth had even dreamed possible. And as it spread unchecked, crossing oceans, continents, ice caps with stunning speed, the evidence that he and the other reality-jumpers had brought it with them steadily mounted—until it was indisputable.

As fate would have it, the seed of the Apocalypse lay scattered not only upon the seemingly infinite copies of Earth, but also across the True Void, the transitional Nothingness, the Null space between universes. And Dr. Huth and his fellow invaders, the would-be conquerors of a hundred parallel worlds, had inadvertently picked up and transported those seeds, that unspeakable contamination, to the first planet that could have sustained them, and which would have served as a launching pad for all their ambitions.

Once the scourge took hold on the tenth Earth, the only defense against it had been force field and battlesuit. There was nowhere else safe to run, nowhere safe to hide, and no way to fight back. Weapons of war intended for intrareality combat—even the warriors' tribarreled laser rifles—had done nothing to slow the mass extermination of the planet's most complex organisms. It wasn't just humans who died—no higher animals were spared, cold- or warm-blooded, large or small. Dr. Huth's mathematical models had forecast a bleak future: When the cycle of slaughter finally ended, only the planet's multicellular plant species and the prokaryotes would be left alive.

The evolutionary clock was running backward.

To escape the global disaster they had set in motion, the reality-travelers had jumped again.

Dr. Huth reached out a black-gauntleted hand and threw back the door flap of the sterilization chamber. He braced himself on the plast-steel frames that held the banks of X-ray generators and stepped onto the low, gridwork target pedestal. The beams were angled to cover every square inch of the suit, even the soles of his boots. He had ramped up the X-ray intensity, hoping that the application of maximum available power would resolve their predicament.

Toeing the marker on the pedestal, he hit the power switch, raised his arms over his head and spread his gauntleted fingers. The battlesuit visor reacted infinitely faster than eyes and brain. Before the latter could even begin to register the blast of energy, the helmet's autosensors opaqued the lens to petroleum-black.

The X-ray pulse lasted one minute, and in theory at least, blasted the suit's external surfaces clean of all living matter. If it worked, they would depart this replica Earth without scourge stowaways.

After his visor cleared, Dr. Huth exited the tunnel's rear and passed through to a second force field—the smaller dome-within-a-dome that enclosed the jump zone. Before him, similarly clad in segmented, gleaming black battlesuits, a dozen surviving warriors set the stage for departure. They were triaging out the most vital gear—weapons, food and medical stores, and scientific apparatus. Behind them stood the mobile, nuke-ore processor, three transport vehicles and a single gyroplane. The rest of their matériel had to be abandoned; the smaller the payload, the less power the jump required.

Beyond the nested containment fields, a pitched, one-sided battle raged. Without the battlesuits' optical enhancements, the seemingly endless legions of attackers were invisible. All that could be seen of them with the naked eye were the corkscrewing aerial wakes they left when passing through smoke or fog or rain—and perhaps that was a blessing in disguise. In his helmet's viewscreen they flew, they floated, they slithered, they massed in thin air like the glowing ghosts of six-foot-long slime eels. The specterlike entities seemed unaffected by planetary gravity, a phenomenon that sorely baffled Dr. Huth. It appeared that although they existed in the current dimension, wreaking havoc as they swarmed and killed, they were somehow not fully of it.

Great luminous blotches of color splashed high on the flanks of the outermost containment dome. Liquid dripped down the impenetrable curtain in rivulets of brilliant lime green.

Hot blood, as seen in infrared.

The gouts of gore splattered the surface of the force field, hung there for an instant, then were gone, vaporized as the barrier shrugged off the insult.

Similar slaughter was raining down upon the planet's entire surface, upon living creatures even less prepared to defend themselves.

Megadeath.

It had followed their leap from the tenth Earth to the eleventh, and now from the eleventh to the twelfth, seemingly homing on the chemistry of their blood and marrow, using them not only for transport, but also as guides to suitable targets, to like-worlds prime for annihilation.

Working frantically in the 18-to-21-day windows of calm between rematerialization and all hell breaking loose, Dr. Huth had gathered a scant handful of facts. It appeared that the creatures first entered the bodies of their hosts as microscopic entities, drawn into the lungs with breath, into the stomach with food and water, and into the soft tissue through breaks in the skin. Like bacterial endospores, their incredibly tough, shell-like outer covering protected them from the hazards of deep space and presumably, those of the True Void. Like endospores, these entities had a lethality threshold.

Under strictly controlled laboratory conditions, he had destroyed them with direct heat in excess of 2000 degrees Fahrenheit, and with maximum-power X-ray exposure. The direct heat method was not applicable in the real world; those temperatures would have flash-cooked the warriors in their battlesuits. Whether the X-ray radiation level and coverage in the sterilization chamber was sufficient to cleanse them of all microscopic contamination was an open question.

Even more unsettling, he hadn't discovered a way to kill fully matured entities after they burst out of their living hosts. It seemed that once they attained quasi-spectral form, they were immune to the effects of radiation, laser, gun shot, explosive, fire and poison. They were as untouchable, and as insubstantial, as they were insatiable for living victims. Dr. Huth needed additional time to unravel the mystery, and once again time had run out.

He glanced down the visor screen's right-hand display, pausing for a second at the function tab he wanted to initiate. The software's Graphic Retinal Interface—GRI—automatically shifted the view mode from infra-red to "normal."

The commander's voice crackled through the com link. "Status report."

"All systems online," Mero replied. "We are ready to initiate jump on your order."

"Close ranks."

At the center of the jump zone Dr. Huth and the black-helmeted warriors formed up in a tight circle facing one another, battlesuits shoulder-to-shoulder.

On the ring's side opposite him, a visor decloaked. Dr. Huth gazed upon milk-white skin, cascading black curls, a full-lipped mouth, strong chin and, even through the visor's polarizing tint, eyes the color of blue ice.

For a split second the whitecoat felt a chill of recognition. Under extreme stress, in his most vulnerable moments, those eyes, that uncanny resemblance, had the power to transport him to the land of recurring nightmares, of savage punishments. And for the thousandth time Dr. Huth came face-to-face with the possibility that a grievous, fundamental error had been made.

An indelible mistake.

The being that stood opposite him had been assembled, egg and sperm, in a petri dish, grown in the belly of an unwilling slave surrogate mother, genetically enhanced and artificially matured on worlds pulled apart at their seams. Auriel Otis Trask had known eight different versions of Earth in her short lifetime, all of them endgame catastrophes. The combination of that unique experience and her altered DNA had made Auriel harder than vanadium steel, harder than either of her gene donors.

Auriel's female component had been harvested from Dredda Otis Trask, the former CEO of Omnico, board member of FIVE, the ruling conglomerate of Dr. Huth's overpopulated, overexploited Earth. Ever the visionary, when Dredda had realized that human life was on its last legs, that there was no hope for her world, she had used Level Four bioengineering technology to remake herself and create a cadre of genetically enhanced warriors, creatures fit to jump universes and conquer entire planets, starting with Shadow World. After Dredda's horrible demise on the eleventh Earth, Auriel Otis Trask had inherited command of the expedition—and the responsibility of leading it out of its desperate plight.

Her plan was to jump back to where the odyssey had begun, back to Shadow World. This in order to gain time, to repower their nuke batteries and recover the gear left at Slake City; and if the specters still followed, to find a way to kill them or leave them behind, once and for all.

Dr. Huth ran the tip of his tongue over the empty sockets formerly occupied by his front teeth. Deathlands was a place he had hoped never to see again. Within hours of his initial arrival there, he had been set upon, robbed of all his possessions, beaten and mutilated. Though the memory of that traumatic event remained fresh, its irony was lost on him.

In a long and storied scientific career he had never once worried about the consequences of his own actions on the powerless. As a young whitecoat, then as director of the Totality Concept's trans-reality program, he had always looked for the Big Picture. The fate of the tens of billions left to starve on his native Earth after it had been scraped clean of sustenance hadn't troubled him. He had seen firsthand what the scourge could do, but he wasn't concerned about the fate of the Shadow Worlders, either. In his experience, other people's suffering was the price of knowledge.

And at that price it was always a bargain.

"Initiate the sequence," Auriel said.

"Counting down from thirty," Mero said. "Prepare for jump."

As Dr. Huth watched the red digits fall on the lower edge of his visor's faceplate, all he could think about were the consequences of failure. If there wasn't enough power for the jump, he was going to slowly suffocate inside the ill-fitting armor. The horror and the unfairness of that fate unmanned him: his lower lip began to quiver and his eyes welled up with scalding tears. There were so many things yet to do, so many discoveries yet to be made, accolades that would be denied him.

When the scrolling numbers hit zero, the double force fields imploded with a jarring whoosh, and the suddenly expanded perspective seared an image deep into the recesses of his brain.

Specters zipped through the air, crisscrossing like flying javelins, streaks of luminous green moving faster than the eye could follow; tightly packed masses of them writhed ecstatically above the mounds of ruptured corpses that clogged the city's plaza. Except for the specters, everything that he could see, for as far as he could see, was dead.

Then the jump machinery engaged and the air overhead began to shimmer, then spin. It morphed into a vortex, flecked with glittering points of light. As the tornado whirled faster, the light from within grew brighter and brighter. Staggered by the blasting wind, Dr. Huth looked across the ring and realized the commander was staring at him. On the cusp of their destruction, Auriel Otis Trask was smiling.

With a thunderclap that rattled his every molecule the towering cyclone vanished; it was the sound of the universe cracking open. A narrow seam, a fissure without bottom, divided the center of their warrior circle, gaping wider and wider like a hungry maw.

Once the passage between realities was established, all struggle was futile; the forces unleashed wouldn't be denied. The ground beneath Dr. Huth's boots dematerialized and he somersaulted into the Nothingness on the heels of Ryan Cawdor's daughter.

Chapter One

"There it is again, lover. And it sure as hell isn't the wind."

Ryan Cawdor glanced over at Krysty Wroth, back-handing the sweat from his brow before it could trickle into his one good eye. Her beautiful face was flushed from the heat and exertion, her prehensile hair had curled up in tight ringlets of alarm—shoulder-length, bonfire-red, mutant hair that seemed to have a collective mind of its own, and always erred on the side of caution.

The eye-patched warrior, his long-legged paramour and their four companions crouched in a frozen skirmish line along the ruined, two-lane highway, their ears cocked. Under an enormous bowl of blue sky, streaked with high, wispy clouds, on the desolate and doom-hammered landscape, they were the tiniest of tiny specks.

The devastation that lay before them wasn't a result of the all-out nukewar that had erased civilization more than a century earlier, in late January 2001; this Apocalypse was vastly older than that. It had come many millions of years in the past, long before the first human beings walked the earth.

Shouldering his Steyr SSG-70 longblaster, Ryan looked over rather than through its telescopic sight, taking in the panorama of destruction, searching for something to zero the optics in on. A volcanic plain stretched all the way to the southern horizon. Countless miles of baking black rock—angled, slick, razor-sharp, unyielding and treacherous underfoot. Eroded cinder cones, like towering molehills, dotted the plain, shimmering in the rising waves of heat. The only vegetation he could see was the occasional twisted, stunted, leafless tree, and clumps of equally stunted sagebrush.

When they had first glimpsed the sprawling badlands, Doc Tanner had remarked that they looked like "the top of a gargantuan pecan pie burned to a how-do-you-do."

After trekking through the waste for a day and a half, the Victorian time traveler's quip no longer brought a smile to Ryan's face.

There it was again, the barely audible sound that had stopped them in their tracks.

Shrill and intermittent, not a whistle, but a piercing, short blast of scream. As the breeze rustled the sagebrush, spreading its sweet perfume, it distorted the distant noise, making its source impossible to pinpoint. And Ryan's predark scope, sharp as it was, couldn't see around the cinder cones or into the innumerable craters, cracks and caverns. Straining, he thought he could make out a second set of sounds, much lower pitched, throbbing, like a convoy of wags revving their engines.

No wags here.

The faint ghost of a predark highway, eroded by chem rain and crosscut in places by five-foot-deep washouts, was only fit for foot or horse traffic.

Ryan turned toward Jak Lauren, who squatted on his left. The albino's white hair fell in lank strands around his shoulders, his eyelids narrowed to slits as he faced into the hot wind. Jak's short stature and slim build made him look younger than his years. Those who mistook him for a mere teenager and underestimated his fighting skills, only did so once. The ruby-eyed youth was a stone chiller, Deathlands born and bred. From ten feet away Ryan could almost feel the intensity of Jak's focus, which was pushing every sense to the limit in order to read the faint sign.

"What do you say, Jak?" Ryan asked. "What is it?"

The albino's reply was delivered without emotion, a death sentence. "Something's cornered," he said. "'Bout to get et."

"Let's give whatever it is a wide berth," J. B. Dix, the group's armorer, said. He swept off his fedora and mopped the beads of sweat from his face with a frayed and stained shirtcuff. "It isn't our problem. Got to keep moving. Don't want to have to spend an extra night out on this rad-blasted rock."

Mildred Wyeth lowered the plastic water bottle from her lips. The freezie, a twentieth century medical doctor and researcher, had taken advantage of the pause in the march to slip out of her pack and stretch her back. Her sleeveless T-shirt was soaked through with perspiration, her brown arms glistened and the tips of the beaded plaits of her hair steadily dripped. "But maybe we can be the ones doing the eating," she countered.

Ryan had already considered that possibility. Their food cache was down to a few strips of venison jerky each.

Two days earlier they had made their way out of an underground redoubt hidden among the 11,000-foot peaks of the mountains of southern Idaho. The deserted complex's armory turned out to be a bonanza: unfired cartridge cases in a variety of calibers, gunpowder, primers and bullets, all kept separate, all hermetically vacuum-sealed, in a temperature and humidity-controlled chamber.

After J.B. and Ryan had loaded and test-fired some sample rounds, they began loading cartridges, assembly-line fashion. They loaded as much ammo in 9 mm, .357 Magnum, .38, 12-gauge and 7.62 mm as the companions could carry. Reliable center-fire ammunition was as good as gold, worth top jack and top trade anywhere in the Deathlands. Unfortunately, the redoubt's food cache had turned out to be unusable. Decades earlier, all the ready-to-eat packets and the canned goods had ballooned up and burst. Foot-high tendrils of dead, gray mold carpeted the contents and floor of the storage room. The seals on the bottled water were intact, though, and it seemed safe to drink.

From the readings on the site's remote radiation counters, the area had taken a near hit on nukeday. It could have been the result of a targeting error on the part of the Soviets, an MIRV inflight guidance malfunction, or a failed attempt to take out the redoubt. Whatever the cause, it meant traveling northwest wasn't an option for the companions. Given the food situation, they would have jumped out with their booty, but before they could do that, the redoubt's power inexplicably failed.

Which had left them on foot, with one open direction of travel: away from the rugged mountain range, onto the edge of the volcanic plain.

Many times in the past Ryan and his companions had taken large prey for their own after others, animal and

mutie, had done the hard work of hunting and chilling—
a case of survival of the best armed. From what Ryan
had seen so far, the biggest critters living on this harsh
landscape were yellow chipmunks. And they weren't
worth the price of a looted bullet. Not that a crispy,
roasted chipmunk-on-a-stick or two wouldn't have gone
down nicely after thirty-six hours of starvation rations,
but a hit by a nine mil or a .38 would have left a scrap
of bloody fur with feet. In the jumble of broken flood
basalt, it was impossible to catch or trap the little rad
bastards. Escape routes, deep cracks and holes were
everywhere.

"Might be a jackrabbit," Krysty said. "They can
scream."

"Bobcat or eagle would make short work of a rabbit,"
J.B. said. "One squeak and it would be over. If it wasn't
chilled on the first hit, it would just jump in a hole and
hide, out of reach. It wouldn't keep yellin' like that."

"There's also the possibility that it's a much larger
animal, more difficult to pull down," Doc said. "A deer
or a stray horse resisting the attentions of a pack of
predators." Perspiration had pasted Doc's long gray hair
to the sides of his deeply lined face and neck.

"Or something much more highly evolved," Mildred
suggested.

"We can't see what it is from here," Ryan said. "And
there's only one way to find out for sure."

"We don't need more trouble than we've already got,"
J.B. said. "For nuke's sake, Ryan, it could be a trap,
something triple-bad luring us in for an ambush—the
oldest trick in the book. There's a million hidey-holes
for things to jump from. If we're caught flatfooted on

a patch of open ground, we're never going to get out of this nukin' frying pan." The short man paused to thumb his wire-rimmed spectacles back in place, up the sweaty bridge of his nose. "We've got a lot of miles of lava field left to cross," he said. "We should stay on the road, swing wide of whatever it is and never look back."

Ryan took the Armorer's point. But as things stood, their lives were balanced on a knife edge, and it was a question of priorities—a decision had to be made as to what came first.

"We need to round up some food," Ryan said. "We won't poke our noses in if there's nothing to gain."

Their stomachs audibly rumbling, Doc and Jak nodded in agreement.

Outvoted, J.B. screwed his hat back down with a flourish and said no more.

Ryan shoulder slung the Steyr and led them offroad, confident that J.B.'s injured feelings would quickly pass, whether or not they found fresh meat. J.B. was a team player, had been ever since the glory days with Trader— that meant honoring a group decision even if he didn't agree with it.

Off the highway there were no trails for Ryan to follow. The jumbled chunks of lava were a solid mass underfoot. Sometimes he was stepping on jagged points, sometimes in between them, and the edges of the rock tore at the soles and sides of his boots. The surface was so rough that running over it without falling would have been impossible. Even walking a short distance in a straight line was damned difficult. Every ten yards it seemed, holes as big as semitrailers and twisting crevasses blocked their way.

Gradually, the vista ahead revealed itself, and it wasn't as flat as it had appeared a quarter mile back—a trick of perspective and of the uniformity of the terrain's coloration. Before them was a dished-out, sunken swath of ground, the top of a huge, collapsed lava dome. Ryan could see the far rim of the crater, a crescent of blacker black, and it was at least a mile away. The deepest part was in the middle, a hundred feet below the rim. The surface looked to be basalt, but the fractured plates of rock were much bigger and tipped up at steep angles.

Ryan knelt at the edge of the drop-off, hand-signaling for the others to do the same. From their new vantage point, the sounds were much more distinct and disturbing.

"My word!" Doc exclaimed. "That scream sounds almost human."

Jak pointed and said, "There."

Ryan caught a glimpse of movement in that direction, but it was too far away to make out details. He unslung the .308-caliber longblaster and uncapped its scope. Seven hundred yards downrange he saw a cluster of four-legged animals madly scrabbling, their heads lowered, their tails in the air, pulling and tearing at something on the ground. The low-pitched sounds he'd heard were their growls and snarls. What with the movement, the intervening heaps of rock, and the heat shimmer it was difficult to see clearly, but he could make out tall, skinny creatures with ribs showing through gray coats, and pointed muzzles and ears. And their heads were all oddly marked: the hair on top, between their ears, was bright orange-red. The violent tug-of-war took the animals and the prize they were fighting over out of sight behind the upturned slabs.

"Looks like a pack of wolves or coyotes," Ryan told the others. "Real big ones. A couple dozen at least. They've chilled something large and they're ripping it apart. Can't see what they've got, but it isn't fighting back."

The shrill cry rolled over them again.

"There's at least one victim still alive down there," Mildred said.

"It appears to be begging for mercy," Doc said.

"Begging the wrong critters for that, from what I saw," Ryan said as he lowered the rifle.

"Guess we won't be eating fresh meat tonight, unless it's haunch of wolf," Krysty said with dismay.

"In my experience," Doc said, "no matter how it's sauced, simmered, or pounded, wolf meat tastes like old boot."

"A boot that's stepped in shit," J.B. added. "Okay, we've had our look-see. We should move on, and triple quick before they catch our scent."

"We can't leave whoever it is that's trapped down there," Mildred protested.

"More likely it's a 'whatever,'" Dix told her. "A scalie or some other mutie. And if it's an ankle-biter, I say more power to the wolves."

Ryan raised the Steyr to his shoulder, dropped the safety and surveyed the kill zone through the scope, waiting for the feeding melee to come back into view. No matter their complaints, no matter how nasty the meat tasted, he knew he and his companions would choke it down somehow, and with any luck it would keep them going long enough to get past the lava field.

Doc and Krysty were still discussing recipes when, a moment later, targets reappeared downrange.

Ryan held the sight post in the middle of the circling animals. He took up the Steyr's trigger slack and held it just short of the break point, slowing his breathing and, by extension, his heartbeat. One of the creatures paused in the pitched battle. Panting hard, it straightened to full height, turning itself broadside to him.

To hit a bull's-eye at the distance and with the twenty-degree down-angle meant taking an aim-point eight or nine inches low. Ryan dropped the sight post that far beneath the animal's chest, and tightened down on the trigger. When it broke crisply, the Steyr boomed and bucked hard into the crook of his shoulder. He rode the recoil upward, working the butter-smooth action in a blur. Fresh round chambered, he reacquired the sight picture in time to see a puff of dust explode on the critter's near shoulder. The .308 round drove it into the rocks hard. It bounced once, ragdoll limp, and stayed down.

The sound of the rifle shot and the echoes that followed turned the other animals into statues, but only for a second.

As they began to scatter, Ryan got off another round. His intended target juked an instant before the bullet struck, and a heart shot became a spine shot. Dust puffed off the animal's back just in front of its hips. Its rear end and tail dropped like a deadweight. Meanwhile, the rest of the pack zigzagged away through the slabs—like the critters had learned how to avoid long distance rifle fire—and vanished into the lava field.

Through the scope Ryan saw the wounded animal crawling for cover on its front legs, dragging the back ones limp and useless behind it. "Two down," he said, ejecting the spent cartridge. "The others took off."

"Think they'll keep their distance?" Mildred said.

"Depends," J.B. said. "On how hungry they are."

"They looked plenty hungry to me," Ryan said, slinging the Steyr and unholstering his SIG-Sauer P-226 handblaster. "Stay alert and stay close."

Weapons drawn, the companions carefully descended the crater rim after him, jumping from block to basalt block until they reached the bottom. Then they began working their way, single file, toward the center of the depression.

They walked in silence, except for the occasional scrape of boot soles. There were no more piercing screams for Ryan to home in on. The screamer had either been chilled by the pack of predators, or it was laying low in the wake of the gunfire, waiting until it sussed out the shooter's intentions.

When they reached the kill zone, Ryan immediately signaled for the others to fan out and secure a perimeter. He and J.B. quickly tracked the wounded animal to a narrow opening in the lava. From the blood trail it had left on the rocks, it wasn't likely to ever crawl out of the hole. Or live long enough to starve.

"Better have a look at this, Ryan," Krysty called out. She and Mildred, wheelguns in hand, stood over the body of his first victim.

"Now that is what I call butt ugly," J.B. said.

The spindly-legged corpse's gray fur was mottled with
yellow; amber-colored eyes stared fixedly into space.
Its bloody canines were a good two inches long, and a
purple tongue drooped out of its mouth. The .308 round
had blown a cavernous hole crossways through its chest,
sending a plume of pulverized flesh, bone, fur, and blood
spraying across the hot rock behind.

Ryan could see things squirming in the puddles of
gore. Thin, wiry things.

Parasites.

None of that was the "butt ugly" J.B. referred to.

Ryan dropped to a knee beside the body. The patch
of color on its overlarge skull wasn't composed of hair
after all. From above the ears and eyebrows to the back
of its head, the creature had a cap of brilliant, reddish
orange skin; naked skin, wrinkled and seamed like a
peach pit. He gingerly poked at it with the muzzle of his
SIG.

Spongy.

The hairless patch rose to a massive sagittal crest,
the anchor for jaw muscles powerful enough to crack
the long bones of an elk.

"Look at the muzzle and the shape of the eyes,"
Krysty said. "It's not a wolf, it's a coyote."

"Part coyote," Ryan said. "Definitely part somethin'
else."

"A four-legged, nukin' buzzard," J.B. spit.

Ryan looked up when Jak appeared from behind a
slab of basalt. He held a battered combat boot by the
toe. It dripped thick blood off the heel; the laces were
still tied and it still had a foot in it. The splintered

end of a shin bone jutted out the top. "Rest over here," Jak said.

The rest was quite a mess, and spread over a wide area.

"Sweet merciful Lord!" Doc said as he took it all in.

Spirit reduced to flesh, Ryan thought. And mercy had had no part in it. He had seen many terrible deaths in his time. This one was right up there with the worst.

The head had been torn from the neck and was missing, no doubt carried away, as were the four limbs, which had been gnawed off at the elbows and knees. The belly-up torso was nothing short of a wag wreck. And the wag wreck was what Ryan had seen the coyotes fighting over. The body cavity was chewed open, neck to crotch, ribs clipped to angry stubs, the organs and guts yarded out through the gaping wound—perhaps while the poor, luckless bastard was still alive. The torso was wrapped in a few bloody rags, the remnants of clothes. Gobbets of bone and flesh, drops of blood and hanks of long brown hair were spread over the ground.

Ryan sensed how quiet it had become in the crater. The weight of the silence seemed to press in on his eardrums. Then he got a whiff of superconcentrated funk. Rotting meat. Vile musk. Ammonia-stinking urine. In that instant he knew the mutie coyotes had doubled back on them, keeping out of sight by following the deep crevices in the rock. Pulse pounding in his throat, Ryan thumbed off the 9 mm SIG's safety.

"They're comin'!" Jak exclaimed, putting his back to the others and swinging up his Colt Python in a two-handed, fighting grip.

There was no time for a further warning.

A unison banshee howl was followed by a scrambling of claws and a concerted rush from all sides and all angles. The coyote pack relied on panic and confusion in a confined space to get the job done. Surprise, overwhelm and dismember. It probably worked champion on dumb animals and lost triple-stupe droolies, but the companions were a different breed altogether.

For Ryan and his companions the ambush drill had become second nature. Even as their weapons were coming up, they moved into a tight, back-to-back circle. This gave them clear firing lanes and reduced the span of those lanes to a mere sixty degrees, ideal for snap-shooting multiple near-targets.

Coyotes launched themselves from the tops of rock slabs. They shot out through gaps in the lava, their fangs bared, their amber eyes gleaming with blood lust. They had no more than twenty feet to cross to reach their victims.

Ryan swung the SIG's sights from left to right, squeezing the trigger as fast as he could. Instant killshots weren't required. The idea was to break the oncoming wave; any incapacitating hit would do.

To his right, J.B.'s M-4000 shotgun boomed as he cut loose from the hip. The high-brass load of buckshot blew an airborne animal off-course, into Ryan's firing lane. As it twisted in the air, he punched a 9 mm round through its exposed underbelly. Before that creature hit the ground J.B. had jacked the pump gun's slide, found a second hurtling target and fired again. With the same result: a sideways-flying coyote, like it had been snap-kicked by a giant's boot.

There was no way and no time to count the attackers. There were too many of them. And they were coming too fast. No time to think, either. Ryan aimed for chests and heads, firing like a machine.

With Mildred, Jak and Krysty similarly cutting loose behind him and Doc blasting away on his blind side, the din of gunfire was deafening.

As Doc's black powder LeMat barked into Ryan's left ear, it sent forth successive gouts of dense gray smoke, which partially obscured the battlefield. The Civil War antique shot lead-ball ammo from its nine cylinder system, and a single shotgun round through a shorter underbarrel. After Doc emptied the cylinder, the shift to fire the shotgun chamber required moving a lever down on the end of the hammer.

Which meant a momentary pause in his stream of fire.

"Release me, you bastard!" Doc howled.

Ryan half turned at the cry and saw a flurry of movement beside him. A coyote had Doc's right boot clenched in its teeth and was shaking its head, trying to tear off the foot at the ankle. The old man stood balanced on his left leg and the tip of his ebony swordstick, which he held behind him. Doc aimed the LeMat point-blank at the top of the animal's garish skull. With a rocking boom, two feet of flame and a tremendous rush of smoke enveloped it.

Ryan didn't know what the hell Doc had packed the shotgun barrel with this time—he usually favored metal scrap and shards of glass—but smidgens of skin, like wet shreds of orange peel spattered the front of the old man's knee boots and slapped into Ryan's thigh. The blast flattened the coyote and set its back and shoulders on fire.

It was the last blast of the battle.

The air was choked with the stench of blood and spilled guts, of burned cordite and flaming fur. Through the haze of gunsmoke, Ryan could see a ring of sprawled, four-legged bodies, a few still breathing laboriously.

They had discharged more than fifty rounds in a matter of seconds.

Ryan's ears were ringing as he replaced the SIG's spent magazine. Behind him, Mildred, Jak and Krysty dumped their empties and recharged their revolvers. J.B. thumbed fresh 12-gauge shells into his combat scattergun.

As the smoke thinned and lifted, Ryan glimpsed a couple of the coyotes making for the horizon. They kept looking over their backs, perhaps to check for pursuit. When the animals neared the crater rim, he shouldered the Steyr and sent a 7.62 mm round zinging after them.

A reminder to keep on running.

"It was almost like they were on a suicide mission," Mildred said as he lowered the longblaster.

"Didn't want to abandon their kill," Ryan told her. "Fresh meat has got to be hard to come by around here."

"It appears we have more than enough, now," Doc said. He jabbed at the remains of the animal smoldering beside his boot with the tip of his walking stick, then added, "Such as it is."

"Nearly blew off your own foot, didn't you, Doc?"

J.B. said. "How many times do I have to tell you, single actions suck."

"I'm alive," Doc said. He gave the corpse another poke. "And that hideous thing is not." From the side pocket of his frock coat, he pulled out the leather pouch that held his black powder reloading gear. He then sat himself down on a nearby rock and with a quick, deft hand began charging and recapping each of the revolver's chambers.

J.B. looked over at Ryan and shook his head.

The one-eyed warrior shrugged. At times, Dr. Theophilus Algernon Tanner could be infuriatingly stubborn and cantankerous. And there was nothing they or anybody else could do about it. The twentieth century whitecoats who had time-trawled him away from the bosom of his family in the late eighteen hundreds, his beloved Emily and his two young children, had gotten so fed up with his contrariness that just to be rid of him, they'd sent him forward in time, to Deathlands. Despite the considerable downsides to the 250-year-old sidearm Doc carried, the truth was, only if and when the LeMat blew up in his hand would he ever consider replacing it.

As Krysty and Jak were finishing off the wounded animals with close-range head shots, a muffled voice called to them. "Is it safe to come out now?"

Ryan and the companions swung up their handblasters, searching for the source of the sound with gunsights.

"Help me, puleeeeeeze!"

It was a man. Very close.

"Are they all dead?" came an even louder holler. "Make sure they're all dead!"

"Keep your pants on," Ryan shouted back.

"I do believe I recognize that voice," Doc told the others.

"How is that possible?" Krysty said.

"More ghosts from your past?" Mildred asked. "An Oxford don circa 1882? Is your merry old brain vapor-locking again, Doc?"

"Neither a supernatural occurrence, nor a mental aberration," Doc said, refusing to rise to the bait, "but certainly a coincidence of note."

"Help me! Puleeeeeeze, help me! I swear I won't run off again."

"'Run off again'?" Krysty said. "He thinks we're somebody else."

"Somebody he's scared to death of," J.B. said, "or he'd have shown his rad-blasted face by now."

Jak moved quickly and quietly toward a vertical fissure in the bedrock about forty feet away, his .357 Magnum ready to rip. Like a bird dog, he stood there on-point. Ryan and the others slipped into position on either side of him, in front of the narrow cave's entrance.

"Come on out," J.B. said. "Now."

"Leave your blaster behind," Ryan said.

"Coming out, got no blaster."

The pancaked crown of a waxed-canvas fedora appeared in the crack in the rock, then a prosthetic right hand—ivory-colored, it had articulated fingers and a big knob on the back of the wrist for tightening them into a fist. The man whimpered mightily as he tried to squeeze his big body sideways through the gap.

He was halfway in, halfway out of the cleft when J.B. said, "Well, I'll be nuked!" and drew a tight bead on him with the M-4000.

"Are you back for another trouncing, you traitorous dog?" Doc demanded, stepping forward and brandishing his ebony cane.

When the wedged-in man looked up and saw who his rescuers were, his jaw dropped. Grunting from the effort, he quickly retreated, squirming back into the fissure, out of sight.

"I told you I recognized that voice," Doc said to Mildred.

Ryan recognized him, too. The man in the hole was none other than Big Mike, also known as Mike the Drunkard, and the "Tour Guide from Hell," a turncoat huckster who had sold his services to the she-hes, the would-be colonizers from Shadow Earth. Riding around in a gaudily painted bus, he had conned gullible villefolk with free joy juice, free jolt, free sex and promises of a much easier life in Slake City. It was a nonstop rolling party until they arrived at the site, then the awful truth was revealed: they had been gathered up to slave until death in the nuke mines.

Ryan, his son Dean and the companions had themselves toiled in the sweltering, poisonous shafts at Ground Zero. Although they had eventually fought their way free, they had been unable to stop the she-hes from escaping this reality and Deathlands' brand of justice. They had, however, waylaid and beaten one of the invaders' vilest puppets to within an inch of his life.

That puppet was Big Mike.

They had decided to let him live because he was

already an amputee. He had only the one hand, which made his surviving in the hellscape a constant, and ultimately losing battle. After all the pain and suffering he'd inflicted on innocent folk, simply chilling him would have been too much of a kindness. Ryan was surprised he'd lasted so long.

"Come on out," the one-eyed warrior said. "We're not going to beat you again."

"Swear to it?"

"Come out now, you tub of shit," J.B. ordered, "or we're going to leave you here to rot. Put your hands up and keep them up."

Big Mike obeyed, moaning as he forced himself out of the cave, holding his arms above his head.

"You seem to have lost something else since we last crossed paths," Ryan said, gesturing with the muzzle of the SIG.

Big Mike glanced up at his left arm, which now ended in a stump. It was cut through clean, like it had been sliced off with a bandsaw.

And recently.

The massive scab was black and the skin around it an angry red.

"In a place as hard as Deathlands," Krysty said, "a man who's missing all you're missing is in one hell of a pickle."

"Hell, pickle ain't the half of it," Big Mike said. "Lookee here." He held out his artificial hand. "Only way I can grip down on something is if I use my teeth on the fucking knob."

"What happened to the other one?" Ryan asked.

"From the looks of that stump, it wasn't mutie coyotes who took it."

"You must've really pissed somebody off," J.B. said, making no attempt to conceal his amusement.

"My former bosses, the cockroaches from alternate Earth," Big Mike replied. "The bastards are back at Slake City, working the mines again, only this time they've cut out the middleman. They're rounding up their own slaves. They took me for a slave, too."

Big Mike waved the blackened stump in their faces. "Getting free cost me this," he said.

Chapter Two

Ryan sized up the double amputee, who sat in the shade of a slab of basalt, drinking greedily from a plastic water bottle death-gripped in his prosthetic hand. The grime caked on the big man's face made his eyeballs and teeth appear much whiter than they were, as if he was peering out from behind a mask. He wore filthy bib-front overalls, a holed-out khaki T-shirt and battered, unlaced boots. His blinding reek reminded Ryan of a bear pit in midsummer.

In the past, Big Mike had proved himself a backstabbing con man, but the evidence of that fresh stump couldn't be ignored. The cut at the wrist and the crust of scab looked far too neat for bladework. The only instrument Ryan had seen that could make such a precise cut—and simultaneously seal off the wound—was a laser. A technology lost in the wake of Armageddon, but perfected to a high degree by the invaders from Shadow Earth.

The last time Ryan and the companions had crossed paths with the she-hes, the combination of advanced weapons and intelligent armor had been more than they could handle. Unable to return effective fire against the battlesuits' EM shields, they had been captured, then marched out to the middle of the hundred-square-mile, Slake City massif—the remains of a once-great, predark city melted and fused into a glacier of thermoglass by a multiwarhead, airburst nuke strike. At Ground Zero they were forced to mine radioactive ore from the maze of tunnels full of bloodthirsty stickies. They had no food but the rats they caught and cooked themselves. And just enough water to keep them working underground until they dropped dead of starvation or rad sickness.

Despite the long odds against survival, none of them had lost heart, and in the end, thanks to ingenuity and luck, they had prevailed. Ryan remembered with pride how his young son Dean had stood his ground, fighting alongside the others, turning the enemy's own weapons against them.

Memories turned bittersweet.

Some time after the nuke mine ordeal, in the dead of night, Dean's mother, Sharona, had stolen the boy away and taken him to who knew where. Ryan smothered the surge of fury that rose up whenever he thought about what she'd done. He couldn't change the past, and dwelling on it only led to guilt and self-recrimination that served no purpose. His abiding hope was that his son Dean wasn't lost to him forever, that he had just gone missing until they somehow, someway managed to find each other again. The boy was never far from his thoughts.

After the encounter at Slake City, it was clear to Ryan and his companions that if the black-armored invaders hadn't come down with a hideous pox, if the disease hadn't forced them to jump universes, the battle for Deathlands would have been lost. Though they were relatively few in number, nothing in the hellscape could stand against them. The battlesuits' shields deflected even point-blank blasterfire. With their all-terrain wags and flying machines, they had the advantage of speed, maneuver and firepower. And the cherry on top, they alone could fully reap the bounty of Armageddon. They ran all their equipment, from the tribarreled laser rifles to the gyroplanes, with reprocessed radioactive waste.

If the she-hes had managed to establish a permanent base at Slake City, within a year they would have toppled the hellscape's baronies, one by one.

While Ryan had no love for Deathlands' brutal feudal system, it was paradise compared to what the invaders offered. And the ambitions of the Shadow Earthlings had no limits.

Ryan knew what the Shadow Earthlings had done to their home world because he'd been there—as proof of their success and the hope it offered the starving multitudes, the first expeditionary force had transported him back to their point of origin. On the parallel Earth he had seen what made the colonization of a place like Deathlands so appealing and so necessary. Shadow World was a planet stripped clean of resources.

At the top of the teeming human population of 100 billion were the CEOs of FIVE, the ruling corporate conglomerate, and their whitecoat minions; at the bottom, in the sprawling underground ghetto known as Gloomtown, the vast, expendable segment of the population was reduced to eating pulverized rock disguised as fast food. While the masses slowly wasted away from a lack of calories, the toxic side effects of "Beefie Cheesies" and "Tater Cheesies" drove them homicidally insane.

A bioengineered agrobacteria, touted as the solution to the global food crisis, had run amok, the resulting

Slime Zone threatening to carpet the entire planet in green slunk. In order to slow the growth of the unemployable classes, the one-world-government's Population Control Service had released a flesh-eating bioweapon into the environment, and like the agrobacteria, the self-replicating carniphages had promptly taken root in the megalopolis. They bloomed at random and picked clean the bones of anyone who didn't reach cover in time.

What the Shadow Earthlings had done to themselves, to their own world, Ryan knew they were hell-bound to do elsewhere.

Big Mike lowered the nearly empty bottle and belched resonantly. "The cockroaches are attacking the nearby villes and sweeping up all comers," he said. "Anyone who can hoist a chunk of ore they're dumping at Slake City's Ground Zero. The folks who can't do a lick of work, the too-young and too-old, they just slice into chunks with their tribarrels. They're leaving the villes empty except for the buzzards. And the buzzards are having a grand old time."

The battle—so desperate, so hard won—wasn't over after all.

Ryan read the grim faces of his companions. He saw anger and disbelief, his own churning emotions reflected back at him. Krysty's beautiful green eyes flashed with something even darker, more primitive—savage hatred. And she had just cause. To ensure the survival of their kind, the she-hes had stolen his seed, not from his loins but from Krysty, violating her like she was a barnyard animal.

J.B. broke the stunned silence. "How many wags and aircraft?" he asked.

"They used three wags where I got scooped up, south of Slake City, over in Burrville off old Highway 24 near Fish Lake. Nuke-powered wags, high speed, with wheels and tires as tall as a man, and invisible-armored like the battlesuits against bullets. I saw one of their flying machines in action—a gunship. It lasered the shit out of a stick-and-mud hut where some of the folks were trying to hold off the ground attack. Lit it up in a green flash. Three seconds later all four walls collapsed and the roof dropped to the ground. Raised a huge cloud of dust. Nobody came out of there alive. After that, the rest of the people stopped fighting back. They just gave up and let themselves be taken prisoner."

"How many she-hes are there?" Ryan said.

"Don't know for sure," Big Mike said. "I saw mebbe nine or ten, but there could be a few more. Hard to say because you can't tell 'em apart in those cockroach suits. When they come and go, you could be counting some of them more than once."

Ryan scratched the back of his neck. Just looking at the bastard made his skin crawl, and his trigger finger itch. There was no telling how many innocent folks Big Mike had steered to gruesome slow deaths in the mines. And now he was confiding in the companions like they were old running buddies. Like he held no lingering hard feelings for their kicking his butt until he could barely breathe. Like they were suddenly, miraculously all on the same side. As distasteful as that prospect was, the con man had information they badly needed.

"How long ago were you taken?" Ryan said.

"Twelve days," Big Mike replied. "I was getting busy in a back room of the Burrville gaudy house. Caught with my pants down, you might say…" Behind the dirt mask, his eyes gleamed at the recollection.

"Just tell us what happened," Ryan said, trying to avert a digression into erotic tall tales.

"Blasters started popping off all around the perimeter berm," Big Mike told them. "Ten-foot-high dirt-and-rock wall meant nothing to those cockroach wags. They drove right up and over it. When I saw that I knew who was attacking us, and there wasn't any point in wasting ammo on them. It was time to head for the hills. But we were already overrun, with no way out.

"After the gunship leveled the mud hut, I surrendered along with the others. The cockroaches lined us up, about thirty in all, and put a laser handcuff on every-one's wrist. They didn't have enough cuffs to do both hands and both feet. They ordered us to collect all the pieces of lasered-up bodies and pile them in a heap. The folks who refused to touch the corpses got their hands whacked off, then and there. Afterward the cockroaches clamped the dropped cuff on their other wrist."

Ryan frowned. He and the others had worn those manacles. They were designed not to be a hindrance to hard labor. The bracelets of silver-colored plasteel weren't connected by lengths of chain. The constant threat of losing something vital was enough to keep the slaves hobbled and compliant.

"Picking up the still warm, cut-up pieces of their relatives broke them folks' spirit," Big Mike said. "After that, they were like walking dead."

"All except you," Krysty said.

"Weren't none of my kin, now were they?" Big Mike said. "When I tried to talk to the cockroaches, explain how I used to work for them, one of them recognized me. That's how I know it was the same she-hes as before. What I'd done for them in the past didn't buy me any slack, though. She-he said I had one good hand and two good legs, I could move nuke ore until I croaked. That's all I was good for.

"Cockroaches trucked us to Slake City in the backs of the wags. About 150 miles, a four-hour ride with no food, just a little water. Took us to the same base on the edge of the nukeglass, only this time it looked a lot different. There were big blast craters everywhere—wags, semitrailers and tractors, gyroplanes, the black domes and tubular walkways all blown to shit. Somebody really did a job on their equipment stash while they were gone. Used high explosive and lots of it."

"Given your predicament," Doc said, "how did you manage to escape?"

Ryan had been on the verge of asking a variant of the same question: "Whose back did you stab to get away?"

"The other prisoners didn't know what was coming, but I sure did," Big Mike replied. "I told them about the mines. Made 'em see that if we were going to make a move to escape we had to do it before they started marching us across the glass."

"They weren't afraid of losing their hands to the cuffs?" Mildred said.

"They were afraid, all right, but they were a lot more afraid of dying. If I was willing to take the chance, seeing as I only had the one hand left, they knew I wasn't kidding about what went on at Ground Zero."

A steady, low buzzing sound behind them made Ryan

half turn. A swarm of fat black flies had discovered the coyote corpses. The scent of spilled blood and guts was riding on the breeze.

"Everyone made a break for it at once," Big Mike said, "heading off in different directions. In the confusion me and a few others got past the base perimeter. Of course as soon as the she-hes saw what was happening they triggered the laser cuffs. All the prisoners lost a hand, including me. It hurt like a son of a bitch, but since there wasn't any bleeding it didn't slow us down. We kept running fast as we could.

"I don't know what the maximum range of those tribarrels is, but I'll tell you this—they were cooking hearts and lungs at better than half a mile. And when those green beams hit rocks, they explode 'em like frag grens. One old boy running ahead of me was hit in the side of the head by some rock shrap, and when he slowed down he got a hole burned through his back and out the other side. Almost cut him in two. The she-hes didn't come after the rest of us, though. Mebbe they figured five one-handed slaves weren't worth chasing down with wags and aircraft. We drove ourselves hard, following the roadbed of old 84 northwest, trying to get as far away as we could."

"How long ago was that?" Dix asked.

"We were six days getting here on foot," Big Mike said. "Lived off rattlesnakes and lizards mostly. Yesterday we made it to the south side of the Snake River. That's when things turned triple ugly again. There's a highway bridge still standing across the river, two low spans, side by side. We should have cut cross-country, gone downstream and tried to raft or swim across, but we didn't know what the heck we were getting into. We were just following old 84. Halfway across the span these coldhearts with white-painted faces like ghosts come after us, yelling and waving blasters. Turns out, it's a rad-blasted toll bridge. Nobody crosses without paying something to the baron. Burning Man is what he calls himself."

"Never heard of him," Ryan said.

"Me, neither," Big Mike said, "but I hadn't been this far north in years. In addition to the war paint, the crazy fucker wears a flamethrower strapped to this back. He isn't shy about using it, either."

"A strange weapon to be hauling around," Ryan said. "Got to be worthless outside fifty yards."

"Not to mention being a waste of good wag fuel," J.B. added.

"Take it from me," Big Mike said, "inside fifty yards that hellfire contraption is nothing you want to mess with. Past that distance his sec men take care of business with bolt-action longblasters.

"Burning Man wanted to collect his toll from us, but we had nothing to give him except cold, cooked snake. When he saw our stumps, everything changed. Right away, he wanted to know how we lost our hands. He was real what you might call 'insistent,' waving that flamethrower nozzle in our faces. A couple of the boys panicked. Couldn't blame them, really. The smell of gas was enough to knock you down. Seeing the baron and that weapon of his, even a triple-stupe droolie could figure out what made all the great big, blackened grease spots on the bridge deck. Our two boys broke ranks and dashed for the other shore. Then we were all running to save our hides. That's when Burning Man cut loose with his pride and joy. He set three of us on fire. One jumped in the river to put out the flames. The others were still alive, thrashing and burning on the deck, when me and that poor bastard over there, what's left of him, made it through the black smoke to the far side.

"Baron's sec men chased us out here into this waste. That's who I thought you were. They didn't waste ammo potshotting, trying to pick us off. Thought they could run us down, maybe. They chased us for the better part of half a day, but we lost 'em in the lava field. Either that or they just got tired of playing the game. Figured being this deep in the badlands would finish us off. It almost did."

The buzz of the flies grew louder.

Krysty let out a yelp and slapped her bare forearm, leaving a gob of flattened bug and a smear of bright blood. "We need to get the butchering done and get out of here," she said. "These bastards are biting chunks."

Chapter Three

Ryan swung his panga in a tight, downward arc and the
heavy blade chopped through the ball joint of the coyote's skinned-out hip. He averted his face as he struck
the blow, this to keep from being hit by flying gore.
Normally, the companions would have throat-slit and
strung up the carcasses to let them bleed out, but they
had a lot more ground to cover before sundown, and
lingering in the collapsed lava dome for long wasn't an
option. The aroma of slaughtered coyotes was certain
to draw buzzards, whose high-altitude circling would in
turn attract other large predators. And there was a good
chance the baron's sec men were still tracking the pair
of grease spots that got away.

Using the razor edge of the panga, Ryan cut into the
still-warm flesh, slicing through the inside of the thigh,
making sure he didn't nick the musk gland near the
base of the tail. Squadrons of black flies buzzed around
his head. They landed on his bare hands and forearms,
lapping up the red splatter. There was plenty of it to go
around—no need to bite into him to get a meal.

Bloody-fingered, he tossed the separated haunch onto
the pile he'd made in the shade of a rock slab. Under his
sleeveless black T-shirt, beads of sweat dripped from
the sides of his chest and along the middle of his spine.
They trickled around his eyepatch and rolled down his

cheek. To his left, Mildred and Krysty were dragging yet another 150-pound, limp coyote corpse over to J.B. and Jak for skinning. They were selecting animals for butchering that hadn't been gutshot. Exploded bowel contents tainted the flesh even worse than butt-gland musk.

Ryan watched J.B. and Jak set to work on the fresh carcass. They had the skinning down to a science. After making incisions above the rear feet, they cut the pelt away from the lower legs. Then Jak held the back paws pinned while J.B. used brute strength to peel the animal's entire skin forward on the torso, turning it inside out as he went, covering the mutie orange head with inverted hide. J.B. stopped peeling back the skin at the middle of the rib cage. There was no reason for them to skin the whole carcass as most of the meat was in the hindquarters. For the same reason, there was no point in gutting the coyotes, either.

Doc kept an eye on the crater's rim through the Steyr's scope, watching for signs of unwanted company, animal or human. The newcomer sat in a spot of shade beside him, fanning away the flies with his prosthetic hand.

"When we get on up to Meridianville," Big Mike said in a voice loud enough for all to hear, "we're gonna be treated like nukin' barons. It's the biggest settlement left on that stretch of the Snake. Busted dams on nukeday washed away old Boise, and Twin Falls took a full-on groundburst—there's nothing left of it but a glow-in-the-dark skeleton. Haven't been to Meridianville for a long time, but I know a lot of folks there, and they all owe me."

When no one responded to the boast, the big man

pressed on. "Me and the whoremaster go way back," he said. "I used to be his gaudy's number-one scout. Grew up in the business, you could say. I traveled the hellscape sniffing out fresh talent for his stable. You know, the daughters of dirt farmers who wanted something more out of life than working their fingers to the bone and turning old before their time. I'd stop by their plot for a cup of water or to ask directions and take the lay of the land, see if they had any female younguns running loose. I could tell by the look in their eyes which girls were ripe for what I was offering, when they wanted some fun and frolic while they still had all their teeth. As soon as their mamas and papas suspicioned I was up to no good they run me off, but by then I'd already talked the talent into meeting me later on in the woods.

"Sometimes I had the whole dirt-farm brood out there, naked as jaybirds, lined up on their backs in the grass, waiting their turn. I'd give 'em all a full, ten-round tryout, and if they had the knack and were eager to learn new tricks, I'd sneak 'em away from their farm after everyone else went to bed. Take 'em on over to Meridianville to get broke in good and proper by the gaudy master and his sec crew. Got top jack per tail as my bounty. Those were the days."

Big Mike reached over and gave Doc a nudge with his prosthesis. "How about you, old-timer? You look like you seen the world and then some. Ever done gaudy scouting? I tell you it's the best damn job in the hellscape."

"So I have heard," Doc said without enthusiasm. "Despite the obvious compensations, it does seem to require rather a lot of repetitive effort."

Big Mike paid no attention to Doc's reply. Ryan

reckoned he'd asked the question just so he could catch his breath.

"Trouble was," Big Mike went on, "I was so good at stealing away younguns that pretty soon I wore out my welcome. Sod monkeys would see me coming down the path and they'd go straight for their blasters. No warning shouts, no warning shots. They just opened fire. Weren't trying to wound me, either. They aimed at my head.

"In the end I had to travel so far from the gaudy to find homesteads where they didn't know me that it wasn't worth the time and trouble of hauling the little sluts back. Got to feed and water them the whole way, you know, and worst of all, you got to listen to them talk. Nearly broke my heart to give up that job, but things always seem to change, and for the worse, don't they?"

Ryan turned the coyote carcass to give himself a better attack angle on the surviving hip joint. He was irked by the bastard's buoyant tone, like he thought the companions were going to swallow his line of crap, adopt him as one of their own and nursemaid him from here on.

Sure, in order to get along they had taken up the causes of other helpless victims in the past, and put their lives on the line in the process, but the people they'd helped weren't accomplices to—and profiteers in—slavery and mass murder. The people they'd helped had done nothing to deserve the injuries they'd received, or the mortal danger they'd been put in. Ryan felt no moral responsibility for the care and safety of the likes of Mike the Drunkard, but he was thankful they hadn't chilled him the last time they'd met. If they had, chances were they would have learned about the she-hes too late to do anything about it.

Ryan stopped listening to the braggart's jabber and concentrated on splitting bone.

TWENTY MINUTES LATER the last, campfire-ready coyote haunch hit the meat pile. As water was now in too short a supply to use on hygiene, Ryan scrubbed his fingers and arms semiclean with handfuls of fine dirt, while J.B. and Jak tied the hindquarters in pairs, foot to foot. Each cleaned haunch weighed about ten pounds. Even though they hadn't discussed it, there was never any doubt as to who would be carrying them. The companions were already toting forty-pound backpacks and weapons.

"Get up," Ryan told Big Mike. When he did, the one-eyed man stepped closer, drew his SIG and aimed it at his forehead. The distance to target was less than two feet.

"Oh, Mama," Big Mike moaned, looking down the barrel.

"Don't move," Ryan said. At his signal, J.B. and Jak started draping paired haunches over the man's shoulders.

"What is this!" Big Mike exclaimed, staggering to keep his balance under the full eighty pounds of dead-weight. "You can see I'm a goddamn cripple!"

"You sure as hell can't shoot a blaster anymore, but your legs work just fine," Ryan told him.

"You're taking advantage 'cause I can't fight back anymore," Big Mike said. "How low-down, sorry-ass is that?"

"As I recall," Doc said, "fighting back never was your strong suit."

"More like, roll up in a ball and beg for mercy," Krysty added.

"If there's more trouble ahead," Ryan said, "that extra weight will slow us down. Mebbe slow us down enough to get everybody chilled. You want to follow along, you want to drink a share of our water, you want to eat later on, you'll carry the load."

"This ain't right," the big man said, but nobody was listening and he didn't try to shrug off the garlands of meat.

After the companions had shouldered their packs, Ryan took the lead, setting off for the crater's south rim.

"Now, wait just a nukin' minute!" Big Mike shouted at their backs. "You're going in the wrong direction!"

"Nobody's holding a blaster to your head," Ryan said. "You're free to break your own trail anytime you feel the urge."

"But not lugging our grub, of course," J.B. added.

"Are you out of your rad-blasted minds?" Big Mike said. "I just came from that way. Nothing over there but Burning Man and the she-hes. You wanna keep on livin' you'll head north to Meridianville." He turned and gestured. "It's thataway."

Even as he pointed, off in the distance, somewhere out on the plain above the crater rim, coyotes yip-yip-yipped. And it sounded like there were a lot more of them than just the two that had escaped.

"You wanna keep on livin'," J.B. said, "you'll shut your trap and get in line."

"I'd stay real close to the rest of us, if I were you," Mildred told him. "You're pretty much a walking banquet."

Big Mike opened his mouth, presumably to lodge yet another protest, then closed it without saying a word. His dirty face twisted into a scowl, he shuffled toward them, pinning the draped haunches to his chest with a forearm to stop them slapping against his bib-fronts.

Ryan figured he'd seen the light. On his own, in this heat without food or water, hiding in a hole from the coyotes, he would last about three days—three very unpleasant days. Ryan didn't waste breath explaining the choice of route. He didn't have to explain it to his companions. They had the same facts he did and they all knew the drill.

The sound of their massed gunfire would've carried tens of miles. If the baron's sec men were still in pursuit, they would be heading this way on the run. While the old highway was by far the easiest path off the volcanic plain, it was also the most obvious. Sec men who knew the terrain could move quickly to the road and cut them off, front and rear. There was no cover along the ruined two-lane, either. They'd be easy targets for a triangulated longblaster ambush.

The lava field, as tough and as slow as it was to traverse, had some definite upsides to it. Because it was the least likely route for them to take, there was a good chance the pursuit, who couldn't cover every possibility, would decide to ignore it. Tracking down a quarry over fields of rock was damn-near impossible unless you had a nose like a coyote, which was probably why the baron's men hadn't located Big Mike and his dead friend, yet. And then there was the chipmunk factor: a million places to take cover and foil an attack.

After picking their way single file across the crater floor, they climbed out of the depression, working their way up the jumble of rock slabs. When they got to the top, Jak took point and set a course for the southeast horizon.

Ryan and the others fell into a familiar rhythm of march behind him. Not too fast, not too slow. A pace they could maintain in the midday heat. A pace that allowed them to constantly recce their surroundings, keeping on the lookout for potentially hostile movement near and far. Every hour or so, Ryan or J.B. circled wide to the rear to check for pursuit.

No coyotes, no sec men.

As the blistering-hot afternoon wore on, Ryan's confidence began to grow. It appeared they'd made the right decision by heading south.

Hours later, when the sun began to dip low on the horizon, the air temperature plummeted. As many miles of wasteland still lay between them and the Snake River, Jak went on ahead to scout some shelter for the night. While Ryan stood watch with the Steyr, the others fanned out and started collecting scraps of wood from dead limber pines that dotted the landscape.

They had gathered plenty by the time the albino youth returned. "Found good cave," he told them. "This way."

It was a few hundred yards to the southwest, down a small sinkhole, maybe fifty feet across and ten feet deep. There was a cleft in the far wall, and it led to a tunnel that angled back into the lava flow. The passage opened onto a low-ceilinged chamber, the result of an air pocket that had formed in the cooling magma. It was big enough to hold them all with room to spare. A sizeable fissure in the ceiling above a side wall let in a shaft of light. It was a natural stove vent.

The companions heaped the wood beneath it and shrugged out of their packs. With a grunt, Big Mike dumped his load of meat on the cave floor.

Jak and Krysty piled up loose rocks, building a long, narrow fire pit against the wall.

"We could get trapped in here," Big Mike said.

"Not get trapped," Jak said. "Picked good cave." Crossing the chamber he pointed at a narrow opening in the wall near the floor. "Back way out," he said. "Hard to crawl in, but cave gets wider after. Winds around, comes out long ways off, far side of cinder cone."

"How am I supposed to squeeze through a little bitty crack like that?" Big Mike said in dismay.

"Better pray you don't have to," Ryan said.

Before the last of the daylight was gone they had a crackling blaze going in the makeshift hearth. The vent worked just fine, sucking the smoke up and out of the chamber. As the fire burned down and the heap of glowing coals built up, J.B. and Doc skewered the coyote hindquarters on to limber pine spits. Once the coals were plenty hot, they leaned the spits over them, between the fire pit border and the wall. Grease squirting from the meat made the fire flare up, but the resulting black smoke shot right up the chimney.

"Aren't you worried something might get wind of that cook fire?" Big Mike said. "More mutie coyotes?

Or those sec men? They could still be prowling around, looking for me."

"No one's after us," J.B. told him. "No one anywhere close, anyway. We made plenty sure of that."

"Even if the sec men could follow the smoke trail," Ryan said, "there's no moon, tonight. Anyone trying to track in this lava field is going to fall into a crack or a pit and break their legs, or worse. Like J.B. said, if the baron's men are trailing us they're still a long ways off. Odds are, they'll hunker down just like we are until right before daybreak. By then we'll be moving on, too."

"Got to take our chances with the fire anyway," Mildred said. "We're not going to eat raw meat, not when we're still at least a half day's hard walk from the river. We get sick on the way there, we get dehydrated from being sick in this heat, we'll never make it."

Despite the constant, grease-fueled flare-ups, the companions didn't bother knocking down the bank of coals. Instead they kept feeding the fire fresh wood to maintain the temperature. After about thirty minutes of frequent rotation, the charring on the meat was uniform. Doc deftly sliced into a haunch with the tip of his cane sword. "Done to a turn all the way to the bone," he announced.

As Doc and J.B. moved the joints out of the fire to cool a bit, Big Mike smacked his lips and said, "You know, that doesn't smell half-bad."

"Wish I could say the same for you," Krysty said, shielding her nose with a cupped hand.

If the fire had warmed the chamber to a cozy temperature, it had also warmed up Big Mike, releasing the full spectrum of his aroma. Even in a time and a place where regular baths with soap were unheard of, his stench was nothing short of spectacular. Before they passed out the food, Ryan made him move to a seat over by the cave entrance. The cold air sucked in by the fire's draft blew most of his pong up the chimney with the wood and meat smoke.

When the joints had sufficiently cooled, the companions tore into them with both hands, hot liquid fat running down their wrists and forearms. Before Big Mike could begin to eat he had to torque down the knob at the back of his prosthesis with his teeth, closing artificial fingers in a vise grip on the foot end of the leg bone.

"Gaia, that tastes vile," Krysty said, making a sour face. Her prehensile hair seemed to agree. It had drawn up into tight ringlets.

Behind the smeared lenses of his spectacles, J.B.'s eyes squeezed shut as he forced himself to swallow. "You know," he said, "this is so bad it makes wolf seem like prime beef."

"I have to breathe through my mouth to choke it down," Mildred said.

"Gamier than roast muskrat," Doc said. "And somewhat more fibrous than armadillo."

"Bear's not so greasy," Jak offered.

"Mebbe we should cook it longer," Krysty said.

"That won't improve the taste," Ryan assured her. The flesh had a definite harsh tang to it already from the burning limber pine resins. It made Ryan's tongue cleave to the roof of his mouth. As he chewed he felt something hard crunch between his back molars. He rolled the gob of meat around in his mouth until he could pick out the inclusion with his fingertips. When he held it close to the firelight, it looked like a lentil bean, flat, circular, but it wasn't. It was the coiled-up body of a parasite cooked to a cinder.

He spit the entire mouthful onto his palm to examine it. There were more little hard tidbits.

Lots more.

"For nuke's sake don't spit out the wire worms," J.B. told him. "They're the best part."

"Nutty," Doc agreed.

Ryan popped the entire gob back in his mouth and gulped it down. Parasites cooked that hard were dead. And their eggs were chilled, too. Protein was protein. Like most Deathlanders, he wasn't all that fussy about food. He just didn't want to crack a tooth on a pebble or a chip of hip bone.

"I've had plenty worse than this," Big Mike bragged, brandishing his half-gnawed haunch in the air like a club. The dripping grease had washed a clean, shiny stripe down his chin. His skin was bright pink under the beard hair. "Worst thing I ever had to eat was a plate of spider stew down in New Mex. Made with hot green chilis and tarantulas as big as your hand."

"Tarantulas aren't edible," Mildred said dubiously.

"Not much meat on them after they're cooked, that's for damn sure, and what little there is you got to suck out of the bodies and legs. Real trouble is, they're covered with all these little hairs that fall off in the stewing. They get caught down your throat and make you gag, so it's hard to keep any of it down. And two hours later I had the squirts thermonuclear."

"Arachnid's revenge," Doc said.

"You'd better believe it was hellfire at both ends," Big

Mike said through a greasy grin. He pressed the haunch to his mouth and greedily tore off another strip of meat with his teeth.

After a dozen mouthfuls of the cloyingly rich meat, Ryan had had enough. The pile of flesh he'd gulped sat like a boulder at the bottom of his stomach. As he had no desire to save the leftovers for breakfast, he tossed the rest of it onto the banked fire for cremation. If all went well, by the next afternoon they'd be off the volcanic plain and along the river where there would be plenty of better forage to choose from.

One by one, emitting various expressions of disgust and discomfort, his companions discarded their haunches as well.

"We've got things to discuss," J.B. said, cleaning the grease smears off his glasses with the tail of his shirt.

Ryan glanced over at Big Mike, who was still chewing happily. Would the bastard betray them if given half a chance? Even without hands? Even after they'd saved his stinkin' hide?

Hell, yes.

"Better do our talking outside," Ryan said. "You stay right where you are," he warned Big Mike. Resting his palm on the pommel of his leg-sheathed panga he said, "Stick your nose out and I'll chop that off, too."

The companions exited the cave and moved away from the entrance, well out of earshot. An overturned bowl of stars lay upon the black blanket of the lava field. It was difficult to see more than a few yards ahead. The clear night had acquired a bone-penetrating chill.

Ryan put his arm around Krysty's waist and pulled her close as they looked up at the brilliant swath of the

Milky Way. He could feel the tension in her body, and though he worried that she was reliving her humiliation at the hands of the she-hes, he didn't say anything, he just gently held her. After a few moments in his embrace she relaxed, snuggled against him and said, "Nice and quiet out here."

"For a change," Mildred said.

"That fat bastard can't stop running his mouth," J.B. said. "You name it, and he's always done one better."

"Or one grosser," Mildred added.

"We have another hellish trek ahead of us tomorrow," Doc said. "Perhaps if we gagged our guest the time would pass more pleasantly?"

"Gagged him and left him behind, you mean," J.B. said.

"We can't part company with Big Mike just yet," Ryan said. "We need the information he's got on the she-hes."

"Why they come back?" Jak asked.

"Mebbe they couldn't find anything better in the alternate universes," Ryan said. "Everything that's missing on their Earth—food, clean air and water, open space, small population—we have plenty of."

"I thought they'd written off Deathlands because of the infection," Krysty said.

When the companions had examined the bodies the she-hes had left behind at Slake City, they found massive, ultimately fatal, bacterial skin infections. The invaders had been caught unprepared by native microscopic organisms.

"They must have found a cure for it off-world,"

Mildred said. "Not unexpected, given the rest of their technology."

"We've got two options come daybreak," Ryan said. "We can either head for the hills or we can take the fight to them, only on our terms this time."

"If we choose to retreat now, dear friends," Doc said, "rest assured these aliens will propagate and then swarm. Like a plague of locusts they will devour the remains of this Earth, just as they devoured their own."

"If we can believe what Big Mike told us," Mildred said, "they've been here at least a few weeks already, setting up their operation. Their weapons, armor and transport are better than anything Deathlands has ever seen. Every day they go unchallenged they're going to get stronger and more difficult to defeat."

"If we run now, we'll be looking over our shoulders until our dying breaths," J.B. said. "I don't like that."

"Then we really don't have a choice, do we?" Krysty said.

"Are we all agreed, then?" Ryan said, looking from face to shadowy face. "We fight them?"

The answer was unanimous and in the affirmative.

"When we last met, the she-hes took us by surprise," Ryan said. "That's why we ended up at Ground Zero in laser manacles. We're going to make sure that doesn't happen again. They still have their tribarrels and EM armor, but from what the Drunkard said they don't have near as many wags as they did before. And mebbe only the single attack aircraft for backup. It doesn't sound like they replaced any of the norm male soldiers they lost, either. It's not going to be easy, no way around that, but we know where they are and they don't know we're coming. We can't let any of them slip away. We've got to chill them all."

After a moment of silence, Mildred said, "They were gone from this universe for a long time. I can't help wondering where they went after they left."

"Wherever it was," Ryan assured her, "we're gonna make them wish they'd stayed there."

Chapter Four

Jak hunkered down on the flank of the ancient cinder cone, making himself as small a target for the wind as he could. In the past hour the breeze had picked up considerably, sweeping across the plain in shrieking gusts, lifting and fluttering his shoulder-length white hair, sandblasting his face with grit. The sawing wail was so loud it drowned out the chattering of his teeth.

His eyes had long since adjusted to the dim light and his perch afforded him a panoramic view downrange, but detail was difficult to pick out. Starshine reflected off planes and edges of rock, and the twisted trunks and branches of limber pines, turning them shades of gray, but the fissures, the rills, the sinkholes—fully three-fourths of the landscape below him—were pitch-black. Occasionally, he caught glimpses of movement, of what appeared to be rolling tumbleweeds—vague, round, silvery shapes that bounded between and vanished into the impenetrable patches of darkness.

He had had the foresight to survey the landscape from this position in daylight, and had mapped it in his mind, marking and memorizing all possible access routes to the cave's back entrance—routes he would have taken if the mission was reversed, if he was the stalker, moving in for the quiet chill. He'd seen no evidence that the cave or the paths to it had ever been used by people, or by animals bigger than chipmunks. Which came as no big surprise. The plain was littered with similar hidey-holes.

As Jak systematically checked and rechecked each of the routes, looking for movement he couldn't otherwise identify and for the glint of starlight reflecting off eyeballs, J.B. was doing the same thing, on the far side of the sinkhole. They had both drawn the second watch.

Despite what had been said in front of Big Mike about their not being followed, nobody had argued when Ryan suggested they post sentries throughout the night. Though pursuit by coyotes and sec men was a longshot, a bivouac in hostile, unknown territory demanded they take customary precautions. They'd been caught off guard before.

If the darkness, cold and wind challenged Jak's skills as a scout, they also challenged his endurance. As strong as he was, as battle-hardened as he was, the effects of exhaustion and lack of sleep, of days of walking under a blazing sun on low rations with minimal water, were taking their toll. His mind kept wandering from the task at hand to his discomfort, and from his discomfort to replays of recent events, including the action plan the companions had discussed and all agreed upon.

They were heading deeper into the turf controlled by the flame-throwing baron and the freshly loaded ammo they carried was a prize he would surely covet. If Burning Man wasn't in a trading mood when they crossed paths, he'd surely try to take it from them by force. Either way, parting with the ammunition wasn't an option. They were going to need every round once they got to Slake City. The only answer was to avoid contact, to bypass the baron's toll bridge and find another way to cross the river to the west.

"Even if we have to build our own barge…" Ryan had told the others.

A buffeting gust of wind jerked Jak back from the vivid memory. He had no idea how long he had been wool-gathering—a second, a minute, five minutes? To wake himself up, he pressed his kneecap into a sharp rock, leaning down with more and more weight until the pain made his red eyes water.

Below him to the right, low on the cinder cone's slope, something moved.

A silent, silver blur against the blackness. There for a second, then it vanished.

There were no straight lines of approach up the cinder cone's slope. Long sections of the winding routes, like the cracks and the gullys, were either sheltered from his view or from the starlight.

Tumbleweed, he told himself. Wiping his eyes with the back of his hand, he watched for it to reappear.

It didn't.

Maybe it fell in a gully, or got pinned against rock slab, he thought.

Holding his breath, Jak strained to hear over the howl of the wind, to pick up the scrape of boot soles, the scratch of claws.

Nothing.

A whole lot of nothing.

Jak found himself wishing for one of the she-he's tribarrel blasters. With one of those babies, he could have lit up the lower slope in an emerald-green flare.

He could have also heated a nearby slab of rock to keep himself warm.

Once again, seemingly of its own volition, his train of thought—and his attention—strayed.

He recalled how the companions had turned captured laser weapons against the invaders. Tribarrels didn't work against the battlesuits' EM shields, so they had used them to alter the nukeglass landscape, to collapse roads that crossed the deep crevasses, taking the invaders down with them.

The captured tribarrels' nuke batteries had soon run out, and with the she-hes having fled to some other universe, repowering them was impossible. Even if they could have recharged the weapons, the tribarrels were designed for one purpose: chilling large numbers of tightly packed human beings. They weren't any good for hunting game. The effect of three laser beams pulsing slightly out of sync produced grievous but cauterized wounds which, if they didn't cause instant death, brought on intense shock. As the animal struggled to escape, nasty-tasting juices were released into the flesh.

A clattering rock slide somewhere on the slope below pulled Jak back into the moment. His hand instinctively dropped to grips of his holstered Colt Python, fingertips tingling from the adrenaline rush.

Fully alert, he strained all his senses trying to locate the source of the sound in the darkness, to pick up the slightest hint of movement. He heard nothing over the wind's wail, saw nothing, smelled nothing. And yet he felt a vague pressure, a presence closing in on him from all sides. His pulse began pounding in his throat and the short hairs on his arms stood erect. The big, predark

Magnum blaster came up in his hand, seeking targets, but there was nothing for him to aim at.

Seconds slipped by and the rush of adrenaline faded, leaving him even more exhausted than before. The sense of building pressure, of being stalked, faded as well. Mebbe he had imagined it because he was so tired? After all, a silent approach over broken, uphill terrain on a moonless night was next to impossible. Must've been the gusting wind that caused the slide, he told himself.

Just as he was about to reholster his blaster, it appeared as if out of thin air in front of him, not five feet away: a face as snow-white, as stoic as his own, blazing reflected starlight. For an instant it was like he was looking into a mirror.

Then the impasto of war paint cracked around a grinning mouth.

The sheer impossibility of it—that someone had scaled the slope, gotten so damned close, without his seeing or hearing *anything*—momentarily froze him. Before Jak could recover and sweep the Python's muzzle three feet to the right, onto the target, the butt of a longblaster came out of nowhere and caught him full on the opposite cheek.

The crunch of impact made lightning flash inside his skull, then everything dissolved into black.

Chapter Five

The naked stickie sprang from a low crouch, its needle teeth bared, sucker fingers outstretched, nostril holes streaming mucous. It hurled itself at Auriel Otis Trask, a blur of lemon-yellow in her battlesuit visor's infrared mode. As the creature reached for her faceplate, it collided with the force field blocking the entrance to its cell. The stickie bounced off the invisible barrier and crashed onto the mine shaft's dusty, thermoglass floor. As it fell it cradled its infant under an arm, taking the full brunt of the impact on its opposite side.

For an instant a smear of snot and sucker adhesive hung in the air like a puff of green smoke, then it was vaporized by the force field.

With its offspring clinging to one stringy teat, the spindly-limbed mutant jumped up and screamed at its tormentors.

Not words.

It emitted a shrill, piping sound, like a blast from a steam whistle. The baby stickie mimicked its mother, adding its even higher-pitched shriek.

Auriel had seen human babies on other replica Earths. Although this infant was bipedal and stereo-optic, it wasn't quite human. There were no cute rolls of fat on its arms and legs; its pale, wrinkled skin sagged in loose folds at the back of its bald head, its buttocks and behind its knees. Its hands and feet were disproportionately large, and the death-grip suckers were already evident on both. As the terrified little stickie pissed a thin arc, Auriel noted the odd—and distinctive—configuration of its male genitalia: a two-horned glans, like a miniature devil's head.

This little mutant had come into the world with a full array of black-edged, needle teeth. Blood dripped along with the clotted secretions from torn nipples, striping its mother's grotesquely distended belly. Because the blood and milk were cooler than Mama's skin, the visor's heat sensors rendered the stripes in bright lime green. There were matching, tiny, circular sucker marks on the flap-jack dugs and upper arms.

The mama stickie drew in a deep breath, preparing to unleash another piercing screech. Under the taut skin of its stomach, Auriel saw movement.

Not the kicking of an unborn stickie.

This was a crossways, sliding movement.

The mutant's black doll's eyes clamped shut, its face twisted in a grimace. Still clutching its infant, the creature doubled over, dropped to its knees and began to moan piteously. The little stickie bawled a counterpoint.

Auriel turned toward Dr. Huth, who stood on the far side of her second in command. Like her, both Dr. Huth and Mero were in fully enabled battlesuits and helmets, self-contained, impermeable microenvironments. Opening the com link she said, "How close are they to hatching?"

The whitecoat handed her a compact instrument with a knurled pistol grip. "Have a look," he said.

Auriel aimed the miniaturized, full-body scanner, holding the four-by-four-inch LCD screen at arm's length so both she and Mero could peer inside the mama stickie and its baby. There was nothing unusual about the infant's innards, but its mother's torso contained something in addition to the expected organs and bones. Something that appeared to be independently alive.

Coils of fluorescent green thicker than the stickie's biceps slid over one another, reversing direction effortlessly—like they had heads at either end.

For the moment, the tightly packed clutch of monsters was contained by thin layers of muscle and dermis, caged by ribs and spinal column. When they were ready to venture into the wider world, they would expand their volume, ballooning in all directions, until the tremendous outward pressure literally blew their host's torso apart. That had been the awful fate of Auriel's mother, while she and her sister warriors helplessly looked on. Once the specters had burst out, once they had unlimited space at their disposal, they would divide, and in minutes the divided segments would regrow to full length, and then divide again. And again. On and on.

In a matter of days, the initial twenty or so specimens could easily become two hundred thousand.

And the air would pulsate with their wakes.

As the commander stared at the enemy through the scanner, not ten feet away, she felt a jumble of sensations: cold fury, frustration and, worst of all, bottomless dread. It appeared that all the pain she had endured while undergoing the Level Four enhancements, all the specialized battlesuit training had been for naught. Maximized physical strength and sense perception, accelerated reaction time, even hard-won technological advancements had proved useless against this unique foe. An enemy that was capable of inconceivable violence, like an asteroid's impact with a planet's surface—merciless, indiscriminate slaughter-to-extinction.

And the bitterest pill to swallow: they had brought the slithering horror upon themselves. They had blindly, inadvertently opened the gates of hell.

Auriel couldn't help but remember her mother's final pronouncement, hissed into her ear through clenched, bloodied teeth: "We are cursed."

She hadn't shared those last words, not even with Mero, who had been Dredda Otis Trask's closest confidante, and was now hers. There was nothing to be gained by the disclosure, and everything to lose. The warriors under her command had already been humbled by the specters, decimated, hounded, chased like rabbits across the realities. Despite calamity and dogged pursuit, their spirit remained strong. Without it Auriel knew they didn't stand a chance. Her sole task was to keep them focused and unified, fighting on until they either escaped this enemy or took their last breaths.

"As you can see," Dr. Huth said, "the specters are about to emerge from this test subject. We will have to abort the experiment momentarily or risk loss of containment."

"Loss of containment" was whitecoat-speak for a repetition of what had happened on the tenth, eleventh and twelfth Earths.

Against her own gut instinct Auriel had agreed to let him bring the seeds of destruction, a tiny sample of the endospores, along with them when they reality-jumped back to Shadow World. In the hectic final minutes on the twelfth Earth, his reasoning had been impossible to argue. They couldn't be certain they had completely sterilized themselves before leaving. The external X-ray treatment might have been insufficient, or they might have already ingested spores, which were so small they were impossible to find. And they couldn't be certain that by jumping universes again, by exposing themselves to the Null again, they wouldn't be recontaminated.

Under strictly controlled, laboratory conditions deep in the mines at Slake City's Ground Zero, Dr. Huth had infected more than a dozen of the indigenous humanoids. If he succeeded in breaking the specters' code with his experiments, if he succeeded in finding a way to destroy them, the warriors wouldn't have to reality-jump again. They could remain on this Earth and establish a permanent power base in Deathlands. If the experiments failed, they would be on the run until their equipment and energy supply were exhausted—one misstep short of annihilation.

"Give me a progress report," Auriel said, lowering the scanner. "Have you found another way to kill them?"

"Tracking the planted endospores with radiation markers hasn't proved as useful as I'd hoped," the whitecoat said. "They appear to locate in the body randomly, whether they are inhaled, swallowed, or absorbed through the skin. Once inside a host, they don't concentrate in any particular organ that can be targeted. They migrate through the tissues and eventually fill all the available empty space inside the torso. This makes removing specters in the endospore stage a very complex, whole-body problem. The level of X-ray radiation necessary to guarantee their complete destruction would certainly destroy the host.

"As we've already determined, the specters are vulnerable after they emerge from the endospores and before they break out of the host's body. If the host is killed while they are still inside it, the specters also die."

"But have you figured out why that happens?" Mero asked.

"The reasons for the simultaneous die-offs remain unclear," Dr. Huth said.

"We've been through all this before," Auriel said, her impatience growing. "Killing every infected host on a planet is logistically and technically impossible. Just as identifying every infected host on an entire planet is impossible. In order to wipe out this threat, we have to be able to destroy the specters in all three of their life stages. To that end what exactly have you accomplished?"

"My attempts to extract tissue and DNA from entities inside the test subjects have so far been unsuccessful," Dr. Huth said. "The samples only contain the tissue and DNA of the host. The specters seem able to avoid a probe inside the host's body same way they avoid laser beams after they break out."

"And what *way* is that?" Auriel said.

"I'm afraid that, too, is unclear at this point," Dr. Huth admitted. He hurried to add, "I do, however, have some working hypotheses…."

Auriel cut him off before he could elaborate further. "Tell me something you know for certain," she said.

"Unfortunately, most of what there is to tell is

negative," Dr. Huth said. "The term 'endospore' that we've been using to describe the protostage is technically inaccurate. The encystation that contains the initial egg form of the specters isn't like the protein coat of a bacterium. Instead of being the organic product of DNA, it's an unusual compound of metallic silica. The fully grown specters appear to have no internal organs or nervous systems, and no external structures such as mouths or eyes. Or at least none that are discernible with the instruments I have at my disposal, and that has become a major focus of concern. These entities are certainly not of this universe, possibly not of any 'universe' that we humans can comprehend. They don't seem to obey the same physical rules as we do. Because of the limitations, perhaps incompatibilities, in our existing technology we may be blind to what's right under our noses.

"For example, I haven't been able to determine how the specters acquire raw materials for growth. From the blood tests I've completed, they don't appear to be taking anything from the hosts except a protected, dark, temperature-controlled environment in which to grow. The incubation time from implantation of endospore to breakout varies widely from species to species, and to a lesser degree from individual to individual. They seem to grow and mature faster inside mutants like stickies. Whether it has to do with their higher normal body temperature or their unique biochemistry is unknown."

"If they aren't taking anything from their victims," Mero said, "why do they go on a kill rampage after they break out and divide?"

"That's another unknown," Dr. Huth said. "Again, it

could be the fault of the instruments. The specters may be acquiring something that I can't yet measure."

It was a poor whitecoat who blamed his tech-gear, Auriel thought.

Her mother had never fully trusted Dr. Huth, perhaps because on their home planet his every breakthrough, his every innovation, had had an unforeseen and catastrophic downside. Auriel had more personal reasons for doubting and despising the man. She could never forget the look on his face was he peered in at her while she, a mere child, lay strapped, helpless in the Level Four isolation tank. The gap-toothed, self-absorbed "genius" had been deaf to her cries of pain and terror as her infant bone, muscle and neurosystem were reengineered, cell by cell. She might as well have been a baby lab rat, or a stickie. And it had been his latex-gloved hands that had excised her nascent reproductive organs. Thanks to Dr. Huth, she would never be a mother, nor even an egg donor.

Thanks to him, she was one of a kind.

Intellectually, Auriel understood the reasons her ovaries had been sacrificed. The male and female sexes each had built-in bioengineering limits, which were dependent upon the amount of body space and chemistry devoted to reproductive functions. Much more of a female's biological potential—hormonally, metabolically, neurologically—was taken up by reproductive duties. If the biochemical obligations of motherhood were removed, there was room for the system to change and grow, and ultimately to evolve. Because a male's reproductive functions took up very little of the body's overall capacity, removing those functions had virtually no effect on biological potential. In other words, the other half of the human species had long since peaked.

Dr. Huth was a normal, genetic male, and that was part of the problem. Biologically, evolutionarily, he was a dead-ender—and he knew it.

As much as the commander loathed the sight of him, he was the only whitecoat they had, and at this point the only whitecoat they were ever likely to find. Whether his scientific expertise was better than none at all, whether it was worth enduring his continued presence, time would tell.

The seated, mama stickie threw back her head and unleashed a bloodcurdling scream. Neck cords standing out, arms locked rigid, heels frantically drummed on the thermoglass. The infant hung on to one breast as the already bloated belly visibly inflated, the skin stretching and stretching until it shined like polished yellow silk. Then the epidermis began to split: a line of bright green along the central seam of stomach muscles. Like the stickie was about to give birth.

Caesarian.

"Time has run out," Dr. Huth said.

"Burn it," Auriel said. "Do it now."

The whitecoat reached a gauntleted hand toward a pair of switches set in the nukeglass beside the cell's opening. One of the switches was a button; the other was protected by a safety cover. He flipped back the cover, exposing a red toggle.

Auriel quickly shifted her visor out of infrared mode to keep from being blinded.

Inside the cell, along the left-hand wall stood three silver-metallic canisters. Hoses ran from the valves on the top of tanks to a rack of stubby nozzles spaced at floor level, knee level and waist level, and they were angled to cover the entire interior, wall to wall, floor to ceiling.

When Dr. Huth hit the switch, mama stickie's cry of agony was accompanied by the mechanical *clack-clack-clack* of the ignition system. The roar of combustion that followed was as loud as a gyro turbine. Its blast of heat penetrated the force field, and slammed the front of Auriel's battlesuit, making her take a reflexive step backward. Inside the cell, temperatures in excess of 2000 degrees Fahrenheit evaporated mutant flesh explosively; the stripped skeletons—one large, one tiny—glowed red for a fraction of an instant, then dissolved. In two seconds mama and baby stickie were reduced to smoke.

Because of its heat-transfer properties, the thermoglass quickly cooled. Auriel surveyed the enclosed space with infrared.

Nothing was left but a deposit of fine ash on the floor and the opposite wall.

No specters.

Farther down the dusty dark of the mine tunnel, the other endospore-implanted stickies began screaming and throwing themselves at their cells' force fields. Like they instinctively knew what had happened even though they couldn't see it, like they were mourning the loss of loved ones.

Which was odd.

As far as Auriel knew, stickies didn't even have names.

Chapter Six

Ryan stumbled over the broken ground, his hands tied in front of him, forty pounds of ammo slapping against his sweat-soaked back. Although seven hours had passed since the surprise attack, his good right eye still wept and it burned like it had been sprayed with wag-battery acid. The inside of his nose and his throat were likewise on fire, and his lungs ached every time he coughed or drew a deep breath.

Similarly bound and burdened, his five companions staggered in a line ahead of him, into the blast furnace heat of the morning.

A dozen armed men with white-painted faces and hair braided in long, single plaits down the middle of their backs herded them along at a rapid pace. The whitefaces moved effortlessly. They seemed to float over the ankle-breaking obstacles of the lava field, and their bootfalls made no sound. Not only had they failed to answer any of the companions' questions since the attack, but they also hadn't spoken a word to one another that Ryan had heard. They communicated with quick touches, nods and hand gestures, giving absolutely nothing away—the sign of a disciplined, seasoned fighting unit. Despite the exertion of the trek and the blazing sun, the whitefaces weren't sweating. And they didn't stop to drink; they didn't even carry their own water with them.

The leader of their captors, a man slightly taller and broader across the shoulders than the others, with a distinctly blocky head, had confiscated Doc's sword stick. Having discovered the hidden rapier blade, he kept unsheathing it and gleefully waving it about, amused by the gadgetry. The companions' blasters had been divvied up, as had all their meager personal possessions. One of the attackers proudly wore Doc's LeMat and its hand-tooled Mexican holster strapped around his waist. Another had taken J.B.'s prized fedora for his own.

The whitefaces all seemed to be enjoying themselves.

And with good reason. Their victory was complete.

They had tracked the companions over the rubble field of the volcanic plain, through a windy, moonless night, and taken them prisoner without firing a blaster shot or sustaining as much as a scratch.

While the companions lay sleeping in the cave chamber, the bastards had dropped gas grens down the campfire vent. There had been no warning because the sentries, J.B. and Jak, had already been taken out. Ryan, Krysty, Mildred and Doc were jolted awake by detonating grens and boiling CS smoke. As the caustic clouds enveloped them, they were blinded by tears and unable to breathe. Somewhere off in the smoke, Big Mike shrieked in terror like a little girl.

Attackers in gas masks had rushed them from both cave entrances at once. In the confusion of jumbled bodies and violent movement, Ryan couldn't be sure who he was punching and kicking, and he couldn't open fire with his SIG in the confines of the chamber without risking hitting the others, either point-blank or with ricochets. Before he and the companions could recover and regroup they were overrun, disarmed, bludgeoned, battered and booted toward the sinkhole entrance of the cave.

Weeping and gasping for air, they stumbled out into the cold night, where they were forced onto their knees. In the starlight, through his streaming tears, Ryan could just make out J.B. and Jak, already tied up, sitting hunched on the ground. Beside him, Big Mike choked and gagged. Then, with a sea-lion roar, he had projectile-vomited every scrap of his greasy, mutie-flesh dinner.

The whitefaces had quickly bound their hands, too, all except for Big Mike, who, of course, had no hands to bind. Still in gas masks, half of the attackers had reentered the cave. They came out carrying the rest of the companions' gear and piled it on the ground.

Ryan and the others had waited for hours huddled together in the middle of the sinkhole, shivering against the wind. The whitefaces didn't seem to notice the chill or their prisoners' racking fits of coughing. They slept in shifts through the night, curled up on the bare plates of lava.

The first rays of daylight had revealed the companions' blood-encrusted noses, split lips and bruised faces. J.B. and Jak had taken the worst of it by far—what looked like repeated club or gun-butt blows to their heads.

From J.B.'s and Jak's expressions, Ryan had realized they were still kicking themselves over what they had allowed to happen. They weren't alone; Ryan was kicking himself, too. He couldn't help but think that if he'd circled wider around the companions' flank on the afternoon recces, that if he'd waited longer on high ground before circling back, he might have seen the whitefaces' dust in the distance, or caught a flash of sun on naked metal. Or if they had set out more sentries, somebody could have at least gotten off a warning shot.

Like J.B. and Jak, like the other companions, Ryan had gone to sleep confident that they'd taken appropriate precautions under the circumstances; that they were, in fact, being extra-careful, all things considered.

The problem was, they had never faced a human enemy with anything close to this level of field skill—tracking ability, night vision, footspeed, stealth, knowledge of terrain—so there was no way to anticipate the danger they faced.

What was done was done.

If they were going to survive the stunning defeat, they had to learn whatever they could from it, bank their anger and focus all their attention on turning the tables and making a timely escape.

Shortly after dawn, the whitefaces had given them each a swig of the bottled water that was left, loaded them down with backpacks and set them marching southeast, in the direction of the Snake River. The pace would have been brutal even without the extra weight, the broken terrain and the lingering effects of CS gas on their lungs.

So far, Ryan had seen no wiggle room in their predicament. No opening to exploit. Not with the weight on their backs slowing them, and their hands tied so they couldn't shrug out of the pack straps. The whitefaces kept their distance, too. And whenever any of them approached their captives up close, they always had at least a half-dozen weapons aimed and unblocked lanes of fire.

They were obviously well-versed in holding and moving groups of prisoners.

None of that boded well for making an escape, or for the companions' future if they didn't get away. In Ryan's experience, Deathlanders this accustomed to taking prisoners were usually in the slavery business, either trading them away for jack or jolt, or working them until they dropped dead.

As he trudged onward, Ryan had to keep glancing down at the ground a few steps ahead, constantly focusing on his footing to keep from falling or twisting an ankle. With his hands tied, he couldn't swing his arms as he walked, which made balance and forward progress even more difficult. The effects of the long march and the day's building heat had begun to take their toll on him as well. His thigh muscles had started to spasm, as if they were about to cramp up. And his tongue felt swollen, too big for his mouth.

Signs of dehydration.

When the whitefaces finally stopped to give them the last of the water, the sun was at its zenith. There was no shade on the hell-blasted plain. The companions couldn't sit on the baking black rock, so they stood in their packs, dripping sweat, and gulped what they were given.

Not enough, Ryan thought as he swallowed the scant mouthful of bathtub-warm backwash. Not nearly enough.

Krysty was glaring at the whiteface dispensing the refreshments, the one with J.B.'s fedora tipped back jauntily on his head. Half-turning to the others she said,

"What's the point of the white paint? Is it to protect them from sunburn? Or is it supposed to scare us because they look like ghosts?"

"No paint on hands or arms," Jak offered.

A fact that Ryan had noted as well. In daylight their exposed skin was tanned a dark, ruddy brown.

"They look like Native Americans to me," Mildred said. "Could the makeup have something to do with the Ghost Dance ritual? I can't recall the details, but I think it originated somewhere around here in the late nineteenth century."

"The Ghost Dancers of my era colored their faces red, not white," Doc informed her, "with black half-moons decorating their cheeks. Unlike these fellows, they wore red shirts, red-striped leggings and tied dead small animals and birds in their hair. They believed that all the natives who danced the Ghost Dance, no matter the tribe, would be lifted into the sky while the earth swallowed up their enemy, the whites. After which the planet would revert back to its natural state, with new soil, sweet grass, running water, trees, and herds of buffalo and wild horses. Then the dancers and the ghosts of all their ancestors would be returned to the earth to live in peace. It appears what we are looking at is either a bastardization of that original vision, or something entirely unrelated."

"Guess the dancing didn't work, then," Krysty said.

"I seem to remember their ghost shirts were supposed to stop bullets, too," Mildred said.

"A claim that also proved false," Doc said. "Based on our location, my guess is these warriors are related to the Bannock-Shoshone. A people whose tragedy was largely forgotten, in part because much of it occurred in the middle of the Civil War, in part because the dominant culture of the day, my own culture sadly, considered their existence nothing more than an impediment to progress and profit.

"Their reservation, to the south and east of here, had the misfortune of being set along the main supply route to the Montana gold rush. Conflicts between miners and natives ended in the Bear River massacre of 1863. Members of a volunteer infantry regiment killed 250 of 450 Shoshone, including 90 women and children. The women who wouldn't submit to gang rape by the soldiers were slaughtered, shot or clubbed to death. The heads of their infants were bashed in. Fifteen years later, starvation forced the Bannock off the reservation. After they killed some settlers, a second, full military campaign was launched against them. The fighting ended when Bannock lodges were attacked and all the women and children were killed."

"Am I sensing a pattern?" Krysty said.

"You are," Mildred said. "It's called genocide."

"Attempted genocide, most certainly," Doc said. "The tribe endured, albeit greatly reduced in numbers. And if my surmise is correct, they managed to survive the nukecaust as well."

"Only now they're all mute?" Krysty said.

"It's been more than a century since nuke day," Mildred said. "Maybe they don't speak our language."

"Whoever these nukin' bastards are," J.B. growled, clearly impatient with both the history lesson and the speculation, "they came out here after big mouth and the one the coyotes ate." Absent his favorite hat, he had a distinct tan line across the middle of his forehead. Above the line the skin was pink from sunburn, as was his scalp.

He leaned closer to Ryan and the others and lowered his voice so Big Mike couldn't overhear him. "That lying pile of crap must mean something to them," he said. "As far as I can see he's the only target of opportunity we've got. I say we all jump his sorry ass, and threaten to chill him on the spot if they don't let us go. They'll understand the sign language if they see me choking the living shit out of him."

Ryan frowned. His old friend was grasping at straws, and that wasn't like him. Maybe J.B. had suffered a mild concussion during the surprise attack? Or maybe it was the combined effect of exhaustion, heat and dehydration? Or maybe he just wanted to get payback, somehow, someway, on someone for the humiliation of being taken prisoner without a shot fired?

Even though J.B. hadn't come right out and said "I told you so," Ryan knew he was damn well thinking it, and that that, too, had to be adding fuel to his fury. No doubt about it, J.B. had been right. If they'd never gone for the look-see, they would have most likely bypassed this fix.

But being right didn't change the present circumstances.

"It won't work, J.B.," Ryan said. "They're not going to let you chill their prize, if that's what he is. The only reason we're still alive is they want us to carry the ammo for them. They don't need all of us to do that, and worse comes to worst, they can always carry it themselves. If you're right about Big Mike, and you make a grab for him, they'll shoot you and as many of the rest of us as it takes to get him back."

Before J.B. could respond, the whiteface who had liberated his fedora jabbed a longblaster muzzle hard into his kidney, making him groan and take an involuntary, stagger-step forward.

The signal for all of them to get moving.

To emphasize the order, the rest of the whiteface crew held their weapons shouldered and aimed, again with clear firing lanes. When the column began to advance, Ryan fell in line behind Krysty and Mildred.

As they continued southeast, toward the low curve of the horizon, Big Mike dropped back from the front of the file until he was lumbering and puffing right alongside Ryan. His arms were free, and he had no load on his back, but the huckster still had trouble keeping up the pace.

"We've got to find a way to escape before they get us to the river," he wheezed. "After that it'll be too late. We'll never get away from them."

When Ryan didn't immediately respond, Big Mike pressed on. "These whitefaces, you know damn well they aren't norms," he said through clenched teeth. "You ever heard of a norm who could follow a trail at night like that, over rocky ground? It must be over a hundred degrees out here, we're dying of thirst, and they haven't broken a sweat or taken a sip of water. I'm telling you they've got to be some kind of mutie. The kind that look norm on the outside, but are all mutified inside. Listen to me, Cawdor, we're nothing but sheep to the slaughter once they get us to the river. I saw their crazy-ass baron up close. I looked into his eyes. He gets his hands on us he's going to cook us alive, every one of us, sure as hell smells like shit."

"Seems to me you're the only one Burning Man is after," Ryan said evenly. "Why would he fry the rest of us? Just for a laugh? We've got both our hands. We can work for him. After he makes you spill your guts, all you're going to be good for is flamethrower practice."

Big Mike glowered at him from behind his mask of grime, but even with arms free he didn't have the stones for a direct confrontation. Muttering a string of profanities under his breath, he dropped further back in line until he was well out of Ryan's sight.

A lot of what Big Mike said made sense, but no way would Ryan ever admit that to him. Not only was he certain that Big Mike would sell them out in a heartbeat to save his own stinking skin, but in a breakout attempt his 350 pounds would also be so much deadweight, at best rolling cover for them, a bullet sponge. Because of that, it was best to keep him in the dark on their escape plan, or the current lack of same.

Notwithstanding the comment about the companions' value as laborers, Ryan knew there was a chance that Burning Man would cook them all for show, for crossing his land, or for something imaginary, and at the first opportunity. He had come across few barons who weren't by nature murdering bastards.

It was also possible that Burning Man was a mutie with a grudge. In the Deathlands, those with visible mutations were not only excluded from all-norm villes, when caught they often got the short end of a rope, or the pointy end of a pitchfork.

That the whitefaces might not be norm had occurred

to Ryan, too. They seemed to be able to do things regular folks couldn't, but in the absence of all the facts, he knew appearances could be deceiving. He saw nothing unusual about their heights or builds, which fell into the standard range—some taller, some shorter, some thinner, some heavier. Their features were hard to make out under the layer of paint and their thick braids concealed the backs of their necks, so an extra ear hole or nose hole or vestigial gills couldn't be ruled out. But without hard evidence to the contrary, it was just as likely that their abilities were the result of centuries of passed-down experience and skills, and intimate knowledge of their home turf.

In the end, whether the whitefaces were muties or norms made no difference. Whatever the source of their advantage, they were in control of the situation.

By the time they reached the edge of the lava field an hour later, his eye had finally stopping weeping. The burning inside his nose and throat was gone as well. The whitefaces had held their distance and maintained their discipline, leaving no opportunity for escape. Ahead of them, the sea of black rock ended and beyond it was a swath of pale, fine dirt stretching all the way to the horizon line—the river's ancient flood plain. At the distant join of sky and earth Ryan could see a thin band of green. Trees and scrub, he guessed, growing along the shore of the river. Maybe agricultural fields, too.

To their right, in the sea of beige dirt about one hundred yards distant, stood a corral. The standposts were made of bark-stripped, limber pine trunks, and they were strung with what looked like bailing wire. The whitefaces changed course, steering their prisoners toward the ramshackle pen. Inside the corral, Ryan could see at least a dozen horses, chestnuts, pintos, all of them unsaddled. There was a water trough and a storage shanty with a rusting, corrugated steel roof.

The whitefaces brought the column to a halt at the corral fence. While the companions waited, their sweat dripping into the powdery dirt, Blocky Head led three of his warriors over to the shanty and disappeared inside.

"Ryan, we're nuked," J.B. said as they stared at the milling animals.

No argument, there.

With the whitefaces mounted on horseback, the prospect of the companions making a successful escape wasn't just remote, it was nonexistent. Horses couldn't be outrun, and blasters were no longer necessary to keep the prisoners under control. The big bodies and hooves would do that nicely.

"Three miles to river," Jak said.

"I don't see these bastards making a mistake between here and there, not on horseback," J.B. said.

"And when we get to the river," Ryan said, "we're going to be even more outnumbered, mebbe separated and probably chained, necks and ankles."

"What are we going to do?" Krysty said.

"We only have one option that I can see, and it isn't good," Ryan told her. "When we arrive at the river, if we get the chance, we've got to go for the highest value target—like J.B. suggested."

"Only this time the target is Burning Man?" Mildred said.

"Nukin' right!" J.B. said. "Separate the baron from the rest of his crew. Take him hostage, get some weapons, then chill him and as many others as we can. We don't want these bastards trailing us again."

"But are you not overlooking one critical point?" Doc said. "How are we going to fight with our hands tied and our backs loaded down like this?"

"They might shift the packs to the horses," Mildred said.

"But even if they don't," Ryan said, "they're not going to roast us carrying all this ammo. It's way too valuable, not to mention the danger of cook-offs. My guess is they'll remove the packs when we get to the river. If they unload us one at a time, we wait until the last pack is off, then go for it. If they unload us all at once, follow my lead. Straight at him. Get control of him, no matter what."

"And if we don't get the chance?" Krysty said.

"Worse comes to worst," Ryan said, "we're just going to have to hunker down. We've done it before. Sit tight and wait for our opening."

"If the whitefaces had all these horses," Mildred said, "why didn't they use them to go after Big Mike?"

"Lava triple hard on horses," Jak said.

"You're right," Ryan said. "Treacherous footing, no trails, no water. Not to mention all the dust a dozen horses would raise, and the noise they'd make on the rocks. Whitefaces on horseback would be too far from the ground to follow tracks at night. They couldn't ride. They'd have to walk the animals behind them, anyway."

The whitefaces exited the shanty carrying bridles and reins. Blocky Head had a long coil of manila rope slung over his shoulder. Half his men held the companions at blasterpoint while he used the rope to cinch the companions neck-to-neck, like shell beads on a string. Ryan was the first bead. The rest of the whitefaces entered the corral and started bridling all the horses.

That done, four of them grabbed Big Mike from behind and bum-rushed him through the corral's gate. He thrashed and fought, trying to dig in his heels, but they hoisted him astride the bare back of a chestnut mare. He looked around, stunned.

He wasn't the only one.

"Perfect," J.B. snarled. "We walk and the lying sack of shit rides."

"They probably don't want to risk him dropping dead before they reach the river," Mildred said.

"Mebbe he'll fall off and break his neck," J.B. said.

When the whitefaces mounted up, one of them had hold of the end of their tether. He walked his horse forward, jerking Ryan and the others along. It was clear the backpacks weren't going to be shifted to the horses.

At a hand signal from Blocky Head, one of the whitefaces dug his heels into his horse's flank and rode ahead at a gallop, toward the river.

Six horses behind the companions, six in front, they began to advance in the same direction as the rider. Blocky Head gripped the reins on Big Mike's mount, leading the animal behind him. Walking on the soft dirt was much easier for Ryan and the others, but they had to move faster or be pulled off their feet. And they had to eat the dust kicked up by the horses in front of them.

Gradually, the tree line came into better focus. Ryan saw stunted scrub in patches amid cultivated fields. Beyond them, to the east across the flatland, was a gridwork of ruined streets and buildings, a predark ville burned and gutted down to the foundation slabs. At what appeared to be the ville's center, all that was left of a large, two-story structure was a disintegrating section of ornate, red-brick outer wall. The skeleton of a high water tower overlooked the destruction.

Ryan couldn't see the river, but caught a glimpse of the far side of the bridge between the clumps of trees. It was a double span, white concrete blazing in the sun, as Big Mike had described. Then it was gone, hidden behind the line of scrub.

They walked the rutted borders of unfenced corn, beans, onions, tomatoes, peppers, all irrigated by a series of shallow ditches. From the size of crop, Ryan guessed the local population was a couple hundred people, at most. An insignificant number pre-nukeday, but a sizeable community by Deathlands standards. No one was working in the fields; the afternoon was too damn hot.

The track between the fields led to a ruined predark roadway. Blocky Head turned the column east on old 84 and followed the edge of the string-straight road-bed to the foot of the bridge. Like the highway, it had seen much better days. Some of the bridge supports were gone, eroded away, washed out or knocked out by debris. The upriver span had a fifteen-foot-wide gap in it, where the deck had collapsed into the current. The downriver span was intact—two lanes, with corroded steel guardrails on either side. In the middle of the bridge a crowd of people had gathered, no doubt alerted to the captives' arrival by the rider Blocky Head had dispatched.

The whiteface warriors were welcomed home with

raucous cheers, whistles and a volley of gunshots fired into the air.

Blocky Head walked his horse onto the bridge, towing Big Mike and his steed after him. The whiteface holding the neck tether rode onto the span as well, pulling the row of captives forward.

From the foot of the bridge, Ryan could see white smoke curling up into the sky on the south side of the river, but any dwellings there were well out of sight. To his right, on the shoulder of the deck near the guard-rail, were a series of man-sized, blackened grease spots. Fragments of charred material were stuck to the surface of the concrete—what looked to be pieces of bone, as well as an empty boot and a dirty white sock.

"By the Three Kennedys," Doc groaned, averting his face.

The overwhelming odor of cooked human flesh forced Ryan to breathe through his mouth.

Ahead, the crowd on the bridge pointed at the prisoners, catcalled, hooted and laughed. Men, women and children were all in whiteface. Whether the paint was ceremonial, dabbed on for the special occasion, or everyday wear, was impossible to tell. Some of the people wore denim bib-fronts like Big Mike; others had on holed-out shorts and T-shirts. All of the men carried longblasters. Most of them were well-worn, bolt-action hunting rifles, but there were a few remade AK-47s and M-16s mixed in.

The crowd parted before the advancing horses, moving to stand on either side of the bridge, and as they did, the boos and the shouts got even louder. The assembled whitefaces pelted Big Mike with small rocks and gobs of spit. He hid behind his prosthesis, trying to protect his face.

The Snake River toll booth was made of piled-up old tractor wheels and tires, and wrecked wags, a crudely fortified emplacement that narrowed the bridge's two lanes to less than one, and offered clear fields of fire that commanded the span in either direction. In front of the barrier a sunshade made from a brown plastic tarp was stretched between a rusting tractor's engine cowl and the cab of an ancient water truck. Under the canopy, on a dais made of stacked wooden pallets, a lone figure lounged on a molded plastic chair, his unlaced combat boots propped up on a 100-quart cooler.

It had to be none other than Burning Man himself.

A flamethrower sat on the dais beside the cooler, close to hand. The weapon looked homemade. Ryan guessed the double, side-by-side steel tanks had once held compressed air. The flamethrower's frame was made of crudely welded scrap metal and its padded, ballistic nylon shoulder straps had been stripped off a backpack. Six feet of armored hose connected the twin tanks to a nozzle assembly consisting of a two-foot length of pipe mounted with clamps onto a metal stock that featured a pair of pistol grips. Silver gauntlets and a matching hood lay on top of the tanks.

Upwind of the stench of carbonized human remains, Ryan caught a whiff of the pressurized wag fuel coming off the dais. Needless to say, there was no open flame anywhere near it. The block lettering on the side of the red truck's tank was badly faded, but legible. It read: Volunteer Fire Dept., Rupert, Idaho. He wondered if the water truck was there to put out the flames of innocent bystanders.

Ryan stole a quick glance behind them and saw that the mounted whitefaces had lined their horses shoulder-to-shoulder across the north end of the span, barring any retreat in that direction. They were trapped between the horses and the barricade. When he looked back, along both sides of the bridge, the crowd was beginning to move. As the women and children deserted the right-hand lane, all the men took positions along the left. Their weapons were aimed low, but held at the ready.

A firing squad waiting for orders.

In a matter of seconds, dozens of longblasters were lined up between them and Burning Man. No way could they hope to reach him before they were shot to pieces. Ryan moved closer to Krysty, shielding her from the blaster muzzles with his own body. As he did so, he peered over the bridge rail, into the river downstream. The channel below the span was very deep, the water green and sluggishly flowing.

Not only couldn't they make a rush for the baron, they couldn't escape via the river. Even if they managed to move as a unit, connected at the neck, and simultaneously jumped the rail without being hit, they couldn't hope to wriggle out of the packs and ropes before they drowned.

The man on the dais called out, "Bring 'em closer!"

As the companions were yanked forward by the horseman, the whitefaced baron rose from his seat. A pair of dark-tinted goggles were perched on top of his head. Under them, his long, graying hair was parted in the middle and braided into twin plaits, which were tied at the ends with strips of leather. His gray beard, braided into short pigtails and likewise tied, only grew on the left side of his face. The right side was completely hairless, no eyelashes, no eyebrows, and covered with a massive, disfiguring scar that ran from chin to forehead. The eyelid caught in the middle was mangled and drooping.

Layers of white paint, no matter how thickly applied, could not hide that half-melted face.

His NOMEX jumpsuit had once been silver; now most of it was blue black from grease stains and ground-in dirt. The suit was unzipped to the navel, and his bare chest bore patches of scar, like splatters of thick, pink candle wax.

The baron jumped down from the dais and strode across the bridge deck.

Ignoring Blocky Head and Big Mike, Burning Man stared at Ryan, and as he did, a broad grin twisted the left half of his face. The right side remained expressionless, immobilized by the rigid plate of scar.

There was something vaguely familiar about the baron, but Ryan couldn't recall where he had seen him before. As the man in the fireproof suit stepped closer, he racked his brain for an answer. If he and the others had run across this bastard, it was something that could potentially save their lives.

Or end them.

Then, still lopsidedly grinning, the baron reached out, clapped a grimy hand on Ryan's shoulder, and said, "Welcome to my world, Shadow Man."

Chapter Seven

Staring hard at the intact half of the baron's face, Ryan finally realized where he'd seen him before. "Captain Connors?" he said.

"Sure as hell is, Cawdor," Burning Man said. "It's been a long time. I guess you could say I've changed a little since we last set eyes on each other."

The baron immediately turned to the firing squad, waving his arms in the air. He shouted at them, "Stand down, stand down! These are comrades." Then to the warriors waiting on horseback he said, "Cut them loose. Do it quickly."

As Blocky Head and the other rider dismounted, whipped out sheath knives and started slicing the bonds from their necks and wrists, the companions looked to Ryan for an explanation.

"You know this guy?" Mildred said.

"Who the hell is he, Ryan?" Krysty said.

"Connors was the geologist for the first Shadow Earth invasion," Ryan told them. "He was there at Moonboy ville with Gabhart, Ockerman, Hylander and Jurascik. You only saw him at a distance, and never outside of his cockroach suit. I saw him up close and personal without the battle armor when they took me prisoner, before they made me jump to the parallel Earth. The way I understand it, Connors was supposed to circle around to the rear of your position and cut off your retreat. Instead, he disappeared from the battlefield. He's the expedition's lost man."

"Don't you mean deserter?" J.B. said, rubbing at his abraded wrists.

Then to Burning Man he said, "You know your fellow cockroaches thought you were chilled?"

"Let's just say I suddenly became aware of other, more promising opportunities," the baron replied.

"So did they, eventually," Ryan said. "They helped us close the passage between our world and yours to stop the invasion."

"I had guessed as much," Burning Man said.

"Only they're all dead for real, now," Ryan said. "Dead and buried."

The baron shrugged. "That's not an altogether unexpected development," he said. "I don't have to tell you folks what a hostile and unforgiving place the Deathlands is, even for the well-prepared."

"We found what was left of their bodies at the ruins of Moonboy ville," Krysty said. "And it wasn't Deathlands that chilled them. It was the second wave of invaders from your parallel Earth."

"Your pals could have used you in the fight," J.B. said.

Burning Man pointed to the wrecked half of his face. "As you can see," he said, "I've had some problems of my own."

"With a wound like that," Mildred said, "you're lucky you didn't die of massive infection."

"The native people hereabouts took care of me after I was injured, and they nursed me back to health," the baron said. "It took a long time for me to recover. We learned about the second invasion too late to do anything about it."

"And precisely what were you prepared to do?" Doc said.

"Destroy them by any means," the baron growled without hesitation. "No matter the cost."

"So you've had a change of heart, then?" Krysty said.

"I can't deny I was on the other side when I first arrived," Burning Man said. "But because of who I used to be, I know what the people from my Earth are capable of, and what their endgame looks like. Their advanced technology would do to this planet precisely what it did to mine—decimate it beyond any hope of recovery. The nukecaust calamity here was horrendous, but on this world—now my adopted world—life and hope still survive. A future of some sort is still possible here. Like you all, I believe that hope is worth fighting for and dying to defend. By the time the warriors and I arrived at Slake City ready to do battle, the base there was already deserted, abandoned." He glanced at Ryan. "Did you have something to do with that?"

"We did our best to encourage them to leave," Ryan replied. "But they didn't jump universes to get away from the likes of us. They left Deathlands to save themselves from something invisible. Turns out, Deathlands' smallest microscopic critters were eating the she-hes alive."

"What do you mean, 'she-hes'?" the baron asked, a frown twisting the mobile side of his face.

"Genetically enhanced females," Mildred told him. "Your home planet's superwarriors."

Burning Man seemed taken aback. After a pause he said, "Years ago, just before my expedition jumped to Deathlands, I heard rumors about ongoing research programs. The speculation was that the CEOs of the ruling conglomerate each had launched their own, ultrasecret lines of inquiry. Only a handful of the top corporate whitecoats knew any of the details, but the general idea was to create a new human subspecies that maximized biological potential—ultimate soldiers who could overwhelm and destroy the armies of the conglomerate's competing members, and who stood a better chance of conquering and colonizing parallel Earths. As far as I know, the programs were still in the experimental stage when we left."

"The experiment worked," Mildred said flatly.

Ryan nodded toward Big Mike. "According to him," he said, "the she-hes have returned to Slake City and are taking another shot at conquest."

"When I got a look at all the clean, fresh stumps on those sniveling cowards," Burning Man said, "the first thing I thought was, more invaders. I saw thousands of wounds just like them on my Earth. The laser cuffs were developed in the run-up to the Consumer Rebellion, a devastating weapon, psychologically and physiologically. The Population Control Service ordered us to use the technology on our own citizens to put down the Gloomtown riots. Not the proudest moment in my military career."

Blocky Head set one of the packs at the baron's feet and whispered something into his ear.

J.B. shot Ryan a look. The one-eyed man knew they

were both thinking the same thing: so the bastards can talk after all.

The baron knelt and opened the pack. He lifted out a gallon-sized, plastic bag filled with shiny 7.62 mm NATO rounds. "These will definitely come in handy," he said, waving the bag at Ryan.

"If we're all on the same team now," Ryan said as warriors picked up and shouldered all the ammo packs, "how about giving back our blasters and blades?"

"That can wait," Burning Man said. "You're not in any danger here, I assure you of that. My apologies for the rough treatment, but I certainly wasn't expecting you to turn up in these parts. The warriors assumed you were part of the fat coward's crew, and acted accordingly. You must all be tired as well as hungry and thirsty. Please follow me and we'll see to your needs."

As Burning Man turned toward the barricade, he pointed a finger at Big Mike and addressed Blocky Head. "Besup," he said, "bring that one along, too. Take him to the stockade. He and I have matters to discuss in private."

Two beaming, whitefaced women picked up the flamethrower by the shoulder straps, hoisting it between them, holding it high overhead, like a trophy. A gang of gleeful children squabbled and scuffled over who got to carry the silver gauntlets and hood.

Ryan and the companions followed the baron through the toll gate. Behind them trouped the rest of the ville. The gate opening was steeply angled, so no one could run or drive straight through it. Foot, horse and wag traffic had to slow to a crawl and present itself broadside to the barricade's hardened firing ports.

The whitefaced kids sitting atop the tier of tractor tires looked healthy and well fed. For that matter, everyone on the bridge did. That was unusual in the hellscape, where bloated bellies, stick arms and legs and weeping sores were more often the tragic rule than the exception.

At the far end of the bridge, ahead on the river flood plain, they got their first glimpse of Burning Man's ville. It was a typical Deathlands defensive compound. The perimeter consisted of a ten-foot-high berm made of pounded dirt and big boulders of river rock. It was topped by crosses of metal I-beams and scavenged wood that held coils of barbed wire in place. A crude roadway of crushed black rock led to the fortified entrance, a steel-plate barrier mounted on a set of wag wheels and frame that could be pulled out of the way by horse or manpower. Three-story-high guard towers overlooked the approaches from the river and from the plain behind the ville, to the southeast. It was as secure a stronghold against conventional weaponry that Ryan had come across.

As they stepped through the gate, they were greeted by a pack of twenty or more snarling dogs. The big-headed hundred-pounders threw themselves at the heavy wire mesh enclosure that kept them penned just inside the berm's entrance. All of them were stamped from the same mongrel mold: short hair in a variety of mixed colors, short curly tails, short powerful legs and muscular bodies. They bared their fangs, drooling, their yellow eyes full of blind rage. Their combined weight bulged the wire alarmingly, but the deeply buried fenceposts held.

War dogs, Ryan thought.

Bred to chill.

Trained to target any scent that did not belong to their owner-handlers. Turned loose on the battlefield, they were silent stalkers and savagely efficient hunters. In the Mutie Wars, similar critters had been used—roaming packs that infiltrated and routed the misbegotten enemy from its hardsites and sniper outposts. Ryan had seen war dogs follow a kill scent for miles through a sewer pipe two feet across.

"Enough!" Burning Man shouted at the animals. And as if he'd flicked a switch, the show of aggression shut off. Ears pricked up, the monsters wagged their curly tails and panted through broadly smiling mouths.

Ahead were rows of closely set, single-story hovels cobbled together with found items—sheet metal, scraps of plywood, concrete block. With no fresh materials to work with, the individual dwellings had a familiar, Deathlands' look to them. But this wasn't the typical, slapdash shantytown. The ville's layout was much better organized: the lanes between huts, although narrow, were set out in straight lines, the paths made of crushed stones and bordered with functional drainage ditches, and they ended, like the spokes of a wheel, in the enclosure's central hub.

At the end of the lane Ryan could see into the wide patch of open ground. Its main feature was a circular building, broad, low to the ground, with scrap plywood walls and a shallowly pitched roof made of limbs, logs, and heaped dirt. A kiva, a communal meeting house. The central plaza was dotted with a few semitrailers sitting on bare rims. Ryan figured they were storehouses. Pigs and goats had their own fenced pens. Chickens ran wild and free. There was also a rock-and-mortar structure that Ryan guessed had to be a well or cistern. The ville had its own protected water supply, which was a strategic plus in case of a siege.

As they headed for the kiva's entrance, Besup led Big Mike around the cistern toward the rear of one of the semitrailers. Women and children followed close behind the huckster-on-horseback, yelling insults at him and throwing not just rocks, but handfuls of horse and goat dung.

"Big Mike really made an impression on them," Mildred said.

"Do not fret an instant over the fate of that wretched bastard," Doc said. "Whatever he gets, you can be confident he has more than earned."

"Believe me," Mildred said, "I'm not worried about him. I just wondered what he did to piss them off so much."

"This way," Burning Man said, waving them through the kiva's entrance, down a flight of steps into the wide, relatively cool room. Sun streamed in through skylights made of scavenged, double-hung windows, and through the building's central smoke vent, which stood above a large firepit. The openings in the roof created brilliant pools of light on the packed dirt floor of the otherwise darkened room. The place reeked of ancient wood smoke—sweet and at the same time sour.

Burning Man gestured for them to sit at the benches that bracketed a long, crude, plank table.

Three gleeful, plump women entered the kiva, bearing jugs of water, which they handed to each of the companions.

Jak tipped back his jug, glugging hard, spilling a cascade of water down his chin and chest.

"Not too fast," Mildred warned him. "Sip it. Pace yourself. Or you'll just puke it back up."

The water tasted real good to Ryan, too. He had to fight the urge to gulp it all down without pausing for breath.

"The food will be along shortly," Burning Man said as the women scurried back up the steps.

After his immediate thirst was satisfied, Ryan set down the jug. Like Mildred, he was puzzled by the ville's reaction to Big Mike's return. The level of hostility didn't fit the story the huckster had told.

"If you really figured the amputees were the victims of a new wave of invaders," Ryan said to the baron, "why did you cook them to cinders on the bridge deck? They were on your side, too."

"And why do you keep calling them cowards?" Mildred added. "Because they ran from the she-hes?"

"They were worse than cowards," Burning Man said. "They were Deathlands scum. They showed up at the ville gate around midday, half-starved, dehydrated and missing their hands."

"The fat one told us you wanted a toll to let them cross the bridge," Ryan said. "He said they didn't have anything of value and that's why you started chilling them. Out of sheer spite."

"If he told you that, he lied to you," Burning Man said. "The amputees came up from the south, from Slake City. They didn't try to cross the Snake River bridge, they came to the ville gate first, begging to come inside for food, water and protection. It was plain from looking at them they had nothing worthwhile to trade. I offered them help because I wanted information about how they got those injuries. Besides, they were in a bad way and it seemed like the proper thing to do. Right after we let them through the gate, the bastards grabbed some of the littlest children as hostages. Toddlers. They did it all at once, on a signal—clearly their plan from the start. While they held blades at the children's throats, the fat one with the artificial hand said they wanted our food, blasters, ammo and horses in exchange for the lives of the babies."

"Dark night!" J.B. spit.

"My sentiments, exactly," the baron said. "Turned out they were nothing but a pack of thieving coldhearts. And from the looks on their faces, after they used our children as shields for their escape, when the babies were no longer of any use, it was clear they were going to get rid of them. Leave 'em in the road to starve or chill 'em straightaway. If the bastards had known anything about recent history in these parts, they would have thought twice about trying a kidnapping. The local folks don't take kindly to the idea of their own being captured and held hostage. Everybody in the Snake River valley knows the rules we live by. Women, children, it doesn't matter who's been taken. We never negotiate for human lives. We chill the hostage takers and bury our dead."

"But you didn't fight them here, in the ville?" Ryan said.

"No sense in shooting up our own home," Burning Man said. "We let them take their hostages as far as the bridge and the north side of the toll booth before we sprung the trap. When the cowards realized the fix they were in, that it was over, that they were going to die on the bridge span, no matter what they did, they panicked, let the children go and turned to run. That's when I cut loose on them with the flamethrower."

"But you didn't get them all," Krysty said.

"I did that on purpose," the baron assured her. "I let a pair of them get away, and then called off the pursuit. One of the two, the fat loudmouth back there, was the ringleader. I figured it was only fair that he and the other coward spent some quality time out on the lava field before the warriors dragged them back here."

"The other one got eaten alive by mutie coyotes," Krysty said.

"That's what I mean by 'quality time,'" Burning Man said.

The baron smiled with the uninjured half of his face, but the light that flashed in his eyes was no joke. It was like the dropping of a veil, or like turning over a slab of rock and finding something coiled and venomous-deadly beneath.

Something all too familiar.

Ryan had seen that same look of delight countless times before, on the faces of other Deathlands' barons, of its coldhearts, of its chiller muties. And he wasn't surprised to see it now. After all, what kind of human being routinely cooked other people, guilty or not, in their own juices instead of blowing out their brains with a single blaster shot, or hanging them from the nearest tree limb? What kind of human being chased other people across a hellish wasteland for the sole purpose of prolonging their suffering?

Burning Man's disfigurement went far deeper than skin and muscle.

His acts of cruelty weren't just calculations, entertainments for the villefolk, a way to instill fear and therefore obedience. Ryan knew his injuries were of the inner kind as well, grievous wounds of the soul. Whatever terrible things had been done to Captain Connors after his departure from Moonboy, the recovery of his sense of safety and power had been translated into outdoing his torturers, into returning the pain he had suffered, and was probably still suffering, a hundredfold and at every opportunity. Under the facade of a generous, caring leader, beneath Burning Man's flaking white face paint, lurked something unpredictable and dangerous.

"What was the local history you mentioned?" Doc asked the baron.

The old man's question appeared to break Burning Man's train of thought. The rock slab slammed back down; the light winked out.

"And what happened to the predark town on the other side of the river?" Mildred added. "Was it destroyed in the nukecaust?"

At that moment the women returned; this time they carried steaming bowls, big metal spoons and stacks of small, woven-reed baskets. As the food was laid out on the table before them, the baron answered one of the companions' questions. "Rupertville survived nukeday without a scratch," he said. "What happened over there is a long, ugly story, and I don't want to put you off your meal."

"Not much chance of that," Ryan said after he took a

whiff of the meat stew. His mouth immediately started to water.

The big chunks of meat were goat, chicken and pork— infused with cumin and cilantro. The thick, red sauce was made of crushed tomatoes and hot peppers, with shelled corn and pinto beans mixed in. A pungent, white soft cheese had been sprinkled and melted on top. The woven baskets held piles of hot, freshly made corn tortillas.

"Please, eat," the baron said. "While you're doing that, I'll go and have a word with the fat coward. If you need more helpings of stew, just ask these ladies, and they'll refill your bowls."

After he left, J.B. hissed to the others, "That's one crazy, hair-trigger son of a bitch."

"That's my diagnosis, too," Mildred said. "Do we really want to throw our lot in with his?"

"Can't trust," Jak agreed.

"We need him," Ryan countered. "There's no way around it. He has trained fighters, transport, weapons and food. And he knows the technology we're up against far better than we do. Without him, our odds go down big-time."

"He could turn on us in a second," Krysty said.

"If that happens, we'll just have to be ready to deal with it," Ryan said.

"This stew smells absolutely wonderful," Doc interrupted. "I suggest we eat it while it is still hot."

The companions ate without speaking, fixated on shoveling down the food. The only sounds in the kiva were groans of pleasure, and occasional belches to make room for more. They were wiping their twice-refilled bowls clean with scraps of tortilla when Burning Man returned.

"Without a doubt that was the finest repast we have had in months," Doc told him. "Most kind of you, sir, and most appreciated."

The baron acknowledged the compliment.

"What did Big Mike tell you about Slake City?" Ryan asked him.

"The coward said the number of she-hes is small," Burning Man replied. "Maybe a dozen of them, in all. They've got a couple of all-terrain wags. And a single gyroplane. He said the old site is now just a staging area where they assemble the newly gathered slaves. They've moved their main operation from the edge of the nukeglass massif to its center, to the mines at Slake City's Ground Zero."

"Funny, he didn't mention the move to us," Ryan said.

"Did you threaten to let a war dog castrate him?"

"We didn't figure he had anything down there to lose," Krysty said.

"The she-hes' high-tech armor and weapons more than make up for our eight-to-one force advantage," the baron went on.

"So, you're saying you're *not* going to go after them?" Ryan said.

From outside the kiva came the sounds of wag engines roaring to life and excited voices.

"We move out tomorrow at first light," Burning Man told him. "It's about 150 miles to Slake City. That will require two full days traveling if we take old Highway 84 to Interstate 15. The road bed is completely gone in many places. No problem for the horses, but it means a lot of detours for the wags. Flash floods have cut some deep gullys through the plain, making for some wicked tricky traverses."

"Even so, two days seems like a long time to get there," Ryan said.

"We'll have to slow down and take extra precautions when we get close to the nukeglass," the baron said. "We don't want to be spotted from the air. If that gyro locates our column, it has the firepower to kill us all."

"What about our weapons?" Doc said.

"You'll get them back tomorrow, before we leave," Burning Man said. "Now, if you're all finished eating, let's find you a quiet, shady place to get some rest."

Ryan and the others followed the baron out of the kiva.

In the central plaza, the preparations for the Slake City campaign were already well underway. A caravan of wags had been assembled in front of the semitrailers. The vehicles were a motley assortment of battered SUVs, all-terrain scout cars and flatbed pickup trucks, all crudely armored with scavenged sections of steel plate. A human chain of men, women and children loaded the flat beds with boxes of gear, food and containers of water. The men carefully rolled fifty-five-gallon drums of wag fuel up plank ramps.

The baron paused beside one of the wooden crates lined up on the ground. He knelt and after rummaging in the packing straw, came up with a rag-wrapped object about a foot long. He stripped off the protective covering, and proudly shoved the thing in Ryan's face.

It was a short length of two-inch diameter, steel

cylinder, threaded and capped at both ends, with a drilled-out fuse hole.

Pipe bomb.

Ryan looked around. There were boxes and boxes of them.

"On my birth world," the baron said, "I learned a good deal about the manufacture of explosives." As he weighed the crude bomb in his palm, that unholy light returned to his eyes. "And about blowing things up."

Chapter Eight

Clad in a helmeted battlesuit, Dr. Huth stood hunched over a makeshift work table, his attention riveted on a monitor and the pair of side-by-side videos displayed there.

Both were of death by fire.

Moving the computer scroller with a gauntleted hand, he compared the same fractions of seconds of recorded time. There was a slight delay as the software interface corrected the blur, interpolating missing pixels.

The recording on the right captured the slaughter of a specter-free stickie, a creature he had sacrificed in order to get baseline, species-normal, biometric values as it expired. An array of remote sensors and cameras had chronicled the physiological effects of immolation. The sequences ended in full-frame whiteouts of total ignition.

On the left were the death throes of a mutant that Dr. Huth had infected with the specters' microscopic seeds. Moments before the entities had burst out of the stickie's bloated torso, he had incinerated it to ash. Again, the sensors had recorded the event in great detail: metabolism values, heart rate, blood pressure, oxygen saturation, kidney and liver function, brain wave output.

As Dr. Huth shifted the controller, moving back and forth between the last instant of life and the precise moment of death, the numerics of the on-screen bio-readouts scrolled up, then plummeted down. Up and down. Up and down. The crawl-speed playback distorted the stickies' final screams, turning ear-splitting shrieks into baritone bellows of pain.

Even though the cries were garbled in pitch and muffled by distance and force field, they still had the power to agitate his other test subjects. A faint chorus of sympathetic wails and moans echoed up from the bowels of the mine shaft.

When Dr. Huth's side-by-side comparison of the readouts revealed no significant differences, right up to the millisecond of termination, he quickly switched computer programs from biometrics to biomass analysis. The spectrographic software detected radiation wavelengths given off by burning materials. From what burned, how brightly, and for how long, it measured bodily raw materials in percentiles.

He blinked at the screen. The spectrographs of both immolations were virtually identical, peak for peak, valley for valley.

It appeared that the specters, right up to the very instant of their breaking out, had taken nothing whatsoever from their victim.

Which was impossible according to the Law of Conservation of Matter.

To grow from microscopic size to more than six feet long, a living creature had to intake and process vast quantities of raw material.

Dr. Huth wanted to rub his aching eyes, but he couldn't because of the battlesuit helmet's face plate. He felt hollow and fluttery at his very core; exhausted not only by twenty-four-hour cycles of nonstop effort, or the confines of the battlesuit he had been forced to live in for weeks, but also by the lack of concrete results and the rapidly closing time window. Every line of inquiry he had tried so far had been for naught. It suddenly seemed possible, even likely, that *this* was the one question he couldn't dent, that he finally come to the limits of his intellectual powers, of his genius for invention and synthesis.

The whitecoat shut his eyes and took a series of deep, slow, restorative breaths. As he did so, his lips began to move. Softly, but distinctly, he repeated the mantra that in the face of defeat had always sustained him: "I am a problem solver. I am a problem solver. I am a problem solver."

Gradually, over the course of several minutes of intense concentration, the self-reprogramming took effect, driving out the negative, counterproductive thoughts. Dr. Huth regained his composure and mental focus.

Without a doubt, he assured himself, this was the scale of problem he had been born to take on. And he had a long track record of success with similar, apparently hopeless challenges. When his overpopulated Earth was on the verge of running out of food, he had helped to develop a strain of energy-rich agrobacteria that, had it ever been industrially cultivated, might have saved billions upon billions of lives. It wasn't his fault that in the rush to put the new technology in place the cyanospores had been accidently released into the environment, where they multiplied out of control, eventually smothering large underground sections of the megalopolis in green slunk.

As catastrophic and disappointing as that outcome had been, Dr. Huth hadn't given up the search for an answer. He had been one of the first researchers to see the potential of converting inorganic rock, a virtually inexhaustible resource, into a form that could be partially digested by, and which would sustain, living creatures. That prolonged consumption of the synthetic fast food drove human beings homicidally insane was an unforeseen—but in his view completely acceptable—side effect. It was a matter for law enforcement and the military to deal with. As far as Dr. Huth was concerned, he had elegantly solved his earth's mass starvation problem.

Twice.

As he stared, his eyes unfocused, at the stop-action images of incineration, he had an "Aha!" moment. In an instant of clarity the experimental design's fatal flaw revealed itself to him. Up to this point he had been splitting hairs with the lives of his test subjects, shaving away the milliseconds between life and death, initiating termination closer and closer to the moment of breakout. This was done in order to test the hypothesis that in the interval prior to their hatching, the specters were harvesting resources from their host.

The potential error was in the experiment's artificial limits, which eliminated the prospect of the specters' release into the environment, but didn't allow a complete testing of the hypothesis. It was still possible that the entities were taking something from their victims, just not in the time frame and under the circumstances allowed by the experiment. As things stood, Dr. Huth was the one doing the killing, triggering the incineration before the entities could burst out. If the specters were harvesting from the host at the precise instant of death, or immediately thereafter, the current experimental design wouldn't catch it. It was also conceivable that the specters had to actually cause the death themselves in order to take their bounty.

The next logical step was dire, indeed.

At least one clutch of specters had to be allowed to come to full term under laboratory conditions, allowed to break out of and kill their mutant host. Remote sensors would record the biometrics of the slaughter, and the burning of the stickie's corpse would yield critical spectrographic data.

The risk involved was off the scale.

Although specters weren't able to penetrate a laboratory cell's force field or pass through the solid nukeglass walls, floor or ceiling, once they exited their host, there was still no way to kill them—at least not that Dr. Huth had discovered. And if for some reason they managed to escape the confines of the cell and the site's deepest mine shaft, if they reached the open space of Deathlands, they would divide endlessly, and swarm by the millions upon the animal life of this world, eventually driving it to extinction. The human slaves at Ground Zero would be the first to die, and when that happened there would be no work force to gather nuke ore for reprocessing.

Dr. Huth and the she-hes would be forced to jump worlds again and quickly, with whatever energy they had stored.

From past experience, the odds of finding another hospitable Earth, or a replica planet with the resources necessary to repower their jump batteries were slim.

So far, it appeared that the X-ray treatments he had initiated on the twelfth Earth had eliminated the spore contamination. If it had spread from encystations inadvertently brought along with them, the mine slaves, who weren't protected by battlesuits, should have already been showing signs of infestation. Barring a documented loss of specter containment, which meant the she-hes had nothing left to lose, Auriel Otis Trask wasn't likely to give him permission for a laboratory-controlled hatching out.

Dr. Huth grinned to himself, grizzle-chinned and gap-toothed.

Accidents did happen, of course.

And a full-blown disaster always had the potential of being a great learning opportunity.

An opportunity that might never come again.

If an accidental release occurred, he would have the chance to study the specters in close captivity, to test their reactions, gauging not just their physical properties, but their behavior. Even if there was no evidence of extracted host material inside the specters, no evidence of specters' organs or bodily functions, there was certainly evidence of what seemed to be organized activity on their part—the simultaneous expansion of volume within the host, a combined outward pressure leading to their bursting free of the torso; subsequent coordinated attacks on their victims and, afterward, the mass, aerial swarming.

The attacks, posthatching, had always followed the same pattern. The specters were able to change their shape, to draw themselves out into the thinnest of threads. In this superelongated state, they entered their victims through any available orifice, pouring into ears or nose, eyes, rectum or mouth. When one of them gained entry, others nearby seemed to home in on the struggling quarry, penetrating it in the same way by the dozens, a flood tide of invaders, whose substance was invisible to the naked eye. Once inside the host, they expanded in volume until the combined hydraulic pressure literally blew the victim apart. Instead of death occurring in a matter of weeks, as was the case in the infestation process, this killing took only seconds. And when it was done, the entities javelined off in search of new lives to steal.

At least superficially, it seemed some kind of communication had to be at work.

The other viable explanations for the *apparent* group phenomena—chemical, magnetic, electrical—needed to be closely examined and eliminated from the equation. Dr. Huth reasoned that an analysis of the specters' behavior—if it was behavior—might provide him a window into what they were, and how they could be destroyed.

Their reproductive cycle was another mystery that had him thoroughly stumped. From a distance, the aerial swarming behavior they exhibited looked like mating, but he had found no evidence that specters produced spores. They increased their numbers after hatching not by sexual reproduction, but by simple division. Which left open the question: What had created the spores? And what was its relationship to the specters?

Dr. Huth caught himself.

His mind was racing in circles.

And he was holding his breath.

He forced himself to exhale slowly, and with an effort, once again managed to clear his thoughts. He faced a complex knot of problems, all of them intimately, perhaps functionally, related. He had to focus on one tightly defined issue at a time, or end up chasing his own tail.

He shut off the computer program and returned the screen to the live feed from aboveground cameras that randomly scanned all of Ground Zero. Moving under the roughhewn ceiling of gray-green nukeglass to the opposite side of the lab, he stepped over the sheaf of power cables that led from a nuke generator to the row of electronics and banks of lights. Rummaging around on a littered sawhorse table, he picked up his hand scanner, then exited the doorless cell.

When his battlehelmet's headlamp swept over the corridor's walls, embedded debris glittered back at him. The millions of occlusions were metallic, fragments of a lost civilization caught up in the matrix like bugs in amber—pull tabs, rivets, washers, crushed aluminum cans. They were objects that the extreme high temperatures of nuclear fission couldn't melt or evaporate. Buried deeper in the nukeglass glacier, at the far edge of the headlamp's penetration, were the hulking shadows of larger, unidentifiable objects.

As he trudged through the drifts of sparkling dust on the floor of the tunnel, the ultrafine material swirled upward, around his knees. When inhaled, the glass dust acted like micro-razors. Since it was highly radioactive as well, it was a toss-up whether the mine slaves would die of shredded lungs or rad poisoning.

Dr. Huth was protected from dust and radiation by his artificially intelligent battle armor, but there were downsides to wearing it for extended periods. Despite the formfitting, bodystocking cushion he wore under the plasteel plates, weeping sores had appeared at the hinge and pressure points. No matter how carefully he walked, the accumulated scabs tore loose from knees, elbows and shoulders. To ward off infection he had to dose himself with antibiotic four times daily. Because of the suit's inexact fit and his inability to fully interface with the controls involved in feeding and excretion, the stench he wallowed in was oppressive.

Exposed nerve ends burning at his every step, Dr. Huth started down a ramp at the end of the passage. The thirty-degree incline persisted for fifty yards, then the corridor took a hard right turn, and began to spiral downward at a much steeper pitch. Texture had been laser-cut into the floor to grip boot soles and cart wheels.

As he corkscrewed deeper and deeper into the massif, he could make out a dim light below. As he descended, the glow grew brighter and the external temperature steadily climbed. When he reached the spiral's bottom and the entrance to yet another horizontal corridor, his visor's temp sensor read 135 degrees Fahrenheit. Sheathed in the climate-controlled armor, he didn't notice it.

Just inside the shaft's entrance, harshly illuminated by a string of floodlights that ran along join of floor and walls, the ceiling was marked by row upon row of three-inch-wide bore holes. Each of the bore holes was packed with a powerful explosive charge. A spiderweb of drooping wires connected the charges, ensuring simultaneous detonations. An identical bank of explosives had been set on the far side of the clustered lab cells. They were the experiment's fail-safe. A breakdown or breach of the force fields blocking the cell entrances would automatically trigger a massive double blast, dropping thousands of tons of nukeglass, sealing off the shaft at both ends.

Because the specters could stretch themselves into thin filaments, sooner or later, like curls of smoke, they would find a route up through the cracks and fissures to the surface. The mile-deep deadfall wasn't a permanent solution to a loss of containment; it was a delaying tactic that bought the she-hes and Dr. Huth time to make good an escape.

This corridor was even grimmer and grittier than the one above: the ceiling a low arch, the walls narrow. It reminded Huth of an animal's burrow. The tunnel stretched off into the distance; past the floor lights, past the force field barrier on the far side of the cells, it disappeared into the bowels of the glacier. Overhead, the sheer volume of the massif was a constant, crushing presence.

It was the darkest, deepest of dark, deep places. And it was blistering hot. Hot as the lowest pit of hell.

Dr. Huth passed by the nuke generators that powered the force-field, illumination and fail-safe systems. When his body moved in front of the string of floodlights, it cast flickering shadows over the entrances to the cells carved into the left-hand wall. The stickies imprisoned inside began to moan.

He strode past the first half-dozen cells. The naked occupants tried their best to make themselves invisible, cowering in the farthest corners. The cells were all the same: bare walls and floor; no bed; white plastic, five-gallon buckets for toilet, water and food. The only other furnishings were the incineration apparatus along one wall and a foot-wide silver dome mounted in the center of the ceiling that held the vid cams and a remote-controlled, wireless stun unit. The rotating dome had a 360-degree sweep of the entire cell. Test subjects were forcibly confined by its robotic stun gun, allowing their safe feeding and watering.

Dr. Huth stopped in front of the seventh cell. On the floor against the rear wall, a pale creature lay curled in a tight ball behind the latrine bucket, its backside facing the entrance. Stickie Number Seven appeared to be the one closest to specter breakout, the prime candidate for an "accident." Dr. Huth shifted his visor to infrared mode and pointed the hand scanner. Blood pressure, body temperature, respirations all registered, but because of the bucket and subject's body position he couldn't see inside the torso.

He turned on his battlesuit's loud-hailer and cranked up the volume. "Get up!" he bellowed at the creature.

The command echoed down the shaft.

Raising its bald head an inch or two, the stickie peered up at him from behind a spindly forearm. Dr. Huth noted the bloody sucker fingers, torn to shreds trying to scratch through the nukeglass. The stickie knew what was coming; by now, they all did. It raised its head higher, the black eyes begging for mercy.

Mercy was out of the question.

Dr. Huth reached for the switches set in the tunnel wall. This time he ignored the covered toggle and pressed the button with his thumb.

The ceiling's dome rotated sixty degrees, then stopped.

A blue arc of high voltage, a mini-lightning bolt snapped from the dome to the creature huddled on the floor. The stickie screamed and jerked like it had been lashed with a whip, but it didn't rise. It curled into an even tighter ball, hiding its head under its arms.

Dr. Huth pushed the button again and held it down. Another blue bolt slammed the mutant. Then another.

The third time was a charm.

The creature sprang to its feet, howling in pain as it hopped wildly from one foot to another. Though decidedly male, it looked nine months pregnant. The massively protruding belly didn't bounce or quiver as the mutant jiggered about, but stuck out rigidly, like it was inflated with high pressure air. The stickie's cries set the other captives shrieking in their cells.

Dr. Huth aimed his scanner at the bloated stomach. Under skin, muscle and bone, three-inch-thick, lime-green oblongs oozed back and forth. As the headless, tailless entities slithered, their entire lengths pulsated, almost doubling in volume before shrinking back to their original size. The throbbing was disorganized, each specter expanding and contracting on its own cycle, each still jockeying position inside the torso to find the necessary structural weak point. Once the soft spot was located, once the pulsations of the entire clutch were synchronized, the simultaneous, rhythmic heaving would blow open the host, gonads to chin. Based on past observations, Dr. Huth guessed that outcome was less than three hours away.

His visor's movement sensor flashed a warning. He turned to his right and saw lemon-yellow, humanoid shapes cavorting in the corridor beyond the last of the cells, on the other side of the force field that blocked off that end of the tunnel.

Free range stickies.

The force field was the only thing that could keep them out. Born with the ability to compress their bodies—this thanks to an unusually high proportion of cartilage to bone—the creatures were able to slip through extremely narrow spaces. And there were plenty of such spaces to be had: the complex fracture planes of the massif were in constant flux, glass screeching on glass.

Dr. Huth had no way of knowing how many stickies were loose in the mines. Dredda Otis Trask had picked them for slaves because they were less susceptible to the hazards of Ground Zero: they had a high tolerance to radioactivity and to inhaled abrasive dust. But the she-hes couldn't make stickies work, and couldn't keep them confined. When they were mixed in with human slaves, they attacked their fellow miners in packs, tearing them apart with their sucker hands, and fighting over the rags of flesh.

Somehow, they had managed to survive and breed in the hellish mines. There was food: rats aplenty, mindburst mushrooms, and the fallen and the weaklings among their own ranks. There was water, too. Cracks in the nukeglass allowed rainwater and snowmelt to penetrate and accumulate underground. Theirs was a very small ecological niche, complicated by isolation, darkness and limited resources. Why hadn't the stickies just left? Most of them probably had. Under different circumstances, those that remained would have been the basis for an interesting research study on adaptation under extreme natural selection pressure.

Looking at the frenzied mob of mutants, a few dozen feet from their imprisoned brethren, Dr. Huth wondered if they were really trying to mount a rescue. If so, were the degraded creatures reflecting human ideals like love, devotion, sacrifice? Or perhaps was he just anthropo-morphizing? Understanding Deathlands' mutant psy-chology hadn't been a priority of the initial Slake City mission. What had been established was that stickies' lust for food and helpless victims allowed them to be easily manipulated and trapped. It was assumed they were ruled by instinct, not emotion.

A little test was in order.

The stickie in cell number seven held its trembling arms raised and spread in surrender, its dead black eyes streamed tears, its nose holes streamed mucous.

Dr. Huth pressed the stun button again.

With a blistering crackle and snap, blue flame spanned the distance from the ceiling dome to the back of the stickie's hairless head. The force of the blow slammed the shrieking creature face-first onto the floor.

At the far end of tunnel, the other muties jolted vio-lently and screamed as if they, themselves, had been zapped.

As he stared at them, Dr. Huth explored his empty tooth sockets with the tip of his tongue.

In blind fury, in apparent desperation, the stickies threw themselves at the invisible force field, which sent them bouncing backward into the darkness. Over and over they hurled themselves at it, with the same result.

Dr. Huth leaned hard on the stun button. Blue arc-light winked like a strobe inside the cell. The silver dome turned, its brilliant bolts nailing the mutant as it tried to flee. No matter how the creature dodged and ducked, the computerized targeting never missed. Booted around the cell by lightning, the stickie waved its scrawny arms and pissed itself.

Dr. Huth wasn't paying attention to test subject number seven, nor was he listening to its screams. He was watching the wild ones jerk in sympathetic pain, watching them fall to their knees, listening to their shrieks of agony and outrage; and as he did so, he got a sudden, pleasurable tickle down in his chest. The paroxysm rippled up his gullet and burst from the back of his throat.

He had almost forgotten how good it felt to laugh.

Chapter Nine

Tribarrel pistol grip in a gauntleted fist, Auriel Otis Trask moved upwind of the clouds of steam pouring off open-topped, fifty-five-gallon steel drums. The caldrons straddled a hissing row of burners that shot flames halfway up their blackened flanks. Three men, naked to the waist, the coating of grime on their hairy backs and arms streaked through by rivulets of sweat, stirred the boiling contents with long-handled shovels.

The camp chefs.

On either side of them stood blaster-wielding, human traitors. A dozen in all, they formed the compound's internal police contingent. For the price of easy duty, for the promise of riches and power in the future, they had turned on their own kind and with relish helped the she-hes enforce slave-camp order.

In front of the cook station, a column of roughly two hundred rag-clad men and women stretched off across the swath of nukeglass, awaiting their morning meal. At the far end of the line, people were yelling; the pushing and shoving had started. Everyone wanted more than what they were about to receive. No one wanted to be last.

Slaves and their black-armored masters stood gathered at the epicenter of the Slake City blast crater, which on nukeday had backfilled with a tidal wave of melted

desert sand and vaporized megalopolis. There wasn't
a scrap of vegetation on the surface of the hardened
massif.

No wildlife.

No soil, just glass dust.

No water source, save seasonal rain.

Without the protection of a battlehelmet visor, the
sun's glare off the gray-green surface thrust straight into
the brain like a dagger.

Ore extraction operations focused on a pancake-flat
depression, five hundred feet across and dimpled like
the rind of an enormous, moldy orange. A battery of
klieg lights ringed three wag-sized holes bored into the
glass—the main shafts of the mine. A cylindrical metal
tank on stilts held the site's drinking water. There was a
railed walkway around the bottom of the tank, and rung
steps up one side to the top. To keep miners from freezing to death when the sun went down, open-flame heat-
ers were stationed near the shallow divots in the surface
where they curled up and slept in piles like prairie dogs.
No one dared spend the night underground because of
the bands of stickies roaming the tunnels.

The ore processor, a self-propelled wag with wheels
taller than a human being, was parked in front of a
sloping mountain of gray-green rubble. Manual labor
transferred the chunks of radioactive nukeglass to the
processor's hopper. A cluster of thick cables connected
it to the gridwork of storage batteries laid out on the
ground. On the far side of the processor, inside a force-
field dome, was the jump machinery, which emitted a
steady, low hum. Since the specters first appeared, their
jump gear was never completely shut down but kept in a

minimal-power resting state to avoid a time-consuming, complete reboot. Beside it were a cluster of black plasteel milspec huts—the she-hes' living quarters.

Auriel looked down the long file. Every slave clutched his or her personal food container: tin cans, handle-less ceramic mugs, cut-down plastic milk jugs, chipped enamel sauce pans. Some of the workers covered the lower halves of their faces with scraps of filthy cloth, makeshift masks to block the abrasive dust from their lungs. Others wore rag masks with narrow slits cut out for their eyes to keep from being struck blind by glare.

The commander, all her sisters and Dr. Huth had turned out for the midday meal, but they weren't there to eat it. In gleaming black battlesuits, they bracketed the column of slaves, five to a side, with laser rifles at the ready and clear firing lanes. The twice-a-day feeding times emptied the shafts of starving workers. A full show of force was required to maintain a semblance of order when the aroma of food hung in the air.

Under Auriel's mother's regime, the miners hadn't had it so easy.

Dredda Otis Trask had made her slaves forage for their own food underground, in the belly and bowels of the glacier. Her rationale had been simple: there was little point in feeding workers who would die in ten days or less from rad sickness, anyway. But foraging the tunnels was no longer an option. Human and stickie predation had driven the radiation-resistant rat population to near-extinction. Although the mind-burst mushrooms that flourished in the humid darkness of the shafts were edible, and the mainstay of the rats' diet, their psychoactive chemicals induced violent hallucinations in Homo sapiens and set the miners attacking one another with pickaxes, shovels and bare hands.

If the gear Dredda's expedition abandoned at the edge of the glacier had survived, Auriel and her sisters would have had other, much better options to choose from. But the wags, shelters and stockpiles of matériel had vanished. In their place deep craters had been blasted into the hardpan, catch basins for stagnant water. Whoever had orchestrated the base's demolition had been thorough. Fragments of plasteel lay scattered for hundreds of yards in all directions.

That destruction had forced Auriel to move their processor to Ground Zero and to bivouac there with her sisters while the batteries repowered. The strategic decision meant that additional supplies had to be transported across thirteen miles of nukeglass. Their surviving gyroplane was of no use. An attack aircraft, it carried just two passengers, including the pilot. The roadbed leading from the southern rim of the massif to Ground Zero was subject to shifting, cracking, or falling away entirely—all without warning. The more round trips to the perimeter their handful of irreplaceable, nuke-powered wags made, the more likely it was that disaster would strike.

Resource conservation had become the central focus of the third expedition to the hellscape.

Twice a day, the miners lined up to eat a watery stew of meat and marrow bones, seasoned with a dash of salt and a mild dose of narcotic painkiller. The protein was harvested from their own rad-contaminated dead, and from the mine's wild stickies, who were hunted down or live-trapped. Humans and muties alike were skinned out and chunked into bite-sized pieces.

The trio of cooks merrily jostled and elbowed one another as they stirred the kettles. They had reason to be happy. Although they did have to butcher their own species, perhaps even people they knew, they didn't have to slave underground, and they got double rations of the narcotic-laced stew. Food was food, whatever the source.

The miner waiting at the head of the line was both skeletal and stooped. A wiry beard sprouted around the edges of his rag mask; grease and sweat matted his long hair to his sunburned skull, his eyes were feverish and bulging. Flying glass chips had inflicted dozens of cuts on his hands, arms and face. Most of them looked infected. Behind him, downwind of the kettles, the other conscripted miners shifted anxiously from one foot to another, furtive eyes on the prize.

They all knew what they were about to consume.

And it didn't matter.

As the shovel blades churned the drums' contents, they revealed not just cubes of indistinguishable, boiled gray meat—swept to the surface of the thin soup before being drawn down by whirlpools were severed human fingers.

The weak of body—and of will—ended up in the cook pots. Those too fastidious to partake of the stew starved to death.

Auriel could muster little sympathy for the assembled Deathlanders; it was more than just the steely resolve of a unit commander, putting the survival of her fellow warriors first. Her experience had given her a unique perspective on life, and its value. Not only was she über-human—faster, stronger, tougher than any man or woman naturally born and bred—but she also had, in her brief existence, witnessed the deaths of entire worlds. And she had glimpsed the apparently endless, distorted mirror images of Earth, the variations on preordained, global annihilation.

In the grand, disinterested scheme of things what did a few hundred more human lives matter?

That said, Auriel didn't eat from the communal stock-pots herself. None of her sisters did, either. The she-hes subsisted on high-energy, low-residue, battlesuit-compatible food pellets they had brought with them from the twelfth Earth.

Auriel looked beyond the column of slaves, at the rad-blasted mountains on the horizon, well beyond the north rim of the glacier. There was more to Deathlands than this island of nukewaste and those distant, barren mounds of brown dirt. Dredda had told her about the data recovered from the initial satellite survey of the planet. Unlike the other eight Earths Auriel had known, this one wasn't desertified. Not a frozen ball of ice. Not entirely poisoned. Not in the midst of an all-out war of mutually assured destruction. Deathlands had many other Ground Zeros from which to mine nuke power. There were vast, untapped concentrations of natural resources, small centers of resurgent human population, and established agricultures and trade routes.

If Auriel felt nothing for the victims of her ambition, she felt the unmistakable pull of this particular replica Earth. A magnetism that was more than simply the promise of a future for her kind; it was more personal, more magical than that, like the discovery of a limb or an organ she hadn't known she was missing—a part of her that now had a name and a reality. Seeing it, touching it, walking it, breathing it, tasting it for the first time she understood the concept of "home."

This was where she belonged.

As she watched, one of the camp chefs attempted to serve the first miner in line with a shovel blade that held nothing but a pint or so of greasy, gray broth and a few rubbery rings of crosscut windpipe.

Quickly pulling back his container, the slave snarled up at the cook, "Dip down deep, you stingy motherfucker! Gimme some nukin' meat!"

Glowering, the chef plunged his shovel into the depths of the cauldron.

After the portion, which now included a few small morsels of flesh and fat, was sluiced into the battered pot, the miner covered it with a forearm and scuttled off toward the shallow, dished-out pits in the surface. As he did so, a half-dozen of his fellow slaves broke from the line and crossed the nukeglass on a dead run toward him. Seeing the pursuit, he immediately squatted down, hunching over the steaming pot, trying frantically to gobble all his grub before it was taken from him, scalding his mouth to assuage his hunger, so that he might live to see another sunrise in hell.

The desperate hope he and the other slaves clung to—for eventual escape, for a return to a normal life— Auriel knew was false. None of them was going to survive the sojourn at Ground Zero.

Six men surrounded the crouching slave, all of them much bigger than he was. The leader of the pack was biggest of all: over six and a half feet tall, with massive shoulders, arms and thighs. Wild hair framed a decoratively scarified face. His jutting, bony forehead, thick neck and bulging biceps looked like they'd been branded by red-hot strands of barbed wire.

Size and strength didn't always translate into more ore in the processor's hopper; often it meant just the opposite. The she-hes couldn't stop friends and relatives taken as slaves from joining together in defensive groups, nor could they prevent packs of coldheart predators from forming. Some of these associations were beneficial to the enterprise—slaves working the mines in teams extracted more ore—but the criminal gangs ran the same operations at Ground Zero as they had in the wider world. They robbed, raped and killed the industrious and the weak whenever it served their purposes. Behavior that stretched an already precariously balanced system to the limit. Conscriptees who actually worked, who mined the ore, needed sufficient food to keep them going until they dropped dead.

The wire-branded pack leader tossed aside the pickax he carried and seized the seated man by the hair, which he used like a handle, to jerk him to his feet. The little fellow let out a howl of pain, tucking the hot pot close to his chest and covering it with both arms. Arm muscles bulging, Barbwire lifted his feet clear of the ground, and held him suspended by his scalp, but the stubborn bastard refused to hand over his meal. Dropping his victim, the big man swung down a balled fist, putting his full weight behind it, pounding the top of the unprotected head.

A potentially neck-breaking blow.

The smaller man's eyelids snapped shut, his knees buckled and his death-grip on dinner weakened. As he slumped unconscious to the nukeglass, blood squirting from between his clenched teeth, Barbwire wrenched the pot away.

Only a little of the stew spilled out onto the ground. Turning away from his victim, Barbwire raised the pot to his mouth by the handle, pursed his lips and blew on the surface to cool it.

Not surprisingly, no one rushed forward to come to the unconscious man's aid, or to take up his cause. The turncoat Deathlanders bracketing the cookpots didn't raise their weapons or move to intervene. Their job was to protect the food, not individual prisoners. The other slaves didn't want to lose their places in line, or be injured in a fight and end up in pieces in the cook pot, themselves.

Auriel grimaced. Wolf packs of predatory cowards and masses of weak-souled rabbits—this was the gene pool that had produced the other half of her DNA. Could her paternal contributor, her "father", be one of these conscriptees? Perhaps Barbwire himself? From what little Dredda had told her about Ryan Cawdor, that was highly unlikely. Though an ignorant primitive like his fellow Deathlanders, he had proved himself a worthy adversary, a hero who had, against all odds, escaped imprisonment on an alternate Earth and recrossed realities to return home—this home. Because of his intelligence, his mental and physical strength, and his fighting skills, Dredda had chosen his seed to artificially fertilize her harvested eggs. Unfortunately, no vid of him survived.

Who he was, whether he was even still alive, remained a mystery.

Having regained his senses, the battered miner, blood sheeting off his chin, lunged up at his tormentor, trying to knock the pot out of his hand.

Barbwire held it out of reach above his head and snap-kicked the smaller man in the chest. It wasn't a full power blow, but it sent the poor bundle of bones hurtling backward, crashing onto his butt and skidding across the slick ground.

"Mero, let's put an end to this," Auriel said into her com link mike.

"I'm on it, Commander," was the reply.

As Auriel and her second in command broke ranks, Barbwire plunged his fingers into the broth, fishing out a few choice chunks, which he popped into his mouth. He tried to pass the pot to the pecking order of lackeys waiting their turns, but they weren't looking at him. They were staring at the two she-hes charging the nukeglass toward them. Turning on their heels, these lesser villains bolted for the mine shafts.

It was already too late for them to get away. Armed with a tribarrel, Mero had cut off their retreat.

There was nowhere else to run.

The five slaves dropped to knees on the glass, their palms on top of their heads, their eyes lowered in submission.

Auriel slowed to a walk as she closed distance on the pack leader. The slaves had learned that their captors would tolerate a range of antisocial behaviors, and that punishments, when they came, usually fell well short of summary execution. This was the gray zone in which predators operated. But every so often an example had to be made, to underscore the boundary and the consequences of crossing it.

Shoulder-slinging her laser rifle, Auriel keyed her battlesuit's external speaker. "You shouldn't have done that," she told him.

The big man said nothing, his eyes narrowed, darting left and right, looking for a way out.

It was laughable.

Some humans couldn't help themselves, it seemed. Even when they knew a course of action would end badly. Barbwire had soiled himself in front of the entire camp, begging to be made an object lesson to the others.

Auriel glanced at the visor's right-hand corner, where battlesuit remote sensors displayed her adversary's heart rate and muscle tension values.

This one was going to put up a fight.

Sure enough, he suddenly lunged for his pickax. As he charged at her, he swung the weapon up and brought it down in a tight arc that put every ounce of his body weight behind it.

Auriel let him come, her boots at shoulder width, her arms at her sides, her hands unclenched. At the very last second, as the ax screamed down, she dodged the blow, twisting in a blur to her left.

The ax's arc continued, the point plowed deep into the glass, sending up a puff of sparkling dust and flying shards. Barbwire let out a grunt as the impact's shock wave rippled up his arms.

Behind them, the rest of the slaves whooped and hollered. It was unclear who or what they were cheering for. The slave taking on the hated master? Or the criminal who plagued them finally facing justice? Maybe they just wanted to see someone's—anyone's—blood spilled.

Barbwire wrenched the pick from the glass and spun to face her. Again he charged, again he worked up maximum momentum, and brought the weapon down two-handed with all his weight behind it.

Auriel didn't move this time. She just stood there, her arms crossed, watching as the point of the ax descended upon her.

The pack leader aimed for the center of her faceplate. His logic was obvious: if he could just split it, he could drive the ax clear through her skull.

It was another futile hope, born of ignorance and desperation.

The point of the pick got to within a foot of its intended target. There it made contact with the battlesuit's EM shield. The weapon's course instantly reversed—like a length of metal pipe shoved into a madly spinning flywheel.

As the ax catapulted backward out of Barbwire's grasp, cartwheeling high in the air, he was thrown off balance, and ended up flat on his butt on the ground, his face twisted in pain.

"Get rid of that nukin' armor, you cockroach coward," he gritted through clenched teeth, his numbed arms held out in front of him. "And I'll pull your stuffing out."

A challenge to her sense of honor? Auriel thought. From this creature?

As delightful as the prospect of a barehanded fight was, she couldn't oblige him. She had to stay in the battlesuit; it was integral to Dr. Huth's quarantine regimen. Instead, she disabled the armor's EM shield. It wouldn't make the fight more fair—nothing could do that—but it allowed her to get up close and personal.

To drive home the lesson.

"I've lowered my shield," she said, waving for him to stand up. "Come on, get up. Let's see what you can do."

Barbwire scrambled to his feet. Quickly closing the distance between them, he tried to grapple with her. For an instant, his hands slid over the black, layered plates, his fingers seeking a hard edge, something to grip. He was four inches taller than she was, and outweighed her by fifty pounds, but her reaction time was exponentially faster. She toyed with him, blocking his clumsy hands, easily stepping out of his reach.

The other slaves started beating their empty pots and pans on the ground and cheering even more wildly.

Barbwire threw an overhand right at her head, which she blocked with an armored forearm. Instead of counterpunching, she circled around his strong side. He caught her with a roundhouse left, his fist banging against the battle helmet.

It didn't faze her; she was moving away from the blow when it landed.

The big man rubbed his skinned knuckles. Realizing that he couldn't beat her in a punch-out, he jumped forward, wrapped his arms around her waist and lifted her into the air.

She let him do it, let him try to crush her with a bear hug, knowing the armor plates would only compress so far. They were almost nose-to-nose, his hot breath fogging the outside of her visor, when Auriel cocked back her right arm and drove a gauntleted index finger into his ear hole to the second joint.

In, and then out.

Barbwire shrieked and let go of her, clutching his ear, stamping his feet, thick blood drooling between his fingers.

When she rushed him, he tried a halfhearted front kick. Auriel grabbed his leg behind the knee and held it up, making him hop around on one foot, turning him, keeping him off balance so he couldn't throw a full power punch.

In a panic, Barbwire head-butted her helmet.

Not a good idea.

It was like head-butting a boulder. Blood poured from a deep gash in his forehead, striping his face.

Auriel dropped to a crouch and executed a perfect leg sweep that sent him crashing onto his back. Straddling his torso, she pounded him with a rain of straight, short punches to the face, bloodying his nose and mouth, breaking his front teeth, sealing shut his eyes and bouncing the back of his head against the nukeglass.

When Barbwire went limp beneath her, she straightened.

The unthinkable was hard to come by in these parts, as awful death was part of daily life, hiding around every twist in the road. It took some creativity, inspiration even, to come up with something that would stick in a Deathlander's mind.

Auriel rounded the big man's body, standing over the head.

The crowd begged and chanted for her to finish it.

"Those who don't work won't be fed," she shouted

back at them, "and they won't be allowed to prey on those who do. Those are the rules here. And this is the punishment for disobeying them."

She put the toes of her armored boots on Barbwire's shoulders, pinning his back to the ground, then reached under his chin with both gauntleted hands. Gripping his jaw, using the powerful muscles of her legs and back, she pulled upward.

Sudden, unimaginable pain brought Barbwire back to consciousness, squealing and thrashing his arms and legs.

Auriel gave his chin a hard wrench to the right, cleanly snapping his neck. His legs no longer mule-kicked, they tremble-danced. Still holding on to his chin, she straightened. Without the spinal column to anchor it in place, the soft tissue of the neck stretched and stretched, then the skin split, the muscle and tendon tore.

With a wet pop, the head came away in her hands. The torso's ragged neck stump spurted blood two feet in the air; it splattered onto her black boot tops.

The slaves' cheers abruptly stopped. It became deathly still at Ground Zero; there was no sound but the hissing of the cookfire burners.

Point made.

Letting the head roll off her gloved palms, Auriel reared back her foot and drop-kicked it in a high arc, gore pinwheeling off the tips of the hair. It landed with an audible splat beside the caldrons.

She reached down and gripped the corpse by the boot heels. As she started to drag it over to the caldrons, trailing a wide smear of blood across the nukeglass, she glanced over her shoulder. The other coldhearts no longer waited on their knees for punishment. They were scattering, trying to disappear back into the feeding line, and a black form was facedown on the glass, laying on top of a laser rifle.

Auriel opened the com link and shouted, "Mero!"

No response.

Auriel dropped the dead man's legs and hurried over to her second in command. She found Mero twitching, head to foot. Turning her onto her back, Auriel stared at her comrade's face through the helmet visor. Mero's eyes had rolled back in their sockets so that only the whites showed. Foam billowed from the corners of her mouth and her jaws snapped together, like a rabid dog.

A chill ran down Auriel's spine as she keyed the com link. "Dr. Huth! Get over here with a scanner, on the double!"

Hampered by his battlesuit, the whitecoat crossed the nukeglass in a shambling, awkward gait. He knelt beside Mero, waved the compact electronic device over her torso, then sat back on his haunches, staring fixedly at the display.

"What is it?" Auriel demanded of him. "What is it?"

He said nothing.

Auriel snatched the scanner out of his hand. The LCD screen showed a jumbled mass of lime-green coils between muscle wall and stomach. At first she thought she was looking at Mero's intestines.

Then the coils started to move.

Chapter Ten

Ryan stood braced in the bed of an accelerating stake truck, squinting through the clouds of dust, a rag mask tied over his nose and mouth. The lavender light of evening spread across a landscape that grew more barren, more devastated, with every bend in the road. Poisoned predark villes and ruined townlets lined this section of the interstate highway, a gridwork of lengthening shadows, the concrete-lined pits and slabs that had once supported sprawling suburbs. Backdropped by low brown hills, smothered in drifts of windblown sand and soil, the dismal flatland was broken only by the occasional, half-standing brick chimney and barely upright light pole.

A landscape hammered into rubble.

A landscape scoured clean of the trappings of life.

It was impossible for Ryan to fully visualize the density and vitality of the communities lost on nukeday. In Deathlands, at least, he'd never seen that many people in one place at one time. On the fateful day more than a century ago, when the MIRV warhead had detonated over the high desert city, it had released a flash of light brighter than a thousand suns and a mile-high blast wave of incendiary heat and incandescent dust. A shock wave rippled through the earth at the speed of sound, jetting out in all directions from the explosion's central point, fracturing roads, deconstructing tall buildings, setting the very air on fire.

Ryan had seen pictures of suburbs like these in crumbling predark magazines. As the wag jounced over splits in the roadway, he imagined what it had to have been like to look up at the retina-fogging flash from fifty miles distant, from a momentary point of safety, from a neatly kept backyard lawn surrounded by a wooden privacy fence, and in the split second before death roared down, to realize that everything that ever was—promises unfulfilled, and promises as yet undreamed of—was over and done with.

He and his companions, all except for Jak, either sat or stood in the bed of the heavily loaded wag. For twelve straight hours they had been breathing and eating the road dirt raised by ghost warriors on horseback, by the dog carts and by the other two wags ahead of them in the convoy.

There weren't enough horses for everyone to ride. Walking would have been preferable to the continual, gut-churning motion, to the wicked jolts to the kidneys as the wag traversed washboards, lumbered over rills and gullies, but on foot they couldn't have kept up the grueling pace.

The companions all had their weapons back, just as Burning Man had promised. Even J.B.'s hat had been returned to him.

The army in which they had enlisted, the army that bounced and zigzagged its way inexorably southward, consisted of fewer than one hundred fighters, most of them either riding horses or driving dog carts. They were going up against an opponent perhaps a tenth that number, but armed with vastly superior technology that could annihilate them all in the blink of an eye. And it looked very much like the chosen battlefield was going to be the dead zone of all dead zones, Slake City's Ground Zero.

Though Ryan radiated confidence when he spoke to the others about a repeat of their previous, successful campaign versus the she-hes, in his gut he knew the companions had only beaten them back because luck had been on their side. At any number of critical turning points, the battle could well have, perhaps should have, gone the other way. He remembered being trapped deep in the nuke mines, cutting off the heads of wave after wave of attacking stickies with a makeshift broad sword, and piling the bloody trophies in an ore cart like pumpkins. His individual act of fury and defiance had turned the tide and rallied the otherwise doomed miners to revolt against their cockroach masters. After that, the flow of combat was one-way: reversal after reversal for the invaders, and with the reversals came a sense of escalating rout.

The sense that Ryan had now, the feeling he would never admit to any of his crew, was of ominous foreboding. Being surrounded by Burning Man's ragtag army gave him no comfort. If not for the trio of wags and the blasters the warriors carried, this could have been the eve of battle four hundred years ago, a campaign ancient even in Doc Tanner's time. And they were going up against an enemy able to jump realities and whose armor deflected bullets, knives and missiles of all sorts.

But there was no turning back, now.

Destiny wouldn't allow it.

At the head of the line, Burning Man drove the lead wag, which was another battered, desert camouflage-painted, stake truck. It was bracketed by a mass of white-faced men on horseback and followed by a half-dozen four-wheeled carts, each drawn by harnessed and muzzled war dogs. Seated on the first wag's stacked cargo, intermittently visible through the swirls of dust, was Big Mike. Burning Man had tied him by the neck to the stake wall. Ryan was grateful that Big Mike wasn't riding in their wag. At least they didn't have to listen to him whine.

The warriors had started out from Rupertville with enough food and fuel to last a week, enough for a round trip to Ground Zero. En route, they had stopped twice to stash fuel drums, water and food in caches off the highway to lighten their load and increase their speed. Even load-lightened, the fastest the convoy could go on the interstate was less than 25 miles per hour. And they managed that only in short stretches of fifty to a hundred yards because the roadway was in such bad shape.

Through the dust, Ryan saw a pair of riders sweep over a low rise on the left. Angling in on the convoy at a full gallop, they merged alongside the lead wag. Besup gestured to Burning Man from horseback. Galloping beside him, Jak straddled a pinto bareback, his long white hair flying out behind his head. They were advance scouts, riding ahead of the convoy, returning to report washouts of pavement, cave-ins, dropped highway overpasses and the safest alternate routes. Slake City was still too far away for them to worry about making contact with the enemy. Because of the condition of the predark road, and the fact that they had to keep detouring off it, they made halting progress. There was nothing static in the path south. The forces of nature constantly recast it—dirt lane detours crosscut or washed away entirely by flash floods.

The warriors, Burning Man included, had adopted Jak as one of their own after the first night's encampment. Ryan knew in part it had to do with their fascination over the color of his skin—or lack of same—but the sudden kinship wasn't just because of Jak's natural "white face." After they had set up camp that evening, the warriors not on sentry duty amused themselves with a knife-throwing contest. Besup beat all comers by repeatedly placing his fixed-blade pig-sticker in the wooden target's center ring from a distance of twenty paces. He was a knife-throwing machine. With his fellow fighters cheering the performance, Besup had reached out to pry his winning throw out of the ten-ring.

From the edge of the leaping firelight, something whistled through the air too fast to follow. Flying across the camp, its impact was a muffled thump. Besup froze, crouched in front of the target, his fingers gripping his knife handle. The top of his outstretched sleeve seemed to be attached to the wood. He tried to free it and couldn't without lifting the target off the ground. He had to release his knife and lever loose the deeply buried staple. Then he held it up to the light for all to see.

A palm-sized, leaf-bladed throwing knife, its keen edge glinting.

Standing at twice the distance to the target, on the far side of the campfire, his ruby red eyes glittering fiercely, Jak held up a matching blade. He didn't say a word.

He didn't have to.

The stoic Besup let out an explosive bellow of laughter, then shouted something unintelligible to the others, who found it funny, too. The entire clan encircled Jak, grinning, backslapping their congratulations. Even Burning Man joined in, and after the ruckus died down, he drew the albino teen aside for a private chat.

Next day, they had Jak riding scout with Besup. And when they spoke to him or of him they used an old familiar name—White Wolf.

Burning Man waved a NOMEX-clad arm out the driver's window of the lead wag. The signal quickly passed back through the ranks and the convoy slowed to a crawl. Behind Jak and Besop's lead, the entire procession turned onto the shoulder, then rattled and rumbled off the interstate, heading overland, in the direction of a pair of barren, rounded hilltops about a quarter mile away.

They stopped in the saddle between the twin hills and began to set up camp for the night, tethering horses and war dogs, hiding the wags and carts under camouflaged tarp shelters.

Ryan and his companions, grim-faced and caked with dirt, bent over their weapons, cleaning them and checking their readiness while it was still light enough to see. As they worked over their gear, warriors came around carrying jugs of water. Ryan used his first sip to wash the grit out of his mouth. He spit pale brown onto the ground, took another mouthful and rinsed again before gulping a drink.

Unlike the night before, no one was building campfires—not now that they were within range of a high-altitude night recon by the she-hes' gyroplane. There was none of the singing and chanting of the previous night, either. The war dogs didn't bark; the horses didn't whinny or nicker. Sound carried a long way in the high desert.

When the grub was distributed, the companions ate their antelope jerky and cold beans in silence. While they were chewing and chewing, trying to soften the hard, stringy meat so it could be swallowed, Burning Man stepped over to them.

"To keep down the dust we're going to have to go much slower tomorrow," he said. "Don't want the gyroplane to catch us stretched out on the plain and give it an easy daylight shot."

"What about an infrared scan?" Mildred said. "We know the battlesuits have that capability, so the aircraft has got to have it, too. Even if we're not raising dust, we're throwing off a heat signature."

"Temperatures midday should mask that," the baron said. "Besides, I can't see our enemies burning fuel on unnecessary, long-distance surveillance with their one and only gyro. Sitting in the middle of the massif, they've got to believe they're safe. They know the sorry state of any military gear in these parts. The reason they're camped at Ground Zero isn't because of outside threats from the likes of us, it's to speed up the repowering of their batteries. As soon as they have enough stored fuel to run their wags and power their weapons, they can get on with their conquest. Come morning, we'll cut across country to reach the ruins at Slake City. We should be at the southern edge of the glacier by tomorrow evening."

"But you told us there's nothing left of the old she-he

base there," Ryan said. "If that's the case, why are we swinging so far south? It's got to add an extra half day to the trip. We could save a lot of time if we started across the massif sooner."

"That's not an option," Burning Man said. "There's only one road cut through to Ground Zero, and we've got to use it. Even the ghost warriors can't break trail on the nukeglass at night."

"We're making the assault at night?" J.B. said in disbelief. "By rad-blasted starlight? Over *that* terrain?"

"Crossing the glacier on that road is wicked dangerous even in daytime," Mildred chimed in. "We know because we've gone that route. The road bed isn't just crudely cut, it's unstable. The ground opens up in cracks without warning. Some of the cracks are big enough to swallow the entire convoy. We've seen whole sections of road slough off into deep chasms. And there are landslides of razor-edged boulders. They either crush you flat or cut you in two."

"To get into position to attack the site we have to cover eight miles of dead zone," Burning Man countered. "We have to do it at night, and on foot. We can't use wags because the engine noise would give us away, and the weight would increase the danger of road cave-ins. For the same reasons, we're leaving the horses and the carts behind. We'll take along the pack of war dogs, of course. And we'll be carrying all the ammunition and explosives on our backs."

J.B. shook his head. "We don't have night-vision gear. If we had a full moon overhead, it might just be doable, but without a moon…"

"I don't see that we really have a choice here," Ryan

said grimly. "We can't count on the slaves at Ground Zero to fight on our side. This time they might decide to run and hide to save their skins. If we don't do something unexpected, if we don't take the she-hes by surprise, they will chill us all, and in short order."

"He's right," Krysty said to J.B. "Surprise is our only advantage. Without it, we don't stand a chance."

"What chance are we going to have if the road opens up under us in the dark or we slide off it into a bottomless pit?" J.B. said. "One wrong step and we'll lose most of our fighters before we get anywhere near Ground Zero."

"You're underestimating the ghost warriors," Burning Man said. "Believe me, you haven't seen the half of what they can do."

J.B.'s persistent scowl told Ryan that his old friend wasn't convinced, and he had good reason to be skeptical. They didn't know much of anything about the men they were going to be fighting alongside, and on whose skills their lives were going to depend. It was a state of affairs that needed to be rectified, and at once.

"You never told us what happened to you after you left Moonboy," Ryan reminded the baron. "How did all this come about—you, the Bannock-Shoshone, the face paint? If it wasn't nuked, what happened to Rupertville?"

"It's a long story," Burning Man said. "Too long to tell standing up." He took a seat cross-legged on the ground and gestured for the others to sit down as well.

"As I said before," he said after they had all gathered around him, "the predark ville on the other side of the river missed the worst effects of the nukecaust. Its isolation and distance from any high-value targets are what saved it from firestorm, shock waves and heavy fallout. Sometime after nukeday, the survivor families of Rupertville banded together. Organized in a loose, paramilitary fashion, they started taking and keeping slaves to work their crops to maximize agricultural production in a world where fuel was suddenly scarce.

"At first they went after members of the Bannock-Shoshone tribe, primarily because they were close by, and didn't have the means to repell well-armed attacks or rescue their loved ones after they were taken. The militiamen bred field slaves in fenced prison compounds on the edge of the ville—and not just for their own use. They sold and traded off the excess laborers, mostly to the eastern baronies. Their biggest profit was in selling people, not tomatoes and peppers.

"About seventy-five years ago, they began using tribal prisoners to scout out and hunt down human trade goods, new slaves for their masters. Anybody and everybody passing through the territory was fair game. Back in those days the warriors had to obey because their families were held hostage, under threat of death in the Rupertville slave pens. The Bannock-Shoshone raiding parties traveled south and east, and they sometimes even stole back the slaves that had just been sold to the barons.

"When I showed up at the foot of the Highway 84 bridge, fresh out of Moonboy, some of the militia were waiting on horseback behind the roadblock to greet me. They all had their blasters leveled. The head man was there, too. They didn't refer to him as baron. He was called General Tidwell. I assume the title was a carryover from the militia's early days. He was a tall, stringy bastard with scarred knuckles, close-set black eyes, weather-seamed, grizzle-stubbled cheeks, and what few teeth he had were streaked and stained brown.

"Old Tidwell's eyes lit up when he saw my tribarrel blaster and ATV. Right away, he wanted to know where he could get his hands on more of the same, said he had plenty of slaves and joy juice to trade. When I told him there weren't any more weapons or ATVs, he invited me to cross the bridge free of charge and offered me his ville's hospitality, which I guessed included taking my gear and dumping my corpse in the river. There were a dozen militiamen spread out behind the barricade with rifles aimed, and I wasn't wearing my battle armor. Even with the tribarrel, I couldn't stand and fight them and hope to win. And they would have had me cold if I'd tried to turn a one-eighty with the ATV and make a run for it. Since I had no choice, I played along. I even thanked the general for his kindness.

"After we crossed the bridge—them on their horses, me on the ATV—and we entered the ville, the whole entourage made a right turn toward the central square. Figuring it was my chance, I broke away from them, throttle pinned. I thought I was going to make it free and clear, but a volley of rifle shots rained down from behind and blew out the back tires on the ATV. I crashed it hard and flipped it, which put me on foot against men on horses, with no cover from the hail of their rifle fire.

"Long story short, they chased me through the streets, between houses, over fences, down alleys, firing away at will. It was like a game to them, especially because I couldn't slow down to return fire without getting hit.

I ended up on the front lawn of a tiny predark house beside the slave pens. As I ran inside, the slaves were all ducking for cover behind the perimeter wire. With bullets shattering the windows and splintering the door I crawled on my belly, trying to find a bearing wall for cover. General Tidwell and his militiamen had me dead to rights. Surrounded. Backed into a corner."

The baron paused for breath, and instead of picking the story right up again, he let the silence drag on.

And on.

Ryan caught himself leaning forward. He could see he wasn't alone. His companions were leaning forward, too. Even J.B. seemed transfixed by the drama of the tale.

"Old Tidwell," Burning Man finally resumed, "was the original Rupertville pyro-fucking-maniac. He collected predark glass bottles that he liked to make into wag-fuel bombs. I guess you could say it was his hobby. Wag fuel was one of the things they got from the east in trade for human beings. Since the general knew he had me trapped, he ordered his men to stop shooting and start throwing fire bombs through the windows and onto the roof. The place was ablaze in a couple of minutes. To escape the flames and smoke I cut a hole in the floor with my laser rifle and dropped down into the dirt crawl space, which was only about two feet high and twenty-by-twenty feet across.

"Over the crackling and hissing of the fire, I could hear Tidwell and his men laughing and yelling taunts at me. Smoke and burning fuel poured into the crawlspace through the gaps in the floor planking, and fire was already curling around some of the joists. Then a fuel bomb must have shattered on the floor right above me, because liquid fire rained down on my head. As I rolled around in the dirt trying to put it out, more bombs exploded, more fire rained down. I heard someone screaming their lungs out—then I realized it was me and I was pissing myself. I could smell my own flesh burning."

The baron paused again, only this time not for breath. He seemed momentarily frozen, caught up in the memory. His eyes suddenly lost the spark of life. Ryan recognized that flat effect, that thousand-yard stare: Burning Man was reliving in excruciating detail the horror that had melted half of his face. Then the instant passed, and the cruel light winked back on in his eyes.

"Something very strange happened to me in the crawl space," he confessed. "I guess you could say my brain overloaded and short-circuited. Rolling around down there in the dirt, I was struck by the fact that I was about to die for a couple of pieces of battle gear, one of which was already wrecked, and the other soon to run out of power. After leaping universes, I was going to die a totally pointless death. That realization and the agony from flames I couldn't smother sent me into a blind rage. Suddenly the pain was gone. All I felt was the driving need to get some payback.

"I kicked out a screen foundation vent and came out from under that burning shack with my hair and head still on fire. I caught the militiamen flatfooted, with their weapons either holstered or lowered, and bunched up like sheep in the middle of the street. Before they could react, I green-lighted the bastards. With one sweep of the tribarrel, I cut every one of them in two, and dropped them, legless, armless, thrashing and screaming into the road. Then I stepped up close and slow-motion lasered off the top of Tidwell's head just above the eyebrows. By the time I was done sawing up the rest of his sec men, the tribarrel's power cell was empty. That's when I let the slaves out of the pens. From the looks on their faces as I stepped up to the wire, they must have thought the devil himself had come to claim them. I guess I was still smoking like a chimney.

"Right after that, I collapsed from my burns and went into a coma. I found out later that the slaves went berserk after I let them loose. Seeing their opportunity for some retribution at long last, they went through Rupertville, torching it street by street, burned it to the ground, and sent the villefolk running for the horizon with whatever they could carry. The freed slaves chased them down and slaughtered them all. Nothing I could do to stop it, even if I'd wanted to. I was in a coma for more than a month. When I came out of it with their help, everything had changed. There was a new settlement under construction on the other side of the river. Most of the slaves who weren't Bannock-Shoshone had already gone back to wherever they were stolen from. And I was a celebrity.

"After I'd recovered, they made me their leader and gave me the name 'Burning Man.' I tried to make the most of it. That's why I put together the flamethrower. There's nothing like a signature weapon and a half-melted face to strike unreasoning fear into your enemies. Fairly simple piece of machinery to assemble—nozzle, igniter, storage tanks—although pressurizing the wag fuel can be a bit dicey."

"And the white paint?" Krysty asked.

"That was the Bannock-Shoshones' idea. I had nothing to do with it. The way they tell it, the paint signifies their spiritual connection to ancestors who suffered and died under the Rupertville militia, and to those who died long before nukeday, the victims of other invading oppressors. Those who survived the slave camps see themselves as living ghosts who walk this world and the next simultaneously, whose spirits abide in both realms. They attribute the skills they've acquired in the process of hunting humans for three-quarters of a century—moving unseen, without sound, tracking their quarry through the darkest night—to this spiritual relationship, which they believe was born out of their agony and their triumph. I'm the religion's poster boy, having 'died' before their eyes, and then returned to life while they watched."

"Given the characteristically pale skins of Western Europeans, there's a certain irony to the facial decoration," Doc said.

"If not an outright mockery," Mildred said. "Are they aware of that?"

Burning Man smiled with the functional side of his face. "The Bannock-Shoshone are a subtle people with a finely honed sense of humor," he said. "After the overthrow of the militia, they shifted the focus of the local economy from slave trade to self-sustaining agriculture. We're no longer dependent on outsiders for anything except wag fuel. And that's the way we like it. Because our nearest neighbors are so far away, we've only had to fight off the odd scouting party. Barons east of us want no part of us because of the distances involved—it's too difficult and too costly to resupply their forces—and because they know our reputation for fieldcraft, night-fighting and short tempers."

The baron rose to his feet and stretched his arms and legs. "Try to get some rest while you can," he told them. "For sure there won't be any sleeping tomorrow night." Then he turned and left them to get on with it.

Ryan didn't ask J.B. if Burning Man's story had made him feel any better about the attack plan. He could see from the unhappy expression it hadn't. That didn't stop his old friend from speaking his mind after Burning Man was out of earshot.

"Ghosts walking the earth?" J.B. scoffed. "Spirit powers? I know a load of bullshit when I smell it."

"That's just the only way they have to explain what's happened to them," Mildred assured him. "They're trying to make sense of gifts they don't understand. It's much more likely that the night sight, superhearing and other acute senses are the result of a unique mutation brought on by nukeday, and refined over generations of the militia's selective breeding program."

"So far it's all talk, isn't it?" J.B. said. "And from a droolie I wouldn't trust to shell peas. Once we get out in the middle of the glacier, in the pitch-dark, it'll be too late to take any of it back."

"Not all talk," Jak insisted. "Seen it. Warriors move like shadows. Follow trail where no sign."

J.B. folded his arms across his chest and shrugged.

Ryan wondered if his old friend was still miffed because the warriors had taken him by surprise. J.B. wasn't used to being so thoroughly bested by anyone.

If pride was the problem, he had about twenty-four hours to get over it.

In the failing light and gathering chill, Ryan and the companions spread out their bedrolls on the ground. Below them, the saddle between the hills was already dotted with curled-up bodies.

A RUSH OF COLD AIR against his back jarred Ryan awake. He turned and opened his eye. Krysty was sitting up. In the process she had lifted the edge of their shared bedroll, letting in the night chill. He guessed it was still four hours until dawn.

"What's wrong?" he asked her gently.

"Can't sleep, lover," Krysty replied.

"Is it what J.B. said? Is that what's worrying you? I don't know why but a very large bug seems to have crawled up his butt."

"Of course I'm worried," she told him. "But thinking about crossing the nukeglass tomorrow isn't what's keeping me up—it's that queen bitch, Dredda Otis Trask."

"What about her?" Ryan asked, somewhat at a loss.

"I've tried to forget what she did to me at Slake City," Krysty said. "Because she was so far out of reach, with no hope of her ever coming back, remembering how she violated me seemed pointless. But now there's a chance—maybe even a good chance—she might have returned to Ground Zero."

"That's true. And it means you'll have an opportunity to settle the score, once and for all. So what's the problem?"

"If she's there, I'll make her pay for what she did to me, but it could already be too late to stop her."

"I don't understand."

"She might have used the sperm she took from me,

from you, to artificially inseminate her eggs," Krysty said. "Ryan, you could have offspring you don't know about out there somewhere on other Earths. Mebbe even on this one."

"I do have offspring," Ryan countered, "and he's gone, taken from me. I think about Dean every day."

"Still, you have to face the possibility that there could be others you know nothing about…."

"If Dredda managed to mix up some children in a jar or some such," Ryan said, "are they really mine when I had no part in raising them?"

"I shudder to think what a she-he would do to a baby."

"A normal child would be of no use to them," Ryan said. "Their goal was to make more creatures like themselves, to propagate their species. Which means any kid they created would be forced to undergo the same genetic engineering as they did. So, if Dredda did make a child, and it was half-mine, would it really be human at this point?"

After a silence, Krysty shifted the subject. "I wish I could give you another son, Ryan," she said. "I'm starting to worry because we've been together so long and I haven't gotten pregnant."

"Mebbe the Earth Mother decided it just isn't the right time for us yet."

"Mebbe I can't ever have children. Mebbe it's part of my mutation, the part you can't see." She touched the ends of her prehensile mutie hair, and its Medusa-like tendrils automatically curled around her fingertips.

"Right now it's better for all concerned that you haven't gotten pregnant," Ryan told her. "Better if that happens after we find a safe place to settle down. If there is such a place…"

She leaned over and kissed him tenderly, then slipped back under the blanket.

Ryan felt her moving against him, kicking off her boots and wriggling out of her jeans. He knew what came next. His pulse pounding in his throat, he sat up and looked around them on the slope. It was hard to see much of anything in the weak light. No one else was moving, though. They were all asleep.

Naked from the waist down under the blanket, Krysty spread her legs wide as he rolled on top of her. He held himself on elbows and knees, poised to strike at the gates of heaven.

In the starlight his lover's flame-red hair turned a glistening black, and it coiled and uncoiled on the blanket like a nest of maddened snakes. Her eyes were wide open, searching, reading his face. Her fingertips traced his lips. Then their mouths met again, tongues touching.

Ryan drove deep into her, as deep as he could go. Then as her long legs wrapped themselves around the small of his back, he plunged over and over into the searing heat, the exquisite softness.

Below his face, the snakes of hair ceased their writhing and began to tremble. Her back arched up from the blanket to meet him and a soft moan escaped her lips. The shock waves of her internal convulsions were galvanic: before he could draw another breath, he was a goner, too.

In the afterglow of their lovemaking, Ryan sensed Krysty's heaviness of spirit had lifted at least momentarily, replaced by sweet, utter exhaustion. Locked in each other's arms they drifted off to sleep.

Chapter Eleven

A handful of milling slaves scattered out of Auriel's path as she advanced on the mine's main entrance. Haloed by the late-afternoon sun blasting off the massif, the crudely hewn, semicircular opening yawned before her. Twenty feet inside the shaft, her battlesuit helmet sensed the dimming light and automatically switched on its headlamp, illuminating the tunnel wall-to-wall and floor-to-ceiling. The battlesuit's external microphone picked up and amplified distant, muffled sounds of pick-axes chinking nukeglass, of shovels scraping rubble and a steady, rhythmic clanking.

As she descended deeper into the throat of the shaft, the clanking grew louder and louder, until it drowned out all the other sounds. Then, from around a bend at the extreme limit of the floodlight, the low gray-steel bow of an ore cart appeared. The cart's wheels bumping over the traction-ribbed floor made the rhythmic noise. At the rear of the cart, Auriel could see the rag-wrapped faces of the slaves pushing it. There was more than just ore in the cargo box—two pairs of human legs hung limply over the sides. They didn't belong to exhausted workers getting a free ride from their sympathetic com-rades. Miners who dropped dead in the traces or were cut to ribbons by cave-ins or ambushed by stickies were carted out of the depths, and summarily dumped beside the cook pots.

The distance between the cart and Auriel rapidly closed. Five slaves struggled with their load, gasping, heads lowered, backs bent, legs driving, pushing it up the shallow incline toward the light of day. Below the laser cuffs, their rag-wrapped hands were encrusted with what looked like dirt, but it was actually dried blood from a profusion of glass cuts.

As Auriel passed by the miners, they glanced up from their toil.

Wary.

Fearful.

Desperate.

But determined. As if to say, any life—even this unthinkably wretched excuse for one—was better than death.

Perhaps a function of her own exhaustion and stress, at that moment Auriel's shield of emotional detachment, of indifference, of physical and mental superiority seemed to waver—the parallel predicament of slaves and master struck home. Her prisoners were doing whatever was necessary, to whomever it was necessary in order to survive to see the next sunrise, just as she was. To keep on going, the miners had to drive the idea that they were doomed out of their heads, just as she did.

There was a significant difference, though.

The slaves' responsibilities were to themselves, to their individual survival, while the fate of all Auriel's sisters, of their unique species, of her mother's legacy, and of the advanced techno-culture that had enabled their creation lay in her young hands. She couldn't turn her back on the burden nor delegate the responsibility to her sisters or to Dr. Huth. It was hers, and hers alone.

Countless times since Dredda's death Auriel had asked herself, why me?

Only two answers had ever occurred to her.

Because there was no other; no one else could lead the sisters to safety. Not even Mero.

Because deep in her heart Auriel knew she had been chosen. This battle was her destiny, win or lose.

Around the turn, the tunnel's downgrade steepened. The light of her helmet's headlamp turned the walls, ribbed floor and the ceiling an opaque, muddy green. With the hard glare off the glass, she couldn't see into the depths of the massif, couldn't see any of the collection of trapped material, the sea of rubbish that hadn't melted or burned to ash on nukeday.

A quarter mile below ground, branching off on either side of the main tunnel, were much narrower passages, winding crevices with just enough room for a worker to swing a pick. These offshoot seams held the richest pockets of radioactive ore, the main shaft having already been mined out. They were also the places where stickies staged their most effective ambushes.

Her helmet's beam lit up an ore cart parked in front of a side seam on the left, about seventy-five feet ahead. The lamp's power obliterated the puddles of weak luminescence cast by overhead strings of widely spaced, nuke-powered lights. The brilliance momentarily froze the crew standing alongside the cart. Then, in unison, they raised their forearms to shield their eyes.

As Auriel approached, the slaves hurriedly resumed work. In the punishing heat, in a twilight intermixed with the blackness of the pit, with heaps of glass dust glittering around their boot tops, they passed ten-pound and bigger hunks of nukeglass out of the cleft. The last miner in the human chain piled them into the bottom of the cart.

That man was very tall and stripped to the waist, a filthy rag tied over his nose and mouth. His hair had been hacked off in clumps close to his head, perhaps with a knife blade. Wounds were visible on his face and skull, a cross-hatching of shallow cuts from flying glass. His well-muscled torso and arms dripped perspiration. When he turned to accept a chunk of ore from the short, buxom female slave to his right, she saw that a blue black shadow covered his left shoulder and draped down his back. Not a massive bruise or a radiation burn—a tattooed dragon. Under a sheen of sweat, the huge reptile was caught in the act of unfolding its leathery wings.

As Auriel passed the cart, the tattooed slave looked up, as did the female, her cap of auburn hair twinkling with tiny glass fragments. Before averting their eyes in customary deference to the masters, they allowed her to glimpse their pure, ravening hatred. It was an act of defiance that jolted the she-he commander.

So far, there had been no hint of a Ground Zero slave rebellion or mass escape attempt, but Auriel knew they were thinking about it. They had to be after seeing a battle-suited Mero collapse in a heap on the nukeglass. They had to sense a weakness that wasn't there before.

Every revolt needed leaders.

Auriel marked the insolent Dragon man and his girlfriend for death at the first sign of trouble.

After another ten yards of straightaway the shaft

veered hard right and began to turn upon itself, a single helix boring inexorably downward. This was the most difficult and dangerous traverse for the slaves, a steeply pitched spiral that ended at the very bottom of the mine. The traction grids cut into the floor minimized but couldn't eliminate runaway or overturned ore carts.

Halfway down, Auriel had to switch off her external microphone. The screams and moans coming from below were too distracting. The noise wasn't from the miners. Captive, specter-infected stickies were vocalizing their misery and terror, and their gathered, wild brethren were wailing along in sympathy.

At the bottom of the spiral, Auriel walked under the explosive-mined ceiling and down the harshly illuminated tunnel. To conserve battery power, her armor's computer automatically shut off the helmet's headlamp.

A person in a full battlesuit stood in front of a cell at the far end of the corridor. Not a warrior—her visor's sensors identified the armor as belonging to Dr. Huth. On the other side of him, fifty feet farther down the tunnel, she caught a blur of movement. Blocked by the force field, free-range stickies were waving their pale, spindly arms and jumping about agitatedly. There were about thirty of them; it was hard to tell precisely because the rear of the mob faded off into the darkness.

To reach Dr. Huth, Auriel had to pass in front of the row of cells—and their occupants. The naked muties, male and female, all lay on befouled floor on their backs. Pinned to the ground by their mountainous bellies, they were incapacitated except for their screaming, and the aimless, futile thrashing of arms and legs. Their cries and the limb thrashing coincided with the rhythmic, outward pulsations of their torsos. Pulsations that were visible to Auriel as skin, muscle and tendon ballooned, stretching just short of the splitting point, then shrinking back.

The unspeakably mutated monsters of this earth were about to give birth to even worse monsters.

These poor stickies didn't have long to live, nor did the horrendous things that slithered among their guts.

A mass burn-off loomed large in all their futures.

As Auriel approached Dr. Huth, she could see his face inside the helmet. The underlighting of its visor's displays accentuated the deep seams and pits in his cheeks and nose, and the heavy bags under his eyes. He smiled a brittle smile of greeting, which made Auriel shudder.

The survival of her species depended upon this grizzled, toothless old man.

Over his shoulder, down the narrow tunnel, Auriel had a much better view of the berserking stickies. With sucker adhesive streaming from fingertips and palms, they hurled themselves at the impenetrable force field, over and over again, like automatons. Maws gaping, they shrieked in a manic pantomime.

Had Auriel had her external audio turned on, it would have been absolute, mind-numbing bedlam in the confined space.

Dr. Huth gestured toward the opening of cell number seven.

Her battlesuit and body stocking stripped off and flung in a heap in a corner, Mero knelt naked on the cell's nukeglass floor. The nine hours that had passed since her initial collapse had wrought a horrific transformation.

Drenched in sweat, Auriel's second in command appeared caught up in the throes of a grand epileptic seizure—her jaws snapping, eyelids rapidly fluttering, powerful arm and thigh muscles quivering in spasm, the tendons in her neck as rigid as cables. And at some point earlier in the fit, her bowels had released. She had soiled herself and the cell floor. After fifteen more seconds of quaking rictus, the seizure finally passed. Still kneeling, her eyes closed, Mero threw back her head and parted her foam-flecked lips.

No sound came forth because Auriel's audio was still shut off, but the sight of her friend, her sister, her battlemate screaming like that was a sword thrust to her solar plexus, an agonizing, transfixing pain straight to her core. And she immediately flashed back to her own mother's death, to the detonation—there was no other word to describe the violence of the specters' mass birthing. When Dredda's torso gave way to the pressure, it was like a frag gren had exploded inside her. The tremendous outward blast had split her in two crossways and hollowed her out all the way to the backbone, reducing her heart, lungs, stomach and bowels to flying gobbets and blood mist.

Death, when it had finally come, had been instantaneous.

Shakily, Mero rose to her feet and slowly turned toward the opening, her pale blue eyes blank with shock, her close-cropped blond curls matted to her skull. Gray ash, the residue from the immolation of the cell's previous occupant, had mixed with her sweat and now ran in rivulets down the milk-white skin of her legs. Mero's pectorals weren't overlaid with fatty breast tissue, but rock-solid muscle. The same for her buttocks. The she-hes' genetic engineering had overbuilt her skeletal structure to support the extra thick sinew and layers of muscle. There was a noticeable bulge in her midsection that hadn't been there earlier in the day; she looked like she was five months pregnant.

But for that ominous bulge, and the color of her hair, Auriel might have been staring at herself in a mirror.

When their eyes met, Mero seemed to come out of her stupor. There was an instant of recognition in Mero's face, then crushing sadness and fear.

She was doomed.

And they both knew it.

The psychic sword in Auriel's stomach twisted, and lances of pain shot down the backs of her legs. Pain, like joy, like love, was part of the invisible bond she shared with her sister-warrior. And this pain was almost unendurable. A true hero—one of the bravest, strongest, most loyal human beings to ever draw breath—was going to live out the last hours of her life in excruciating agony, in this utter shithole beneath the ground, amid the din of mindless, gibbering mutants.

Grief-stricken though she was, Auriel couldn't dwell on her own anguish. As commander, that luxury was denied her. There were the others to think of. Her sisters still looked to her for hope, for a way out of their predicament, even though it looked like the window of escape was rapidly closing. In two more days they would have stored enough battery power to put Shadow Earth behind them, but only if Mero's infestation was an isolated incident would they leap universes again.

Otherwise, there was no point to it. They couldn't escape what was already growing inside them.

If the contagion had spread among their ranks, this was where—and how—everything would end.

"We are cursed" is what Dredda had said.

Because they had tinkered with the mechanisms of their own bodies? Because they had cheated fate by leaping realities? Because in their hubris they had violated some basic underlying principle of existence?

With her mother's last words echoing in her head, Auriel forced herself to look away from Mero's face. She keyed the suit-to-suit com link. "How many of us are infected?" she asked Dr. Huth.

"I have scanned everyone," the whitecoat replied. "And I found no sign of specters. But that falls well short of what I consider to be definitive evidence. It is impossible to locate individual spores inside the body without first tagging them with radiation markers."

"Can you control Mero's seizures with medication?"

"No, the convulsions are a result of the tremendous internal pressure exerted by the specters on her organs and nerves. I can dull the pain somewhat, but you do understand that she is going to die harder than any of the stickies because her altered physiology is much more resilient—heavier bones, larger muscle mass. Chances are, it will contain the specters longer before they eventually break out and kill her."

"So she will suffer like my mother did?"

"Precisely."

"I can't allow that. Make her unconscious and incinerate her, now."

"You're not thinking this through," Dr. Huth said.

Auriel stared at the old man. He was smiling that phony, gap-toothed smile of his. It made her want to throttle him until his tongue turned black. Had Mero somehow been contaminated by his precious spore samples and experiments on the stickies? She knew that was highly unlikely given the test protocols—and the sister-warriors had been sealed up in their battlesuits ever since their arrival on Shadow Earth. Apparently, their efforts at sterilization and isolation on the twelfth Earth had been in vain. Either that, or reinfection had occurred during the Null space transit.

"What else can we do for her?" Auriel demanded.

"We can't stop or slow the specters' maturation process," he told her. "In her case it seems to be picking up momentum at record speed. Mero's end is inevitable, and it will come very soon. As you suggest, we can put her out of her misery before they break out, but if we do that, her death will have been for nothing. If she has to be sacrificed, shouldn't it be for a greater purpose?"

"What do you mean?"

"We have the option of letting the specters come to term and hatch out of her," he said. "We can confine them in the same cell. They can't penetrate the force field and escape. I've never had the opportunity to run tests on them outside of a host. Those tests may give us the information we need to destroy them."

"You could do that with the infected stickies, instead."

"Yes, I could," he admitted, "but not with as reliable results. I know very little about the normal physiology and functioning of those mutants. On the other hand,

I have a great deal of information on the expression of Mero's virally altered genetics. As I told you before, discovering what the specters are taking from their victims is the critical element here. Given our failure to destroy them up to this point, understanding what these entities are doing, and why, is probably our last remaining hope. If we euthanize Mero now to ease her suffering and then reality-jump as soon as we have sufficient power, wherever we materialize next we will face the same insurmountable problem, with the same limited set of facts to work from. You can't let yourself be swayed by emotion. You can't let this opportunity slip through our fingers."

Auriel glared at him. True to form, the whitecoat was leaving out a significant downside. If after the monsters burst out of Mero, Dr. Huth couldn't find a way to kill them, he, Auriel and the sister-warriors could still jump away, leaving Shadow Earth to the specters, who would divide, spread and feed until there was nothing left.

Ceding victory once more to those hated enemies was a bitter pill to swallow. This abundant, relatively unsullied replica Earth by rights should have been hers and her sisters' to harvest and to husband.

There was also another, even graver possibility: that they were all infected by the spores and didn't know it yet. The initial error compounded exponentially.

Fatally.

At that moment, seemingly on-cue, the stabbing pain in her gut transformed. Instead of being spread over a wide area, it became centered, a tightly focused pinpoint of sensation. It felt like something was moving, something wriggling inside her.

A chill raced down the length of her spine, and adrenaline rush made her heart pound and her face burn.

With an effort of will she shrugged off the uncharacteristic wave of panic. Merely the power of suggestion, she assured herself. Battlesuit sensors could trigger tiny muscle spasms; it happened all the time.

Besides, she knew that even if it turned out she was infected like Mero, even if they were all infected, it didn't change anything. For the sake of her ten other sisters she couldn't give up. They were the first and last of their breed. Her only family. Her only future.

Auriel shut off the com link and turned away from Dr. Huth.

Mero was staring at her through the shimmer of the force field, her naked body trembling, her belly protruding, her eyes pleading for mercy.

Mercy that couldn't be granted.

Although she had no reproductive organs, Mero was going to give birth. She was going to suffer horribly for the good of the warrior-sisterhood, and the edification of Dr. Huth. Auriel couldn't explain that to her now, not with all the stickies yelling. Maybe when it was quiet, after they were burned to ash…

In the meantime, standing ramrod straight, Auriel raised a clenched, gauntleted fist to her beloved sister.

The universal sign for "stay strong."

Chapter Twelve

Over the low rumble of wag engines and the squeak of leaf springs, Ryan heard a droning sound. Distant. Intermittent. The widely spaced wags, horses and dog carts were crawling through the broiling, late afternoon. Minimum speed and maximum separation distance helped to keep down the telltale dust. Burning Man's wag rolled at the head of the long column, controlling the pace.

Brake lights flashed, and the convoy came to a halt.

Whitefaces on horseback pointed to the north, at the source of the sawing noise.

From the back of a stake truck wag, Ryan saw a darting shadow against the backdrop of brown hills and green-gray massif. The sleek, black ship looked like it was skimming over the surface, only he knew that was impossible because it was moving way too fast. An optical illusion, Ryan realized, because of the distance. It was at least five miles away. The gyro was flying very low, less than two hundred feet above the ground, and angling away from them at high speed toward Ground Zero.

Because the gyro had no altitude to speak of, because it was going in the opposite direction, apparently it couldn't pick them out against the background of desert. Or maybe its sensors just weren't looking southeast.

Either way, there was no reason for the column to take evasive action.

"Isn't flying recon," J.B. said. "Got to be a transport mission."

"We lucked out," Mildred added.

Ryan seconded that. If they had been caught out in open, they had no defense against the black ship's firepower.

The column held position and waited. It didn't take long. A minute later the gyroplane disappeared over the curve of horizon.

Then the grinding tedium of their advance resumed.

IT WAS EVENING by the time they arrived at their destination. For hours they had paralleled the border where the barren hardpan ended and the thermoglass monolith began. The hundred-square-mile backwash of nukeday was like an unnatural growth, a vast, alien landscape dropped down onto the high desert plain.

When the wag engines shut off, it got very quiet. Quiet enough for Ryan to hear the sounds of babies crying, babies screaming. Not real babies, of course. The wide disparity between day and nighttime temperatures caused the massif to expand and contract. Its manifold imperfections, its embedded material, became focal points for fractures and tectonic shifts, and the friction of glass scraping against glass made the piercing, desperate noises.

Like a burning orphanage.

Ryan and Krysty jumped down from the wag bed. J.B., Mildred and Doc followed. As they all hopped to the ground, Jak rode up on his pinto. After dismounting and tying the horse's reins to the wag rear bumper, the albino teen joined the others, surveying in silence what little was left of the she-hes' Slake City encampment.

Before them was a series of tightly-clustered craters blown into the beige hardpan. It looked like the aftermath of an exquisitely targeted artillery barrage. Some of the holes were deep enough and wide enough to swallow four wags abreast.

What had happened here occurred years earlier, Ryan knew. Even so, the detritus of that demolition was still in evidence, scattered all around them. Twisted fragments of black plasteel—some bigger than a person, the rest a confetti of splinters and shards—lay on top of brown earth and the dull green nuggets of glass, the remains of molten hail that had pummeled the earth on nukeday.

When Ryan and the companions had departed this place, there had been wags here. Colossal, 6x6 land-dreadnoughts, armed with laser cannon. There had also been rows of milspec huts connected by enclosed passageways.

The one-eyed man stepped up to the nearest crater and looked over the rim. It was about ten feet deep and twice that across. The bottom was obscured by a puddle of stagnant water. Half-submerged down there was a wag wheel and half an axle. The wheel's tire was seven feet in diameter.

Burning Man approached them, with Big Mike in tow. Big Mike's arm stumps and legs were free, but he had a rope noose tied around his neck. He didn't look at all happy to be there, and certainly not on the eve of battle. Ryan figured it was a case of the glass being half full: Big Mike should have been counting himself lucky there wasn't a tree in sight to toss the end of the rope over.

"You did all this?" Krysty asked the baron, gesturing at the craters. "Blew up the wags and everything else?"

"Took every gram of explosive I had on hand," Burning Man said. "But it was worth it."

J.B. gave him a hard look. "Why did you destroy everything?" he said. "You understood the technology. Couldn't you have used it?"

"You folks were here long before I was," Burning Man countered. "Why didn't you just drive off in the wags? You left them here."

"They stopped running after the she-hes reality-jumped," Ryan said. "Out of battery juice. We couldn't figure out how to repower them. The she-hes didn't leave any operating manuals behind."

"You didn't answer J.B.'s question," Mildred said to the baron. "Why did you blow up all the wags? They came from your own home world. You had to know how to repower them."

"That would have been like taking poison," Burning Man told her. "Because that's what was left behind— techno poison. To use the technology myself and the tribe, even to leave it intact risked its eventual resurrection here. And advanced technology isn't what this world needs. If you want to see what the marvels of applied science can do, it's right in front of you. It's called Slake City."

"I do believe our host is something of a Luddite," Doc said.

"You're the one to talk," Mildred said with a smirk.

She pointed at the holstered, black powder LeMat. "Pot calling kettle. Come in, kettle…."

"As you well know," Doc said, "I do not go around destroying modern weapons because I think they are the work of the Devil. I just prefer not to use them myself. It's a matter of personal taste."

"'Prefer'?" Mildred said. "'Personal taste'? Sorry, Doc, but with you it's more like a crackpot religion."

"I refuse to dignify that remark with a response," Doc said, turning on his heel and walking away, down the line of parked wags.

"The geezer's kind of a prima donna, isn't he?" Burning Man said to the others.

"He's just a little sensitive about his antique blaster," Ryan said.

"If he's not careful touching off that piece of junk," the baron said, grinning with the mobile half of his face, "he and I are going to look like twins."

Glancing up at the purpling sky and the first stars of evening, Burning Man said, "You'd better call grandpa back. We've got just enough time for a last meal before we move onto the glacier."

After the companions shared a quick, cold, high-energy supper of venison jerky and dried fruit, they were passed cloth bags of ammo, marked by caliber—for their own weapons and for the mixed caliber blasters of the whitefaces—and a handful of rag-wrapped pipe bombs. In the fading rays of daylight, they knelt on the hardpan and started loading their own backpacks.

Ryan waved one of the pipe bombs at the others. "No friction, no rattling around," he warned them. "We don't know how stable the homemade explosive is."

By the time they had shouldered their burdens, the stars were out in full force and limit of visibility had dropped to fifty feet, at most.

Jak looked up at Ryan, his pale face and red eyes lost in the deep shadow. "See later, down road," he said.

A typically terse, supremely confident goodbye.

"Watch your step, Jak," Ryan told him.

Without another word, the albino teen turned and joined Besup and the other three whiteface advance scouts. They melted into the darkness ahead like wisps of smoke.

The rest of the warriors had finished watering the dogs, which were shoulder-harnessed, but not muzzled. They had wrapped the animals' feet in leather booties to avoid glass cuts and give them better traction. The only sound the war dogs made was the occasional excited whimper, as if they knew what was coming, and that there would be plenty of blood for all. Their high-pitched shrills were indistinguishable from the groans and moans of the rapidly cooling massif.

The twenty dogs and their individual handlers set off up the road.

"Move it," Burning Man said. His flamethrower strapped to his back, he booted Big Mike ahead of him, toward the path.

"Why do I have to go with you?" Big Mike whined. The whitefaces had strapped a heavily loaded pack onto his back, and he still had the noose around his neck. "You don't need me in this. I can't fight the cockroaches without hands. And I told you I've never been to Ground Zero before, so I can't help you recce the site…."

"You're coming along because you haven't paid your debt to the tribe in full," the baron said.

"You mean because I'm still alive?"

"Start walking and shut your mouth," Burning Man said, his gauntleted hand reaching for the flamethrower nozzle's pistol grip, which was clipped to his belt at the hip. "I'm not going to tell you again."

Wisely, Big Mike chose not to argue his case further. He did just as he was ordered, shuffling his feet forward, shoulders slumping under the weight hanging from his back, trailing the end of the noose on the ground behind him. If, in the process, he rolled his eyes toward heaven or pulled an anguished face at the injustice of fate, it was too dark for Ryan to see it.

He and the companions brought up the rear of the file, moving quickly to maintain visual contact with Burning Man and his captive. Under a blanket of stars, the nukeglass turned to mottled shades of gray, feathering off on all sides to pitch-black. The blackness at the very edge of sight was as devoid of color as the overturned bowl of night sky, the only difference being, there were no stars in it. Focusing too far ahead was disorienting; sky and earth blended and became inseparable.

And as they advanced it was growing noticeably colder, too.

Taken together, it was the opposite of their first visit here, under blinding sun and withering heat.

The weather-pitted glass immediately ahead of Ryan's boot-falls, virtually under his nose, had a dull sheen to it. It almost looked wet, but it wasn't. In the spots where the surface had recently spawled off from the weight of vehicle traffic, where fresh glass was exposed, it was as slick as snot. With the low light it was difficult to estimate the depth of depressions and cracks in the roadway. Because of that, the blackest of black transverse shadows had to be stepped over or jumped.

"Never in my wildest nightmares did I consider the possibility that I would be treading this horrid path again," Doc admitted.

"You and me both," Krysty said.

"Isn't it always what we don't consider," Mildred said, "that sneaks up and takes a bite out of our butts."

"Wyeth's Law of Unpleasant Surprises?" Doc said.

"In another lifetime, Doc," Mildred said, "before the nukecaust, I could have built a multimillion-dollar writing career on a self-help book with that title. In Deathlands, it's a definite no-go. For one thing, it assumes a Deathlander's life consists of things other than unpleasant surprises. That would be a very hard sell, even to a triple-stupe droolie. And what kind of advice could I give to a Deathlander audience? Kill yourself while you still have the strength?"

"Not to mention the lamentable fact that there are no books being printed anymore," Doc said.

"And even if there were," Krysty added, "not a lot of people have the skill to read them."

Ryan didn't join in on the banter. Their task was looking more and more difficult, if not impossible. He caught himself clenching his fists as he walked, waiting for, maybe even expecting to hear, a resounding crash and human screams from the impenetrable wall of blackness ahead.

A disastrous road cave-in.

They had already put the first quarter mile of the

massif behind them. That part, the outer edge of the monolith, was much thinner than the rest. As the tidal wave of liquefied quartz sand surged away from Ground Zero, its force gradually diminished. The still-molten backwash of that surge had filled the vast cavity of the nukeblast crater, a man-made chasm that was close to a mile deep. But the glacier's enormous mass didn't make it any more stable. In fact the reverse was the case—the sheer weight of it caused vast sections to fracture and shear off.

Without warning.

For close to a mile they followed a bluff wall on the left, an elevation that was created when the Ground Zero road had been cut. Its top was higher than Ryan's head. When he looked into the darkness on the right, he got a sense of sprawling open space, and a faint breeze brushed his cheek. From his experience years ago, he recalled the massif's landscape of fantastical shapes. Twisted, tilting spires. Collapsed calderas. Glass-encased tops of skyscrapers, their flagpoles pitching mad carny tents. A hurricane-tossed, frozen sea that had engulfed and entombed the ruins of a great city.

Krysty walked a few steps ahead of him. Mildred, Doc and J.B. were in single file behind. Around them, the glacier shrilled and creaked.

When the road made a hard bend to the left, Krysty stopped dead in her tracks. Ryan paused in midstep, too, his scalp tingling from adrenaline rush. The tight, cutback turns were the most dangerous sections of the route because that was where the roadway was undermined by avalanches.

Then a disembodied floating head appeared out of the

gloom on the right. The whitefaced warrior was waiting for them, a human signpost to steer the tail end of the column away from a precipitous drop-off.

To be able to navigate in this enveloping darkness, under these hazards, Ryan reckoned the warriors had to be some kind of muties—maybe it was their eyes, or some other mutation-heightened sense, or a combination of altered senses. Either that, or it was as Burning Man had said: the whitefaces were guided by the spirits of their departed ancestors who ran alongside them.

The smiling whiteface marked the route to safety. Krysty and Ryan were five feet from him when the ground beneath their boots shuddered violently. With an ear-splitting scream of cracking glass, a huge section of road dropped away. The warrior's face vanished in a heartbeat, falling into the blackness, right before Ryan's eye.

A millisecond later, Krysty was falling in front of him, too. Ryan reacted instinctively, lunging forward, reaching out. His fingers closed on one of Krysty's back-pack straps. Then her deadweight came down on his outstretched arm and dropped him to a knee. His arm rigid, he was bent over the chasm.

From below came a thundering crash of glass on glass, followed by a cloud of upwelling dust.

"Gaia!" Krysty cried. Suspended over the abyss, she kicked her long legs, trying desperately to get a toehold in the wall of glass.

"Don't struggle," Ryan warned her. "Makes it harder for me to keep my grip. I'm not going to drop you, lover."

As he spoke, her prehensile hair rose from her head in snakelike coils and wrapped around his wrist.

Summoning all of his strength, Ryan lifted her far enough to catch hold of the other backpack strap with his free hand. Then, bracing his legs, he gave a mighty grunt and pull, and at the same instant threw himself backward, swinging the upper half of her body onto the edge of the roadway.

J.B., Doc, and Mildred grabbed her arms and pulled her the rest of the way up.

"Are you cut, Krysty?" Mildred asked. "Are you cut?"

"No, I don't think so," the redhead said, looking at her hands, then her legs. "A few scratches is all."

"We can't stay here," Ryan said. "It's too dangerous. Let's move."

As they climbed the low bluff, this in order to circle around and regain the road on the far side of the cave-in, Ryan could hear J.B. behind him, muttering a string of curses under his breath.

Chapter Thirteen

Jak and Besup and other three advance scouts moved up the dimly visible road, leaving the others behind at the remains of the encampment. They weren't carrying loaded backpacks, just blasters and knives.

Despite his excitement to once again be on the hunt, Jak found himself hanging back from the warriors, uncharacteristically wary, maybe even a little skittish. He knew what dangers lay ahead in the dark, but he had no idea how they were going to find their way through them.

Besup seemed to sense his unease and confusion. "Don't try to think," he said gently. "Just let yourself feel. The guiding spirits are all around. If you let them, they will lead you."

"Lead me?"

"Close your eyes, White Wolf."

"What?"

Even though Jak had been riding scout with the white-face for several days, that experience hadn't prepared him for the strangeness of the suggestion. For sure, Besup's trailcraft was beyond anything he'd ever seen. His tracking ability was like a sixth sense. He could pick up trail where Jak was certain there was none. But that magic had been performed in the daytime, and death wasn't waiting for them on all sides.

Besup rested his hand lightly on Jak's shoulder. "It will be all right," he said. "Just close your eyes."

Jak did as he was told, though the order confused and dismayed him. "What happen now?" he said.

"Wait," Besup cautioned.

Wait for what? Jak thought. There was nothing. All he could see was the blackness on the inside of his eyelids.

"Don't try to look forward, through your eyes," Besup said, firmly squeezing his shoulder. "Don't use your eyes at all. You must look the other way, White Wolf. Look backward. Look inside your mind."

Jak tried to do that. Straining for something he still didn't understand.

"Not so hard," Besup advised him, squeezing again. "It's not a reaching, it's more of an opening up."

And so it was.

When Jak let go of the striving, of all the effort, and simply *looked back,* like a switch had been thrown, without aid of his organs of sight he became aware of his surroundings. They formed a detailed, 360-degree picture in his mind. How it happened, why it happened, what had happened, Jak couldn't explain, nor fully comprehend.

It was suddenly just there, inside his skull.

The road of glass lay before him, as did the unfolding desolation of the massif, and the other four Bannock-Shoshone scouts standing, watching him intently, and waiting for his response. He recognized each of them. He could even make out the cracks in Besup's face paint. Was this what the warrior meant, he asked himself, or was it just his imagination playing tricks on him?

"What I see in head real?" Jak said, his eyes still closed.

"Come with us, now," Besup told him. "It's time for us to run."

"Run?"

The idea of doing that in the dark, of running blind over this man-chilling terrain, made the gooseflesh jump out on his pale arms. It was an insane idea, a terrifying idea, but there was an unmistakable thrill to it. An electrifying thrill.

This was wildness taken to the nth degree.

When Jak opened his eyes, he saw the warriors were already running away from him. Before he could call out, they had vanished into the blackness.

And he stood there alone. His shoulder still tingled from Besup's touch.

After a split second of indecision, Jak took a quick breath, shut his eyes again and looked backward.

The inner landscape clicked on as if it had been waiting for his return.

It felt like he was standing in two different universes at once, the inner and the outer. And he could "see" the warriors sprinting ahead. As he started to run after them—the tips of his hair whipping against his shoulders, his boot soles slapping the roadway—the sense of exhilaration was like nothing he'd ever experienced.

Jak was by no means a deep thinker, a philosopher. He lived in the moment, for the moment. And always had. He was a doer, not a talker. Besup was also a man of few words, but in the two days that they had ridden together he had taught Jak that the Bannock-Shoshone believed the spirits of the dead constantly surrounded and interacted with them. And that the whitefaces inhabited two worlds, the human and the spirit. Their sacred religion, their visions of the other reality had nothing to do with prayer or sacrifice—Jak never saw them do either. They didn't smoke fuddlestick or drink tea made of mind-burst mushrooms. Their faith accepted as truth that normal human senses were constantly deceived, that there was much more to existence than what they revealed; that there were in fact worlds within worlds.

The time Jak had spent with Besup had allayed his natural, born-in-Deathlands suspicion of rad-tainted blood. If the whitefaces were muties, then that mutation was buried deep inside them, in their brains, their hard-wiring. It was something they couldn't or wouldn't bring themselves to speak of or analyze. When he opened his heart to the Bannock-Shoshone, he realized they meant no harm to him or his friends. More than that, he wanted to learn from them, to travel where they traveled. To experience what they experienced. To share their connection to what lay beyond.

The bond between Jak and these strangers had nothing to do with the fact that his white skin matched their facepaint. He was rooted, as were they, in the warp and weave, and the mystery of the present.

His footfalls hardly made a sound on the road. High-kicking, joyous, energized, he raced onward.

Now, he, too, danced with the spirits.

Jak didn't dare open his eyes, didn't dare break the trance that held him enfolded. He knew if he looked outward all he would see before him was dead black emptiness. Looking with his mind, looking inward, he had a stunning vision: he saw himself running in a circular pool of incredibly intense light that revealed every pebble, every crack, every dip, every slight turn in the road to Ground Zero. He ran faster, but realized it was impossible to outdistance the pool of light because its source was from within him, and it hung like a blazing lamp above his head.

Not dead yet, not dead yet, Jak thought as he sprinted to catch up with the others, drawing on reserves of power and stamina even he didn't know he had. Not dead yet, not dead yet. Kicking hard, arms pumping, that mantra of astonished disbelief quickly transformed into: not gonna die, not gonna die.

Which then became: damn, this is fun.

Jak rounded a bend and saw the four warriors ahead of him, and that he was rapidly gaining on them. He couldn't make out their individual circles of inner light, but they were well-illuminated by his. As he closed the distance, he noticed their forms slightly blurred around the edges. Unidentifiable stuff seemed to be coming off their heads, backs and legs. Gauzy, wispy, pale stuff, like steam or smoke, but as he got nearer he realized it was neither. It appeared to be some kind of particulate matter, but without weight or substance; it was like fine ash streaming off their bodies. Bits of it hung suspended in the air for a split second, then as they fell, they disappeared. The closer Jak got to the whitefaces, the heavier the off-pouring of this melting ash became—clouds of it, raining down, vanishing before they touched Jak or hit the ground.

When he was within twenty feet of the warriors he started to see the moving shapes behind them. Human shapes, outlined by the steady flow of this strange, insubstantial matter. Even as he looked, his perspective switched; it was like seeing a perfectly camouflaged and motionless prey animal make the tiniest movement, and suddenly taking in its full shape, detail and identity. In that way, in that instant, the vague outlines in front of Jak took on solid form. And he saw that the warriors were no longer journeying alone, but had been joined by five, six, seven strangers, who were keeping pace behind them. From the rear, they looked like people, real people, with real skin and muscle and bones. These newcomers wore their hair braided like the whitefaces, and had on the same kinds of tunics and boots.

Jak reasoned that these had to be the whitefaces' summoned ancestors.

As he followed the living and the dead, the roadway under him rose and fell, descending in long straightaways through low, flat valleys, up over crests crowned with forests of glass spikes, winding through a series of climbing curves. The road's course was dictated by the topography. And the topography was dictated by hardness of the underlying strata—the skeletal remains of the ancient megacity—and networks of fracture planes that constantly reshaped the surface.

As the distance to Ground Zero narrowed, Jak's zone of illumination gradually expanded, until he was "seeing" past the edge of the road, fifty, then a hundred yards in all directions. In the harsh light of his mind's vision, the landscape of the massif didn't look any the less hammered, grotesquely twisted and unreal. But a new element had been added: a population. For better or worse, Jak's brain seemed to have mastered the trick of seeing through death's camouflage. Thousands of human forms, presumably of people who had been lost on nukeday, now wandered among the glass-encased spires and frozen waves. The groans of the slipping fracture planes underscored their weeping. Their spirits as entombed in the matrix as the material debris of Slake City.

Jak turned his vision to the rear, to see if he, too, was shedding the strange ash. To see who, if anyone, was running behind him. He saw nothing—no flow of ash, no pursuing spirit forms. Above all, no Christina, his dead wife, and no Jenny, their dead sweet baby girl. But even as he felt the crush of disappointment, he sensed that loved ones lost were somehow still with him, gathered inside of his ring of light.

Hearing the cries of the trapped souls on all sides, seeing in his mind's eye their anguished faces, their pleading hands, Jak's instinct was to withdraw, to pull away from their suffering, from their bottomless anger, their sense of being cheated out of the glory of their lives. It was either that or be overwhelmed.

Jak concentrated on his vision of the road directly ahead, and of the warriors and their ancestors leading the way.

But the nukeday dead were unavoidable. The ghosts gathered in mobs, clustered around bases of the massif's prominent landmarks, as if drawn to the highest points on its surface. The "why" of this behavior came to him in a flash, like the answer had been projected into his head. Unable to ascend higher, to rise above this desolate graveyard, it was as close as they could come to finding peace.

Jak and the scouts had run maybe an hour and a half

straight when Besup and the others suddenly slowed
to a walk, then stopped altogether in the middle of the
road.

It wasn't a rest stop.

The warriors didn't need it; neither did he. Jak wasn't
thirsty or out of breath. He wasn't even sweating.

Besup knelt in the road, then waved for him to come
closer.

"What is it?" Jak asked.

"Ahead, a trap," Besup whispered. "Can you see
it?"

Their mission was to clear the road of obstacles for
the force that followed. Up to this point there had been
no obstacles to clear.

Jak made the mistake of opening his eyes and was
plunged into darkness. He closed them immediately, and
the light clicked back on.

"Trip wire," Besup said. "Stretched across road. Kill
zone beyond."

Jak could see it clearly, a thin, single strand at ankle
height, attached to a spindle of nukeglass on the left
side of the road, crossing it, and then running off into
the wasteland on the right where the nukeglass formed
a row of steep-sided peaks. He drew deeper into himself
and the circle of illumination broadened on all sides. But
not far enough to see the other end of the trip wire.

"Where lead to?" Jak said. "Where enemy?"

"Higher," Besup said. "Go higher."

Without his conscious volition, Jak's perspective immediately began to climb. Like he was in an elevator.
Like he was flying straight up in the air. His viewpoint
hovered for a moment, then below him, he saw the faint,

red glow on top of an elevated, rounded pinnacle—the roof of a ruined building shrouded in layers of thermo-glass—that had a clear overlook of the road.

Dropping closer, Jak could make out a cluster of human figures. Six of them around the banked coals of a warming fire. Not members of the ghostly dead unless the dead snored while they slept. Three were curled up on the rooftop while the others stood watch. They weren't she-hes in battlesuits, either; these were Deathlanders. Traitors to their own kind. They weren't armed with tribarrel lasers. A tripod-mounted, heavy-caliber conventional predark machine gun controlled a 150-foot section of road.

Jak could visualize the trap being sprung. There would be no cover from the searching autofire. Nuke-glass slabs were no match for full-jacketed ammo, new or reloaded.

The sentries couldn't see the road on a moonless night; that's why they had rigged the trip wire.

Jak felt a hand on his arm. When he opened his eyes, he could barely see Besup's painted face.

"How far Ground Zero?" he asked the warrior.

"Less than a mile, we figure," Besup said. "Can't use blasters to take out the gun post crew, and we can't let them get off a shot. It would alert the main compound of trouble, and we lose element of surprise."

"Blades only, then," Jak said.

"Blades only," Besup confirmed.

With eyes closed, Jak followed the scouts and their ghost ancestors off the road, across the uneven surface of the massif. It was like walking over a field of jumbled lumps of refrozen snow or ice. Only more treacherous—these lumps were brittle and razor sharp. The scouts moved cautiously and without a sound, circling wide right to approach their target from the rear.

The top five stories of the predark skyscraper protruded from the surface of the massif; the rest of the enormous structure was hidden beneath it. On nukeday, as the tidal wave of liquefied sand had receded back to Ground Zero and the deepest point in the crater, the surface of it that was exposed to the air had rapidly cooled and stiffened, and the dripping, gelling mass had clung to the sides of the rectangular structure, encasing the exterior walls and windows in a sloping tent of dirty green glass many feet thick. And it was even thicker at the bottom, where the downward flow collected then hardened.

As they neared the base of the pinnacle, Jak could see the surrounding landscape was occupied by more of the ancient ghosts. Legions of them, people of all ages, milled aimlessly until Besup and the others approached, then they parted like a breaking wave, opening a wide path.

Jak saw their faces up close, heard their wretched cries, imagined that he felt their dead breath gusting against his face. For more than a century they had been trapped in this wasteland limbo, their existence ignored, their wailing falling on deaf ears. The gun-post sentries on duty above couldn't hear them, or if they did, they couldn't distinguish the lamentations from the sounds made by the shifting glacier.

Jak didn't want to look at the ghosts, didn't want to share their pain, but the only way he could avoid it was to open his eyes. And if he did that, he couldn't find his way in the dark. Hot tears slid down his cheeks.

"You must steel yourself, White Wolf," Besup whispered in his ear. "You cannot help them."

Jak focused his attention on the problem at hand, craning back his head to take in the summit of the towering mountain of glass. To eliminate the gun post they needed to reach the peak, and they had to do it without raising an alarm. Though there were creases and rills all over the pinnacle's surface, it was far too slick to scale in a free climb. And hacking foot- and handholds into it would give them away.

One thing was certain: the sentries had to have a way to get in and out themselves.

Something pushed against his back. And he felt a feathery light pressure on his arms, insistently urging him to move to the right, around the base of the mountain. The other scouts were moving that way, too. The ancestors were doing the pushing.

Jak scanned the irregular blobs and pillows of glass at the bottom of the slope, looking for anything that might pass for an entrance, and seeing nothing.

Then one of the ancestors broke ranks and ran ahead, waving and pointing.

Jak saw it at once. Maybe four feet off the ground, nestled in a cleft between two massive enfoldings. A rat hole gnawed in the glass, a rat hole big enough for a person to crawl through.

Chapter Fourteen

Under the blaze of klieg lights, Auriel Otis Trask hurried across the Ground Zero compound. In front of the mine entrance, about seventy slaves slept packed into a series of bathtub-sized, natural pits or depressions in the nukeglass, their bodies covered with piles of rags, trying their best to keep warm and out of the night wind. If any of them saw her walk by, they kept their heads down.

And that was a very good thing.

Armed with a tribarrel laser rifle, Auriel was in no mood for curious stares. Mero lay on the brink of death; Dr. Huth had just notified her of that fact via com link. It was a message that she had been expecting—and dreading with all her heart. She had to be there, on-station, when Mero died. Standing witness to a fallen sister was her duty as commander, and her honor as a loyal friend.

Before Mero had been sedated, between seizures while she was still lucid, Auriel had explained the dire situation to her. That there would be no mercy killing in her case. That she wouldn't be euthanized like the stickies before the specters hatched out so Dr. Huth could perform analyses he had up until now been denied. Analyses that might be the key to their survival, and that were in fact their last hope for same. Auriel had explained that the fate of all the sisters hung in the balance.

Ever the stalwart soldier, Mero had responded through clenched teeth, "I would've gladly given my life on any of the other worlds to save even one of my sisters. I'm going to die on this one anyway, I know there's no way around it. This way I might be able to save my sisters. At least my death will have some meaning."

Mero's acceptance of her fate didn't make it any easier for Auriel to bear. Under the circumstances, what else could Mero have said? The situation was no longer in her control. And even though she loathed Dr. Huth as much as Auriel did, she was never one to whine or complain about a tough assignment. Of all the warriors for Auriel to lose, Mero was the least expendable.

It had been a profound relief when Dr. Huth had finally rendered her semiconscious, when Auriel didn't have to keep looking her in the eye.

As the commander stepped through the mine's brightly lit entrance, she asked herself for the thousandth time if she was doing the right thing here. For Mero. For the others. Did she have any choice in the matter? Could she trust Dr. Huth not to make a bloody mess of it?

The options were few; the good options were none.

Auriel didn't blame herself for what had happened up to this point. She had inherited a situation that was a tightrope-walking over disaster. But this decision was all on her.

Unbidden, her mother's horrific last moments flooded her mind. A recurring flashback that she always did her best to smother. Now she let the tape run in its awful entirety. Auriel had never dreamed she would ever see Dredda, the bedrock of the unit, fall apart so utterly. At first, her disintegration was emotional, due to the pain, then it was physical—and impossibly violent. The lesson Auriel had learned was a hard one, and it struck deep: sisters might well be superbeings, but they were still subject to human doubt and suffering. They were still all too mortal.

About twenty yards inside the entrance came the first of three newly installed chokepoints. Made of piled, laser-cut blocks of nukeglass, they narrowed the tunnel from both sides so it was just wide enough for a single ore cart to pass down the middle. This created defensible, hardsite emplacements for the sisters who were standing guard belowground. The strategically positioned sets of barricades had become necessary precautions because of the shift in mine operations since Mero had fallen sick. The looming catastrophe of a mass infection had significantly narrowed Auriel's time window. She and her sisters had to have sufficient fuel to jump realities, and as quickly as possible. Which meant the gloves had to come off. Now two-thirds of the miners toiled underground around the clock. They were allowed just four hours of sleep in every twenty-four, and fed once a day.

The new bottlenecks didn't impede the steady flow of radioactive ore to the mobile processor aboveground, but they divided and funneled the slave force, eliminating the possibility that in the close quarters of the mine, with their 40-to-1 advantage in numbers, the laborers could surprise and overwhelm their masters, despite all their advanced weaponry and body armor.

As Auriel passed through the gap in the barricade, the sister stationed there shifted her tribarrel rifle to her left hand, decloaked her visor and raised a black gauntleted fist in solemn salute.

There were tears in the sentry's eyes. Tears she couldn't brush away because of the battlesuit helmet.

Auriel felt a twinge of sympathetic pain in her gut. Bright, stabbing pain. Despite their technology, despite their genetic alterations, the sisters weren't machines. They were mere flesh and blood. They loved. They suffered loss. They grieved. All the sisters had been informed of Mero's sacrifice; they knew she was dying agonizingly for the cause. That her death was now imminent had been inadvertently broadcast through the com link by that thoughtless bastard Dr. Huth.

Auriel picked up her pace. The knots of miners pushing carts in both directions yielded the center of the tunnel to her, either moving out of the way or bringing the carts to a stop so she could walk around them.

Deeper below ground, past the second chokepoint and under the watchful eye of the sister manning the third, the slaves were hard at work, reducing the massif's hot spots to portable-sized rubble. Pickaxes in the side seams crashed into walls in a resounding, constant clatter, human chains handed out chunks of ore, and dumped them into the carts lined up on either side of the tunnel. Under the string of widely spaced, overhead lights, the air in the main shaft glittered from the suspended glass dust.

A tall man with an ax stepped through the sparkling cloud, partially blocking her path. He had a rag mask tied over the lower half of his face, and he was naked to the waist. Behind him stood a diminutive woman with short-cropped auburn hair. She, too, wore a face mask and held a pickax.

Normally, Auriel didn't permit the features of individual slaves to even register in her consciousness. Given the certainty and unpleasantness of their fate, any form of contact with them was counterproductive. But she *did* remember this man with the enormous dragon tattoo on his shoulder. She remembered his little auburn-haired friend as well. And looking at them now she sensed they had some kind of personal connection. Were they lovers? Brother and sister? Or maybe they had just joined forces in the slave camp in order to survive?

Her visor's sensors remotely measured Dragon Man's pulse rate and blood pressure. That information confirmed what Auriel read from his body language: murder was on his mind.

Her murder.

From the way the corded muscles in his arms and chest were flexing and twitching, he wanted nothing more than to rear back and clobber her with his pickax. But the futility of a one-on-one attack was giving him pause.

Seeing his indecision, Auriel knew that the tipping point hadn't been reached yet. Sometime soon, though, this tattooed slave and all the others would realize that they had nothing to lose by turning on their masters. That they were going to be either worked until they dropped dead, or dragged into the superheated dark and pulled to pieces by packs of stickies.

At present she had more pressing issues to deal with. Because even in the confines of her battlesuit, Auriel could move so much faster than the male slave who threatened her, he had no chance to step out of the way or deflect the full power of the shoulder strike she delivered to his midchest.

The stunning blow bowled him off his feet and sent him flying backward, spread-eagled. He slammed into the side of an ore cart with his butt, and tumbled head over heels into the half-full cargo box.

The display of sudden violence froze the other slaves close by, turning them into masked, glitter-dusted statues.

Before Auriel could move past the knot of bodies, Dragon Man climbed out of the cart and attacked her, still clutching his ax.

Her patience long gone, she thumbed the tribarrel's power button. The compact weapon system came to life instantly, emitting a faint vibration that registered in her fingertips even through the battlesuit's gauntlets.

Ax cocked back, Dragon Man closed the distance. Above the rag mask, the whites of his eyes were a shocking pink, enflamed by the mine's corrosive dust.

Auriel didn't particularly want to kill him because she couldn't afford to lose any more workers at this critical stage of the operation. But she didn't want the other slaves to get the idea that their lives had somehow gained value, and that because of that they suddenly wielded a new power to influence events. Bottom line, it was pretty much of a toss-up whether or not she cut loose with the laser rifle.

"Out of my way or you're going to die where you stand," she told him, her voice booming through the battlesuit's external speaker, the tribarrel aimed rock-steady at his chest. "Move aside or I'll cook your heart to a cinder."

"No, Ronbo, don't!" the woman cried, throwing down her pickax and stepping between her friend's chest and the black weapon's clawlike flash hider.

A touching display of selfless bravery, but Auriel didn't allow herself to be moved by it.

"You do realize that you're not protecting him from anything," she informed the woman. "The beam from this weapon will slice through both of you like you're made out of paper."

"I know that," the woman said, holding her ground.

"Get out of my way, Ti," Ronbo snarled. He was bleeding from a nasty two-inch cut on his left temple. When he tried to move her with his free arm, the little woman locked her legs, and lowered her center of gravity, and despite the disparity in size wouldn't be budged.

Auriel knew at most the pair had another four days of exposure before the rad sickness took hold and killed them. With any luck long before then, the sisters would have safely jumped to another replica Earth.

"I'm going to let you two live," she told them, "but only if you get out of my way, now."

Whirling, little Ti pushed Ronbo backward with both hands, then caught hold of and trapped the arm that was still wielding the ax.

Auriel walked past them and as she did so, the other miners averted their eyes and hurriedly resumed their labor so they wouldn't incur her wrath. She followed the main tunnel to the helix and took the spiral ramp down to the bottom level, and the entrance to the cramped corridor that housed the row of experimental cells.

The shrill, animal sounds echoing down the burrow made her skin on her neck crawl, but she knew they weren't from Mero's death throes. Mero was too weak at this point to cry out. At the far end of the corridor, beyond the force field, wild stickies danced and leaped about in apparent celebration. The noise was them mimicking—and mocking—her sister's suffering.

A battlesuit-clad Dr. Huth stood in front of Mero's cell, fidgeting nervously with a hand scanner.

The intervening cells were empty but for drifts of ash and pieces of charred long bones, the remnants of Huth's still-born experiments.

When Auriel looked into the cell and saw the state of her friend, a galvanic shock shot through her. Mero lay on her back. Like the late-phase infected stickies, she was pinned to the floor by a boulder of massive, jutting belly. The skin of her stomach looked shiny, like an overinflated balloon; it had already begun to split, lengthwise, from the tremendous internal pressure. And worst of all, Auriel could see full grown specters moving under her tight skin, sliding back and forth, pulsating in near-unison. Though Mero was unconscious, her eyelids were open and her eyes grotesquely bulged from their sockets. Mero's face and lips had turned a dusky blue.

Her mother's face looked like that, right before the end.

"She can't breathe," Auriel said to Dr. Huth. "She's suffocating."

"The specters have compressed her lungs and are squeezing down on her brain stem as well," the whitecoat said dispassionately. "I've observed this same series of events in my other test subjects. It's part of the entities'

ingenious hatching process. Slack muscle is much easier
to delaminate and split than contracted muscle."

"This is unspeakable…"

"Any second now," Dr. Huth cautioned, his voice
quavering with anticipation.

There was still time to change the course of events,
Auriel told herself. To end this. To destroy the wretched,
evil things that were killing her sister.

She reached for the incineration switch set in the
tunnel wall. She flipped open the protective cover, and
her hand hovered over the red burn toggle. Before she
could act, flesh and blood exploded.

It rocked Auriel back on her heels. There was no
impact from flying matter; she was jolted by surprise
and shock. Red liquid splashed the inside of the force
field that blocked the cell entrance.

Mero's substance dripped ceiling to floor.

No longer able to contain his excitement, Dr. Huth
fairly squealed, "Infrared mode! Infrared mode!"

Auriel used the helmet's GRI to shift her visor
view.

The bright arterial-red curtain instantly turned brilliant chartreuse.

A fraction of a second later the force field shrugged
off the liquid insult, and what Auriel saw inside the
narrow cell dizzied her. Dozens of lime-green specters,
like flying eels, whipped around and around the walls
and ceiling. They moved in a churning blur, elongat-
ing themselves into thin threads, reversing directions,
searching every square inch of the cell for a way out.
Or for something they could kill. Their frenzy and their
ravening hunger were palpable.

Under the frantic light show, Auriel could see what they had done to poor Mero. She was blown virtually in two, a ghastly, gaping wound from throat to groin, from hip to hip, from armpit to armpit, the stubs of her shattered ribs sticking out. Though Mero's pain was clearly over, frozen on her dead face was a look of astonishment and horror.

Auriel spun on her heel and seized hold of the white-coat's battlesuit around the throat. "What have you done?" she demanded, shaking him about inside the armor like a marble in a can. "What have we done?"

"It was necessary," Dr. Huth assured her.

"If they ever get out…"

Dr. Huth finished the sentence for her: "We will have to jump realities again, and very, very quickly."

In disgust, Auriel shoved him away. She stared at the captive, lime-green whirlwind. "Will they replicate while sealed up in there?" she said. "Will there be even more of them soon?"

"That's one of the things I hope to find out," Dr. Huth told her. "Understanding and breaking their cycle of reproduction could be a way to eliminate them. I also need to analyze the before-and-after data to see what, if anything, was taken from Mero upon the instant of her death."

"And if nothing was taken? Then what?"

"Then I have to start over fresh, with a new set of hypotheses, rejecting the premises I've employed so far. Premises that were based on a detailed understanding of the mechanisms of earthly biology. Ultimately though, I may even have to reject the application of biology to this problem."

"You've lost me, Dr. Huth," Auriel said with impatience.

"From the beginning," he went on, "I have been proceeding on the assumption that these entities bear some faint resemblance to ourselves. That they process some kind of raw material for the energy to power themselves. That they reproduce with some variant of or alternative mechanism comparable to our DNA. That they grow in the same sense other living creatures do—from a few cells to many, from simple to complex internal function. So far, I've been unable to find evidence to support any of those assumptions."

"If all of those assumptions are wrong," Auriel said, "what are you going to replace them with?"

"I have to think in a completely different direction," Dr. Huth said. "And I have already begun that process. For example, the endospores we have identified as alien may not be these creatures' eggs after all."

"Why not?"

"Because I can find nothing inside their protective shells. No genetic material. No DNA. No RNA. They aren't bacterial. They aren't viral. They aren't, in any sense I can understand, alive. Nor do they seem to have the capacity of ever becoming alive."

"Then how are they connected to the specters?" Auriel asked. "What purpose do they serve?"

"They may not be connected at all. Their presence could merely be coincidental. They could be unrelated artifacts."

"Then we are left with nothing."

"Not quite," Dr. Huth said. "I first assumed the spores were living entities like the bacteria we are familiar with, but constructed of compounds of metallic silica instead of carbon. It is also possible that they are much simpler than that, in structure and in function."

"Simpler?"

"It has occurred to me that the spores' relationship to the specters may have more to do with direction than point of origin."

"Spit it out, Dr. Huth."

"They could be some kind of microscopic tracking or targeting devices."

"That makes no sense to me at all," Auriel said in exasperation. "Where are the new clutches of specters coming from, if not from inside the spores? How are they getting inside their victims?"

"Those are the questions I need to answer."

"And you had better do it fast," Auriel warned him.

As she turned to leave, a skewering pain doubled her over and dropped her to her knees. It was like being run through with a lance. Burning, tearing pain.

"Are you all right?" Dr. Huth said, hurrying to kneel beside her.

For a moment she couldn't answer him. She had no air. Then as the initial wave of agony subsided, she felt it—the same sensation she'd felt before. Only this time it wasn't a faint wriggling, a vague twitching. This was no muscle spasm. This was no sympathetic fantasy. There was something inside her, something alive and it was moving, crawling around in her belly, pushing aside her organs, poking around blindly, curiously, indifferent to the excruciating pain it caused her.

"What is it?" Dr. Huth said. "What's wrong?"

A second locus of pain, this one much higher, blossomed just under her heart. Electric pain spread across her chest and shot down the insides of both arms. The vagus nerve, was her panicked thought. It was nudging on her vagus nerve. As the paralyzing intensity of the ache slowly subsided, there was a sliding pressure across the front of her right lung. When she inhaled she could feel the hard outline of the intruder, she could feel it slither, momentarily trapped between her lung and chest wall.

"Answer me!" Dr. Huth shouted.

Her heart thudding, Auriel swallowed her panic and her nausea and snarled back at him through gritted teeth. "Scan me, you asshole. Scan me quickly."

Dr. Huth drew his hand scanner and waved its sensor back and forth over the outside of her battlesuit.

Auriel watched his expression stiffen as he took in the results. In the yellow backwash of his visor's GRI, the whitecoat suddenly looked a thousand years old.

"Well?" she demanded.

"You're infected," he replied woodenly, as if shellshocked. "I counted more than a dozen of them inside you."

For a second, Auriel thought he was actually mourning her fate. Then he spoke and shattered that illusion.

"There's a good chance we're all infected."

Dr. Huth's concern, as always, was only for himself.

As if they had heard, as if they understood the words and the consequences, the mob of wild stickies on the other side of the force field danced their joy, mock-weeping and moaning even louder.

Chapter Fifteen

Jak, Besup and the other three scouts cautiously moved closer to the blaster position's entry hole—a vertical slit, less than three feet across at its midpoint. When they were within ten feet of it, they were enveloped in a pungent, all too familiar odor. The scouts exchanged looks of utter disgust.

"Triple nasty smell," Jak whispered.

"Roof is sentries' shitter," Besup hissed. "Watch where you step."

"And breathe through mouth," Jak muttered.

The traitors in the blaster emplacement above were using the lip of the predark roof as their privy, probably because climbing up and down from the five-story perch was such a time-consuming hassle. They were tossing—or excreting—their solid waste off the summit and letting it fall straight to the ground. Maybe they thought the addition of a little personal fertilizer might encourage plant growth and embellish the landscape.

At least they had enough brains not to let fly directly above the hardsite's only entrance.

The ancestral ghosts took point, disappearing one by one into the hole in the buried building's flank.

When Besup started for the opening, Jak followed close on his heels. Before dropping to hands and knees and ducking his head to enter, the albino teen opened his eyes for a split second. Even though the lip of the hole and the side of the pinnacle were within easy reach, all he could see front of him was a wall of solid blackness. Jak closed his eyes and crawled forward, into a passage so narrow that it brushed against both his shoulders and grazed the top of his head.

Under his fumbling fingers and sliding knees, the floor and walls of the tunnel felt ridged or striated. In his mind's eye he could actually see the linear tool marks left behind by its construction. The sentries—or more likely some unlucky slaves—had pickaxed and chipped their way into the heart of the ancient tower block.

The other scouts crawled in after him. Jak could hear their whistling breath in the enclosed space. He hoped no one else could. The five of them were jammed into the passage in a daisy chain, like a cork in a bottle. Once inside it, there was no easy or quick way of going back. Not only was there no room to turn, but there was also no way to coordinate a unison retreat. The scouts were at the mercy of whoever or whatever was waiting for them at the far end.

At least, Jak thought, the Bannock-Shoshone ancestors could give them some warning if there was trouble ahead.

He followed Besup up what seemed like a gradual slope for forty or fifty feet, then the tunnel ceased to be a tunnel, and opened onto a much wider, much taller space. As Jak crawled forward, he "saw" Besup standing full upright. In front of him were the bright edges of a flight of steps. These steps weren't crudely hacked into the glass. And they were trimmed in metal. Definitely original; definitely predark.

It made perfect sense. The rat hole passage led to a stairwell entrance, and the stairs led up to the roof.

The nukeglass inside the well amounted to little more than a thin coating, a solidified ooze over the walls and stairs. Jak guessed that air pressure in the stairwell, and perhaps some substantial interior doors, had impeded the influx of molten liquid. The lower door had since been removed from its hinges and was left leaning against the wall of the landing. Above it, hammered into the wall above the staircase, was a crude metal stanchion that held an unlit torch.

Jak pushed up from his knees and got to his feet. At least the climb to the top was going to be easier.

With the seven ghosts in the lead, and Jak and the four scouts following, they moved upward to the next landing. Figuring two landings per floor, they had eight more before they reached the roof.

Everything went smoothly until they approached the third floor above ground. The ancestors stopped on the steps, then turned, blocking the way.

Jak leaned around Besup's hip to see what was going on. The ghost closest to the landing was waving a finger at them. A "no-no" finger. He then pointed at something on the deck of the landing.

Whatever it was, Jak couldn't see it from his vantage point.

"Danger on the landing," Besup said, addressing Jak and the scouts below him. "Walk only in my footsteps."

Then they started up the stairs, in a tight single file.

When Jak saw the white stones, or eggs, all of the same size and shape, arranged in a careful pattern on the landing floor, he knew exactly what they were. Though he had never encountered the jump-up, laser antipersonnel mines in person before, Krysty and Mildred had. It happened years ago, during the first invasion. And after their narrow escape they had warned the other companions about them.

Instead of being armed with a conventional explosive and ball-bearing projectiles, these AP mines combined laser beams, reflective mirrors and the ability to hop in sequence to various heights above the ground. When one of the cluster of white eggs' infrared sensors was triggered, they all jumped up in the air and discharged their cutting beams, which created a multiblade, multiangled, bandsaw effect that turned the unwary into a pile of steaming, bloodless chunks.

The path Besup took was the one laid out by the ancestors. Jak stepped precisely where he stepped, moving up the inside of the stairway, climbing onto the bottom rail of the steel bannister, then swinging over to the far side of the landing.

The rest of the stairway was undefended. The scouts moved quickly and without incident to the uppermost landing, where again, the door had been taken off its hinges. Jak heard voices coming through the doorway, from out on the rooftop. He was straining to make out what they were saying when Besup lightly touched his eyelids.

Jak flinched at the contact, then opened his eyes.

It took a second or two for them to adjust. A faint, flickering light filtered into the top of the stairwell, through the doorless doorway.

When he regained his focus, he saw that Besup had

his back pressed against the wall not two feet away, and was grinning at him, wide-eyed with excitement. The whiteface warrior then reached down to his waist-band and unsheathed a long, slender shadow. He held it up for Jak to see. The predark dagger's six-inch-plus blade was coated with a black substance, probably titanium nitride—all but the razor-sharp double edge, which caught and reflected the weak light in a fine, bright *V*. This wasn't the same knife Besup had thrown campfire target practice with. This blade had only one function: piercing living flesh and bone. It was designed for chilling.

Jak stuck a hand under his shirt and palmed a pair of leaf-bladed throwing knives.

There would be no blasters. No noise in this fight, if they could help it.

The warrior ancestors were nowhere to be seen, with eyes open or closed. Jak figured they were already out on the roof, walking among the blaster emplacement's oblivious sentries. While the ghosts could be observed and heard by their own kind, and could touch their flesh, they were invisible to everyone else. They couldn't directly interact with the objects of the living world.

The way the light from the rooftop kept fading in and out, Jak knew it had to be from the fire he'd seen with his mind's eye. The voices outside the well continued their dialogue. He counted three men talking. Jak carefully edged closer to the stairwell's opening, so he could make sense of what was being said.

"We're sitting in the catbird seat," one man announced with pride. "There aren't anywhere near enough she-hes to try and run all of the Deathlands. Them cockroaches are going to have to use homegrown folk to govern and police and milk the sweet stuff from their new territory. They're going to have to use people like us, who have proved their loyalty from the start. The rewards are gonna be bigger than any of us ever dreamed possible. Imagine skimming the cream off every ville in Deathlands."

"Question is, what are we gonna to do with all the cream that we skim?" said a second sentry.

"It's gonna be a string of gaudies, for me," the third man said. "Stocked with only the best, hand-selected talent. Set up my stable of sluts in old semitrailers all up and down the interstate. Ring the compounds with barbwire. Charge an arm and a leg to get in the front gate, but from then on everything's free. Take as much as you want, any way that you want. Do it until your damn pecker falls off."

"You know," the second man said, "starting a high class jolt-a-teria has always been in the back of my mind. Not one of those dirt-floor, cardboard shanty, puke-in-a-puddle dumps. I'm talking about the kind of place where an ordinary sodbusting shit-kicker could go, kick back and get himself petrified with the best brain-melter in the land."

"Me," the first speaker said, "the first thing I'm going to do is open up a traveling fun fair, like a carny only featuring games of skill and complimentary joy juice for old and young. My philosophy has always been, if you're old enough to swallow, you're old enough to get hammered.

"I'd go from ville to ville in a caravan of monster-big wags, give the folks a once-in-a-lifetime chance to chill caged and helpless muties for a price. You know, scalies, stumpies, stickies, the odd droolie—anything that looks so comical butt ugly that you'd pay good jack to kill or maim it. I'd charge so much per bullet. So much per arrow. So much per whack with a nail-studded club or stab with a blade. I tell you, folks are going to damn well eat it up."

Warm holes, jolt, joy juice, blasters and wags.

The familiar hard currency of Deathlands.

To Jak, the sentries sounded like nothing more than run-of-the-mill, coldheart chillers. The kind of road scum who would sell out their own mothers for a bit of strange tail, a few hits of jolt and a quick peek from the top of the shit-heap. He transferred one of his knives to his left hand. The other he positioned between his thumb and first two fingers, ready for instant release.

Because his eyes were open, if the ancestors gave a signal to begin the attack, Jak didn't hear or see it. Besup nodded to him and the other scouts, then ducked through the empty doorway.

Jak flew out after him.

The campfire threw plenty of light to fight by. It was built in a cut-down, fifty-five-gallon steel drum, which was positioned near the emplacement's machine gun. The M-60's bipod front legs were resting on the edge of the roof, muzzle pointed downrange toward the Ground Zero road. The buttstock sat on the holed-out, foam seat of a predark office swivel chair.

Three of the six sentries were curled up in blankets, asleep on the sheet of nukeglass on Jak's side of the fire. The other three—the talkers—were sitting in swivel chairs on the far side of the drum, with their backs to the M-60 and the road.

"Yeah, it'd be like therapy for them," one of them cackled.

"You should charge extry for blastin' them really big, flab-ass scalies," the guy beside him said. "Three-hundred-pounders and up."

"Yeah, I'll charge 'em by the squeal."

All three brayed with laughter, which caused the sleeping men to stir and groan in complaint.

Because the talkers were looking right into the flames, they couldn't see anything beyond the red glow. This allowed Jak and the scouts to advance unnoticed across the rooftop toward them.

Although the fire blinded the sentries to their approach, it gave the attackers a perfectly illuminated view of the intended targets. The trio was bundled up to keep off the night's chill. They had black caps pulled way down low over their ears. They wore layer upon layer of clothing, fingerless gloves and had makeshift, insulating lap robes of black plastic bags. Their boots propped up on chunks of nukeglass so they could absorb the fire's heat. The boot soles and tops were wrapped with, and presumably held together by, overlapping turns of silver duct tape. Beat-up, rust-barreled AK-47s rested against the sides of their chairs, close to hand. The guy in the middle, the carny man, had a remade handblaster laying across his lap.

As four disembodied white faces suddenly appeared in the fire's glow, not ten feet from where they sat, their laughter faded away and the row of nasty grins turned to

slackjawed astonishment. Snarling curses, they pushed
back their chairs and lunged for their blasters.

But it was already too late for that.

As Besup's arm shot forward, Jak also let fly.

The leaf-bladed throwing knife struck first. The head
of the man in the middle jerked back from the stunning
impact of the steel blade into his left eye socket. A point
of the half-buried, four-lobed blade penetrated the weak-
est spot in his skull, spearing deep into his forebrain.
The crunching wallop sent him and his wheeled chair
rolling backward in a blur. The blaster he was trying to
raise tumbled from his fingers. When the chair's rear
wheels hit the lip of the roof, its seat-back tipped over
the edge, spilling out its occupant. The silver tape on
his boot soles flashing in the firelight, the middle man
backflipped off the rooftop.

Only then did he start to scream.

Like a steam whistle.

A scream cut off short when seconds later he crashed
into the ground.

Even as the head of the man in the middle was
slammed by the leaf-bladed knife, Besup's pinwheeling dagger sank to the hilt in the chest of the man on
the left, just beneath his sternum. His eyes slitted with
pain, he flopped back onto the seat of his chair, clutched
the knife's grip in his gloved hands and began pulling
on it with all his might. In a rush the dagger came free,
and when it did, it released a spray of arterial blood
that hissed and steamed when it hit the side of the fire-
drum. His heart pierced by a diamond-shaped wound
that would never close, he lost consciousness at once,

and was dead in seconds. Besup's bloody knife clattered to the rooftop.

The third seated man took a knife hit at the base of the throat as he swung up his AK, trying to bring the muzzle to bear. The muzzle dropped as his mouth gaped open, then opened and closed, opened and closed as if he was trying to say something, or to scream. But the blade had severed his vocal cords. Blood pouring from his lips, he fell to his knees, then his face on the ground beside the firepit.

The sleepers meanwhile had been awakened by the curses and the scream, and reacting to the sounds of alarm, rolled for their weapons.

There was no question of taking any of them prisoner. Not under the circumstances. Not when the success of the mission depended on keeping the baron's approach to Ground Zero a secret. They all had to die.

A knife thrown by a scout on Jak's right speared one of the remaining men from behind as he bent over, trying to scoop up an assault rifle. The blade penetrated the base of his skull by a good three inches, and the impact sent him flying forward, arms and belly over the lip of the cut-down barrel, headfirst into the fire. Already dead on his feet, he just hung there over the coals and burned.

Unwilling to test his arm on a moving target, a second scout dashed forward. He caught a sentry from behind and locked an arm around his chest. With a quick crossways stroke of his blade, he slashed the front of the man's throat from ear to ear. As the sentry turned and tumbled away, falling to his knees, blood sheeted down from his neck and onto his chest.

In the meantime, the last of the sleepers made a desperate low dive around the base of the fire can, using it for cover so he could reach the M-60. Snatching hold of the machine gun's buttstock, he lifted and pivoted the weapon to turn it on his attackers. As he did so, his bared teeth glistened in the firelight.

Jak had already switched his blade to his strong hand. His arm whipped forward in a blur and the steel star swished through the air, arcing ever so slightly as it closed on the target. With a solid *thwock* of impact, it struck the lower half of the man's face. The blade crashed through his front teeth, shattered them top and bottom, sliced through his tongue and slammed into the back of his throat.

As the sentry let go of the machine gun's stock, frantically trying to spit out teeth and metal, blood squirting from between his lips, a fixed blade knife caught him in the side of the neck, just below the jawline in front of his ear.

Before he could recover and maybe put up a fight, Besup and a second whiteface grabbed him by the arms and legs and in a single coordinated heave, pitched him headfirst off the edge of the roof.

Three seconds later, a muffled splat came from below.

The scouts moved quickly among the fallen, recovering their blades, cutting throats to make sure the sentries were all dead. As they were doing that, a dense, sickeningly sweet smoke began pouring out of the fire can and spreading across the rooftop. Jak reached over, pulled the dead man out of the fire and let him drop to the ground.

Besup picked the M-60 off the deck and hefted it in his hands, testing its weight and balance. "Nice blaster," he said. "Full-auto. Heavy caliber. Way too good a trophy to leave behind." He slung the weapon across the top of his shoulders, like a yoke. To the scouts he said, "Get those ammo belt cans. We need them, too."

Jak and the scouts then backtracked their route out of the tower, avoiding the cluster of jump-up laser mines, this time with open eyes and the help of torches lit from the fire. After they climbed from the rat hole tunnel, when the stars were once again overhead, they extinguished and tossed away the torches. Giving the base of the building a wide berth, they closed their eyes and headed across the nukeglass toward the road.

The ancestors were again with them as they began to recce the last mile to Ground Zero. They were about halfway there, when Jak noticed a low, grinding roar. And the closer they got to the site, the louder the background noise became.

As they rounded a turn, he saw light through his closed eyelids. When he opened his eyes, ahead of them was a bowl of radiance blazed against the backdrop of the night sky. It was created by the rows of klieg lights that illuminated the slave camp. A low ridge of overturned slabs and rubble, a ridge that curved off into the distance in both directions, blocked their direct view of the site. Twinkling clouds of dust rose up through the glow, cast off by the rumbling nuke ore processor. When they peered over the ridge, Ground Zero was almost exactly as Jak remembered it—the mine entrance was located in a broad, shallow depression in the massif.

Having determined that the road was clear of hazard

right up to the perimeter of the camp, they silently withdrew, retreating down the road to await the arrival of Burning Man's main force.

Jak, Besup and the other scouts took shelter out of sight behind a jagged, hundred-foot-tall, glass pinnacle. They hunkered down in the darkness, eyes tightly shut, surrounded by nukeday ghosts whose wails no one else could hear.

Chapter Sixteen

Carrying heavy packs and moving over the difficult terrain, it took Ryan and the others more than four hours to cover the eight miles to their target. It was well past midnight when they caught up to the war dogs, the other whitefaces and the advance scouts.

Above the rise in the ribbon-straight road, Ryan could see the ominous glow of Ground Zero, the broad dimple in the center of the massif, which was only a quarter mile away. And he could hear the ore processor's roar sawing in the distance.

Jak hurried over to them out of the dark.

"Any trouble?" Ryan asked him.

The albino youth shook his head, no hesitation. "Piece cake. Road to mine clear."

Ryan craned his neck back and looked up at the night sky.

"We've got plenty of time," said a voice behind him.

Ryan turned. The dim light was kind to Burning Man's face. In half shadow, the baron looked almost unmelted. Even if he couldn't quite make out the man's features, Ryan could feel the waves of intensity and excitement he was radiating. On the verge of a desperate battle, Burning Man was way-pumped.

Maybe too pumped.

J.B. gave Ryan a gentle nudge with his elbow. He, too, immediately sensed the problem and its scope. Who was going to ride herd on a superjuiced baron, when the baron was in charge of the op?

"It'll be at least three or four hours before it starts to get light," Burning Man continued. "Come along with me. We need to do a recce of the site, get all our ducks in a row."

Ryan and J.B. fell in line behind the baron, Jak and Besup. They left the road and moved in a low crouch, angling toward the landscape's prominent feature: the irregular rise that was the backside of the broad but relatively shallow sinkhole's rim. The baron stayed on-point, leading them toward the dome of light, through the maze of shattered blocks and uptilted, fragile plates.

When they reached the barrier and paused, Burning Man reverted to his previous role in life, as a white-coat.

"This ridge is as old as nukeday," the former geologist told them. "It was created by the backwash of molten, but rapidly cooling thermoglass. After the initial tidal surge reached its outer limit, that wave rebounded to the center. When it surged forward again, it had less momentum and had already begun to stiffen. The second wave solidified into this ring of ridge, which has since fractured and deteriorated."

The baron then carefully took hold of the glass and inched himself upward. Ryan and the others followed suit, peering over the ridge top and down onto Ground Zero.

Burning Man pointed to the left. "The living quarters for the she-hes, and maybe their labs, are in those black domes," he said. "We've got to figure at least some of them are occupied this time of night."

Beyond the domes, Ryan saw the nuke ore processor. From its hopper a column of glass dust rose like thick smoke into the glare of the klieg lights. Its roar was much louder, and it was constant. A gridwork of massive storage batteries was lined up on the ground, the batteries connected to one another and the processor by thick cables.

As they watched from concealment, slaves pushed a steady flow of carts from the mine entrance to the hopper, and back. There were no cockroaches in sight, but a quartet of men with whips and blasters urged the workers onward.

"Turncoats," Ryan said in disgust.

"Sellout, backstabbing fuckers," J.B. agreed.

"They're really driving those slaves hard," the baron said. "The she-hes' power supply must be dangerously low, or else they're building up their resources to get ready to make another reality jump."

"If they're in a big hurry, they don't have the slaves all working at once," Ryan said, indicating the dark forms huddled in the pits in front of the mine entrance.

"Resting them in shifts, probably around the clock," Burning Man said. "Squeeze more out of them that way."

"Another couple of sellouts, over by the mine entrance," J.B. said. "See the guys standing on either side of the opening, arms folded, not working. If I'm not mistaken, they both got long blasters on shoulder slings."

"There could be a whole lot more turncoats on the

site," Ryan said. "Down the mine shaft, mebbe in the huts."

"They're not our immediate concern," Burning Man said. "Before we deal with them, that gyroplane's got to be put out of commission."

The sleek black aircraft sat unattended on a makeshift landing pad behind the row of domes.

"If we can't keep that thing grounded," the baron continued, "we don't stand a chance in hell. Once it's airborne and it's got its EM shield up, it can do whatever it wants to us, whenever it wants. There'll be no escape. With its infrared sensors, cannons and pilot-guided missiles, it can hunt us down. I'm talking to the last man, even in the pitch-dark. Once it's up in the air, we won't be able to make a dent in it with bullets, and we won't be able to hit it with pipe bombs. I'm going to take a dozen warriors and half the explosives, and decommission it, opening salvo."

"What about that water tower down there?" Ryan said. "It's the highest point on the site. Conventional rifle or tribarrel shooting from that platform could command the whole battlefield."

"You're right, that's a potential threat, too," the baron said. "While we have a go at knocking out the gyro, Ryan, you and your sawed-off friend there can keep any tower snipers pinned down. Use that sweet, scoped, predark longblaster of yours. After the gyro's taken care of, on the way to the mine, we'll blow up the water tower, too."

Burning Man seemed to be settling down. As a result, Ryan's concern about his ability to plan and execute a successful attack started to fade.

"Besup, you will lead the second wave of the attack, pushing toward the mine entrance," the baron went on. "But I want you to hold back until after we blow up the gyro, and after the she-hes come out of their huts and move onto the glacier. That's your signal to attack, and to release the dogs. If we can drive all the she-hes into the mine shaft we can deal with them there. We can demolish the entrance and seal them inside. Or even better, chase 'em way down deep, and *then* blow the shaft. Put a hundred thousand tons of nukeglass between them and the surface. Once we get them down that stinking hole, we've got control of their power supply, the batteries, the processor, even their jump zone—which, if you look hard, you can see over there, on the far side of the water tower. That squat black box is the jump generator. No force field around it, either."

"How can you tell that from here?" Ryan said.

"All the glass dust in the air would reveal the protective dome's outline, even at this distance," Burning Man said. "Since the jump zone is unprotected, we can hit that, too. I'm keeping a third wave of attack in reserve, this to sweep in after Besup and the dogs have done their work, and make a final push for the mine entrance."

"I don't see how we're gonna make the she-hes back down," J.B. said. "I mean, we've got surprise and superior numbers on our side, but they've got tribarrels and EM-shielded body armor."

"Believe me, I know how to fight opponents in battlesuit armor," the baron said. "In my other life, I wrote the book on it. Especially in tight places. My best advice with tribarrels is, don't get hit in the head."

"Speaking of that," Ryan said, "there're a lot of

bystanders down there. And if what you say about the slaves being worked in shifts is true, there are even more of them in the mine…."

"Nothing I can do about them," Burning Man said. "The poor luckless bastards got captured at the wrong time, in the wrong place. Once the shooting starts and the pipe bombs start popping off, they either make a break for it across the massif, or they get whipsawed in the cross fire. No way am I going to let them be used as hostages, or as human shields. We can't give this enemy any advantage and still hope to win."

As the baron scooted back from the viewpoint, he said, "Besup, you're taking the fat liar with you. Put the bastard out in front of your force and let him soak up some of that she-he firepower. And Ryan, I want White Wolf with me. Your boy's got a hell of a throwing arm, and we're going to need his help taking out the gyro."

When they returned to the road, under the baron's direction they divided the ammo and explosives and reloaded their packs. That done, Burning Man began separating his forces into three columns.

"See you on the other side, lover," Ryan said, quickly taking Krysty in his arms. She kissed him hard and held him crushingly tight for a fraction of a second.

Pulling back and smiling, Krysty said, "On the other side."

The other companions' farewells were just as brief and matter-of-fact. A hug, a handshake, a slap on the back. None of them felt the need to dwell on what might happen next. Considering who and what they were going up against, the downsides were all too obvious.

Besup took charge of the dogs and half the main force, about forty-five men, which included Doc.

Eleven warriors and Jak made up the baron's demolition team. Krysty and Mildred, along with the remainder of the force, prepared to sweep in to complete the rout and form the pursuit down the mine shaft.

After Ryan and J.B. had said their goodbyes and set off across the road toward the glow of Ground Zero, the one-eyed warrior turned to his old friend and asked, "You mind spotting for me this time?"

"Nope."

"Let's go find us a hide and something to shoot."

JAK STOOD in the middle of road, hefting twelve inches of pipe bomb in his hand. The crude device was heavy and compact, capped at both ends. He reckoned it would windmill through the air nicely.

Burning Man was making his way down the row of warriors, pairing them up in two-man fire teams. They were all burdened with packs full of explosives; he was burdened with his trademark flamethrower, and wore his NOMEX hood and gauntlets.

As the mutilated man stepped up to him, Jak got a strong whiff of the weapon's leaking fuel. The baron didn't seem at all concerned that a random spark might make him the epicenter of a thirty-foot fireball.

"White Wolf," he said, "you and Washaskie are a team. He'll light the fuses, you do the tossing."

Washaskie was one of the four whitefaces Jak had blind-run the road with. Stoutly built with short legs, the perpetual delight on his face hadn't wavered even while he was slitting a sentry's throat.

Washaskie accepted the clutch of wooden matches and the hand-twisted cheroot the baron handed him.

After Burning Man finished the pairings and duty assignments, he addressed them all. "When we get within arm range of the gyro," he said, "I want you to set out your explosives, line 'em up on the glass. As I explained, one of you will light all the fuses, the other will do all the throwing. You've got plenty of extra pipe bombs in your packs so don't worry about the misses. Mistakes don't matter as long as you manage to get the explosives at least forty or fifty yards downrange. And as a last reminder, make sure you both duck after you chuck. These puppies fling shrap a long way."

Burning Man then led Jak and the rest of his force overland, circling wide to the west to come upon the gyro and its landing pad from behind. It was a distance of more than a half mile over brutal terrain, but their elevation and the intervening arc of ridge concealed them from the compound's view. The continual noise from the ore processor covered the cracking and crunching sounds as they broke trail on the massif's brittle surface.

Right away, Jak tried closing his eyes and "seeing" the landscape with his mind, but this time it didn't work. The light cast from Ground Zero played on his eyelids and ruined his concentration. Though faint, the wash of reflection off the billowing dust clouds made it possible for he and the warriors to see where they were going with eyes open.

Except for the heavy weight of the pack on his back, Jak found it fairly easy going. That all changed when they reached their destination. Burning Man made them fan out at intervals of thirty or forty feet before they started over the ridge. Keeping low, careful not to slash his hands on the razor-edged rubble, Jak crested the rise in the crust and looked onto the brilliantly floodlit depression. One hundred fifty yards away, down the gradual slope, near the center of the concavity, was their target—a slender, black airship thirty feet long, one huge, main propeller mounted amidships on the cabin roof, one secondary propeller aft on the fuselage. Twin weapons pods hung like massive testes under the front of the chassis. The pods bristled with cannon barrels and missile tips. The airship had no windows that Jak could see. No doors, either. Its surface was as smooth as polished black stone.

The domes where the she-hes were supposed to be sleeping stood to the left another fifty yards. Between the ridge and their target, the nukeglass was mottled in shades of greenish gray, with harsh glare reflecting off the places where the surface had recently spawled off. Elsewhere, it was marred by cracks, pits, gullys of various widths and depths. To reach their attack position, the warriors had to crawl to it on their bellies, under the bright flare of the kliegs.

Jak's first thought was, who was watching them? As he advanced, inching along on elbows and knees, scanning the landscape downrange and downslope, the answer came to him.

Nobody.

The she-hes had set up their base eight miles from any sign of life, in the middle of a rad-poisoned hellhole. They had superior weapons and armor. They had the cloak of a moonless night. Complacency had set in.

Either that, or maybe they didn't have enough personnel to keep a proper watch around the clock.

Spread out across the nukeglass, the warriors descended in pairs from one point of concealment to the next, a zigzag route that followed radiating gullys to shallow pits, and avoided the patches of glare where they could be silhouetted. It was impossible to keep from being cut in the process. The fractures in the surface were like serrated blades that sliced through clothing and skin.

Jak's knees and elbows were bleeding badly by the time he and Washaskie reached the flat bottom of Ground Zero and Burning Man hand-signaled a halt to their advance. They were about fifty yards from the gyro. Jak figured he could throw a pipe bomb that far with some accuracy, but only from a standing position, where he could really rear back and chuck it.

Standing up would expose him to fire from deeper in the compound, but the risk was minimized because they had circled around. The aircraft itself now blocked a direct view of the assault.

Washaskie hurriedly began pulling pipe bombs from his pack, setting them out for Jak to grab. Then the stocky warrior lit his cheroot with a wooden match, puffing mightily to get the tip of it glowing.

Spread out in half circle, the warriors awaited the baron's signal.

When he jumped to his feet and chucked the first bomb, the others followed suit.

Jak held out the fuse end of the bomb and a kneeling Washaskie applied the end of his cheroot to the jutting, twisted-paper stub. The second the gunpowder inside started to sputter and spark, Jak turned his head, located his target, then rotated his hips, and from the soles of his feet let the sucker fly.

Burning Man's bomb exploded with a blinding flash, about three feet short of the target, but with enough force to rock the aircraft on its skids. The baron's shrill cry of triumph hung in the air for an instant before being smothered by a ragged string of similar detonations, retina-burning flashes and rocking concussions. Glass shards and hot shrap sizzled overhead. Gouts of cordite smoke briefly obscured the target.

Jak and Washaskie immediately fell into a rhythm.

Light and chuck, then duck.

Light and chuck, then duck.

The ground underfoot quaked from consecutive volleys of explosions, and new seams opened up, racing across the surface.

In the one-sided melee, some of the bombs fell short, some actually hit the aircraft and bounced off. And others skittered across the smooth glass, skittered beyond their target and dropped into the pits where the slaves had been trying to sleep. As the bombs exploded in the pits, plumes of ragged flesh and severed limbs flew skyward, like they were shot from a cannon, black gobs against the flame orange and fire red, falling back as gruesome rain upon the massif.

Though Jak's ears were numbed by the explosions, he could hear the screaming, and the whine of the shrap.

The unfortunate overshoots and their spectacular consequences didn't dent Washaskie's mood one bit. Grinning like a triple-stupe droolie, he puffed hard on the cigar to heat the glowing coal.

The string of explosions continued. Fifty yards ahead of them, the aircraft shuddered again and again, swallowed up in enormous flashes. The rearmost propeller sheared off. Shrap gnawed holes in the edges of the main rotor.

Then all of the warriors found the distance, Jak included.

Six pipe bombs bounced under fuselage and exploded nearly simultaneously, blasting the gyro off its skids. Heat and shock enveloped both of its belly pods, and the fireball ballooned as a cluster of red-tipped missiles self-launched with a roar. Three feet above the surface, they chased one another across the diameter of Ground Zero, just over the heads of the slaves cowering in the sleeping pits, then plowed into the ridge on the far side and exploded in interlaced balls of light.

Washaskie seemed to get a big charge out of that, his eyes full of glee as he clenched the butt of the cigar between his teeth. Then his head snapped back, his chin suddenly pointing skyward, like it had been mule-kicked. And all the stuffing came out of him. He slumped onto his back on the glass.

Jak thought he'd been clipped by a piece of flying shrap. He knelt over the warrior and looked at his face. There was a hole in his cheek directly under his left eye. A round, black hole. Blood began to pour from it.

Washaskie's eyes opened. They were glazed with shock. He was still alive, but he wasn't smiling anymore.

The echoes of the pipe bomb explosions were still rumbling in the distance when something kicked up a bright puff of dust beside Jak's boots and ricocheted across the massif.

Not shrap, he thought.

Jak grabbed hold of Washaskie's collar and started dragging him away, across a landscape that offered no cover. As he did so, bullets smashed into the glass five feet ahead of him and then three feet to the right.

The sniper was bracketing his shots, trying to zero in on a moving target.

Chapter Seventeen

Ryan and J.B. beelined for the lee of the ragged ridge. The one-eyed man hadn't paid much attention to the landscape feature when they had been brought here against their will the first time. As prisoners of the she-hes at Ground Zero, the companions had spent the daylight hours slaving deep underground, and when they were released topside after dark, they had had other, more pressing things to worry about, like starving or freezing to death. The change in tactics, from defense to offense, had altered the perspective. Now the eroding structure had strategic value. Nukeglass boulders couldn't stop full-metal-jacketed bullets or tribarrel blasts, but they did conceal the assembled attack force and its movements.

Turning to the right, Ryan and J.B. followed the curve of the barrier. They were searching for a gap, a notch, a hole in the concretized rubble that would give them a protected shooting platform. The harsh glow from the kliegs streamed over the top of the sawtoothed ridge. The backside they paralleled was cast in a pit of hell darkness. Traveling at a slow walk they traced four hundred yards of the circumference before they found what they were looking for.

A beam of light speared out of the side of the ridge.

It cut through the surrounding shadow, angling up and fading into the night sky.

Close inspection revealed two overturned slabs of nukeglass, each more than a foot thick, and ten times that long, cemented crossways into the ridge matrix. The slabs formed a long, low tent bordered and mounded on each side by melted and congealed quartzite rubble. The light poured through the apex of their joining.

Ryan and J.B. began to carefully clear the loose material that blocked entry. The far end of the break in the wall looked down on the site. With the rubble removed, it had a relatively flat floor. And there was just room enough for the two of them and the Steyr to fit inside. There was also a back way out in case they had to stage a quick retreat.

A perfect hide.

They crawled into position on their stomachs, Ryan first, and ended up shoulder-to-shoulder on the edge of the overlook. His upper body propped on his elbows, J.B. thumbed back his fedora and peered through Burning Man's binocs. Ryan uncapped the Steyr's scope and likewise began to survey downrange.

From this vantage point he could see both sides of the ore processor. One battlesuit-clad she-he was overseeing the loading of the hopper and operation of the processor. It was the only sign of a cockroach aboveground that he could find.

Though Ryan had a shot he could make on the she-he, there was no point in targeting that enemy. He knew that the Steyr's 7.62 mm rounds would have no effect. The battle armor's EM shield would deflect them a foot or so before they made contact, sending the rounds ricocheting harmlessly into the night.

He shifted his field of view to the right, taking in the camp turncoats who were laying into the ore-cart-pushing slaves with boots and occasional gun-butts. The guards were urging the miners to move faster.

In front of the mine entrance, sleeping slaves outnumbered their oppressors at least ten to one, but no one stirred from the pits in the nukeglass to come to the aid of the beaten and kicked. They either were too tired to put up a fight, or too afraid their comrades wouldn't back their play, and that they'd be hung out to dry. Or maybe the she-hes had taken their loved ones belowground, splitting up family groups, holding them as hostages in order to maintain control of a large workforce.

Ryan lined up the gyro in the scope's viewfield, then elevated the sight to look beyond it to the ridge's opposite rim. The combination of glare of the kliegs, the residual heat shimmering in waves off the massif's surface, and the distance, which was better than half a mile, made picking out man-sized targets difficult. With the scope held steady, it took him a minute or two to search out and verify pinpoints of approaching movement. It would have taken him a lot longer than that if he hadn't known the direction Burning Man and his bomb throwers were coming from.

Half-hidden by the shimmer, the whitefaces advanced, paused, advanced, moving on their bellies from scant cover to scant cover.

Ryan swung his sights back onto the compound, checking in turn the gyro, huts, ore processor and mine entrance. "Don't see any threats to them yet," he said.

"Nobody's looking their way," J.B. agreed without lowering his binocs. "Better get ready to rip. They'll be in arm range soon."

Ryan dropped the bolt action's safety, but kept his finger outside the trigger guard and his eye peering through the scope. The first explosion came a couple of very long minutes later, a thunderclap and flash that sent a geyser of smoke, shrap and glass jetting up into the night sky. The rocking concussion rolled through the massif; Ryan could feel the grinding rumble against his stomach muscles.

Before all the debris had fallen back to earth, a shower of glass fragments still glittering in the klieg lights, a flurry of subsequent explosions blossomed around the gyro, ringing it in fire and smoke.

The noise of the overlapping blasts was deafening. And their shock waves rippled through the glacier.

There was no answering response. As had been hoped, the sudden attack and its ferocity had taken the camp by surprise.

From Ryan's elevated viewpoint it looked like the compound was being shelled by artillery.

Plumes of thick smoke swept across the nukeglass. Then came the bark and squeal of simultaneous pipe-bomb detonations, explosions that lifted the gyro into the air.

A cluster of red-tipped projectiles burst out from under it, out of the billowing smoke and flame, a slow-mo horror that suddenly speeded up as the rockets achieved full thrust, heading in a straight line right for them.

"Oh, fuck, oh, fuck," J.B. groaned.

Clutching the Steyr in his left hand, Ryan grabbed his old friend by the back of the collar and hauled him bodily out of the rear of the hide.

No time to run, they dropped to their knees and covered their heads.

Overlaid explosions 125 feet away lit up the night, jolted the ground and sent up a towering spray of hot metal and shattered glass. A hail of chunks and slivers rained down on their backs.

As the concussion faded away, Ryan thought he heard the crack of assault rifle. Single shot.

J.B. had heard it, too. "That's an AK," he said with conviction.

Then a burst of autofire rattled up from the compound.

The defenders of Ground Zero had definitely come out of their stupor.

Ryan and J.B. scrambled back into the hide. Looking through the binocs, J.B. said, "Got a shooter on the left side of the water tower."

Ryan swung the Steyr's sights onto the structure. A lone rifleman stood on the elevated platform, long-blaster shouldered and aimed toward Burning Man's force. Through the scope Ryan saw the rifle bucking. A fraction of a second later he heard the gunshot clatter.

To compensate for the difference in elevation, Ryan put the sight's post two feet low of center chest. As he struggled to get his breathing and heart-beat under control, he rested the pad of his finger on the trigger, tightening down to just above the break point.

"Nukin' hell! Ryan, take him out!" J.B. exclaimed.

But before he could do that, the shooter in the view

field moved five feet farther away on the platform, spoiling the shot. Ryan released the finger tension and let the trigger spring back.

The man on the tower resumed rapid-firing at the warriors caught without cover on the nukeglass.

Ryan reacquired the target, which had now turned sideways to him. He put the top of the post on the shooter's waist and smoothly broke the trigger. The Steyr boomed and bucked hard against his shoulder.

Riding the recoil and regaining the sight picture, Ryan saw the man slammed against the side of the tank. He lost hold of his rifle and it tumbled off the platform. Then the shooter slumped, his knees buckling, and rolled off after it. He hit the ground headfirst beside one of the supporting legs and didn't move.

"Another one," J.B. announced as Ryan worked the longblaster's bolt action, flipping out a smoking hull, then chambering and locking down on a live round. "On the ladder, on the right…"

A second potential shooter, AK slung over his back, was scrambling up the ladder that led to the tower platform.

"If he gets around to the rear of tank you've got no shot, and from there he'll still command the kill zone," J.B. warned.

Ryan held the sights on the middle of the man's back, a foot below his head, and dispensing with the niceties of breath and heartbeat control, got off a shot. Even though he got the scope back on the target as the bullet struck, he couldn't see the point of impact. The man suddenly stopped climbing. He stood there for an instant, frozen, clinging to the ladder's rungs, then just let go with both hands. He toppled off the ladder backward and crashed to the ground at its foot.

Then the shit totally hit the fan. And it happened so quickly, there wasn't time to think, it was all Ryan could do to react.

A wave of superintense heat slammed the front of the hide, making him jerk back his hands and groan a curse. The emerald-green laser beam was so hot it remelted the nukeglass like slabs of candlewax. An instant later a volley of bullets smacked into the face of the ridge inches from their position.

Ryan heard a sizzling sound, and his nose was struck by a nasty smell. When he looked beside him, he saw that drops of melted glass were burning holes through the brim of J.B.'s treasured fedora.

"Fuck!" the Armorer exclaimed, ripping the hat off his head as they scooted backward, out of the dissolving shooting blind. Slapping the fedora on his hip, he snarled, "The bastard fucked up my hat."

As they ran low and fast back the way they'd come, to try and join up with Besup's forces before they began the main assault, Ryan put together the chain of events in his mind. He guessed that the she-he standing by the ore processor had used her battlesuit's infrared sensors to locate the hide after he touched off the first shot. And that the emerald-green laser beam the cockroach fired had worked like a pointer, lighting up the target for the conventional weaps of the turncoats.

"Whoa!" J.B. said, catching Ryan by the shoulder. He pointed in the direction of the road, which crossed their path at a right angle. "Over there, who is that?"

Whoever it was, he was running away from Ground

Zero, his head lowered, legs pumping hard. Even in the dim light, without the aid of optics, he looked hefty.

Ryan swung the Steyr to his shoulder and looked through the telescope. Beside him, J.B. raised the binocs.

The runner had no hands.

Chapter Eighteen

Doc stood near the pack of war dogs, waiting out of sight of the compound with the rest of the force for Besup to give the signal to attack.

From over the ridge came the booms and flashes of the pipe bombs detonating and the shrill screams of shrap and those caught in its spray, sounds that set the huge animals to leaping, snarling, snapping, struggling against their restraints. With extreme difficulty their handlers kept them from joining the fray.

Madness, Doc thought as he looked around him.

The grinning whitefaces.

The century-old weaponry.

The dogs of war.

The horrendous migration to a hostile, alien battle-field.

This was absolute madness.

The Oxford-trained part of his mind rejected what he knew was about to unfold as unspeakable. But his uneducable lizard brain, like the brains of the ravening canines, had registered the scent of blood in the air, the scent of blood and the sounds of pain, and that had triggered his memory and an avalanche of instinctive drives.

If war and battle were to some men like a drug, then close-quarters combat was the drug of all drugs. To be lost in the frenzy, in the fury, was to forget everything else, to realize the transcendence of slaughter.

And I am not immune to its call, Doc thought, staring at the fingers of his own right hand, which trembled with excitement.

He drew out his sword and let the cane-scabbard fall to the ground. Shifting the long blade to his left hand, he pulled the LeMat from its hand-tooled, Mexican holster.

At the front of the formation, near the backside of the ridge, Besup let out a shrill war cry. And everyone and everything broke into a dead run.

Caught up in the whooping, shouting mob, Doc rushed through the gap in the ridge that had been cut for the road, onto the down tilting glass plate of Ground Zero, into the glare of blinding lights.

And chaos.

The warriors sprinting before him immediately fanned out, to make themselves more difficult targets. Those leading the formation opened fire with longblasters, shooting from the hip as they ran. The raucous clatter of one-sided, massed blasterfire filled the shallow bowl.

Who or what they were shooting at, Doc couldn't immediately see. He kept running though, as fast as he could, both to keep up with those ahead of him and to keep from being trampled by those coming from behind. He held the LeMat in his right fist, and in his left, the sword raised point-first toward the night sky.

Under other circumstances, against other adversaries, with his assortment of nineteenth century weapons, Doc might have felt as useful as a vestigial tail. But against EM-shielded battle armor, his Civil War-era black-powder pistol and tempered Toledo steel was no less ineffective than the late twentieth century rifles of the Bannock-Shoshone.

Doc held his fire, saving the LeMat's lead balls for targets he knew they could damage—the turncoats.

Over the bobbing tops of heads, in the gaps between the whitefaces' backs, Doc saw a quartet of battlesuited she-hes barreling out of the row of gleaming black huts on the left, and more of the cockroaches popped out of the mine entrance, on the far side of the sleeping pits, directly ahead.

The turncoats guarding the slaves stood their ground and returned fire at the attackers.

Bullets whined through the throng, and in front of Doc, whitefaces here and there dropped to the glass, struck multiple times in midstride, their misted blood hanging pink in the air, clinging to his face and hair as he hurtled through it.

Two hundred yards of all-out sprint under fire brought Besup's force to the edge of the pitted area where the slaves took their rest. Those too paralyzed by fear to flee the onslaught were caught in a withering, conventional cross fire. Any hope of their turning on their masters and using superior numbers to overwhelm them was baseless.

The rising stench of gore and plundered bowels, and the sense that their release was near set the pack of war dogs to howling. Half-dragging their handlers along, they snapped their jaws at the air.

From beside the black huts, emerald-green beams sliced into the formation's flank. Even as more whitefaces began to fall, legless, headless, the ground rocked under Doc's boots and the left side of his face was struck by a blast of heat that made him flinch. Pipe-bomb explosions, one after another, lifted the four she-hes off their feet and hurled them into the air like black puppets. Evidently, although their EM shields could turn away multiple, small projectiles, they were no match for such a powerful force. They couldn't keep boots on the ground.

The she-hes scrambled to their feet, only to be blown off them again. And again. And again. They were tossed through the flash and smoke, and sent sprawling onto the glass.

The merciless barrage of Burning Man's pipe bombs, momentarily at least, took the she-hes and their tribarrels out of the battle and drove them inexorably toward the mine entrance.

Besup led his warriors into the ranks of huddled slaves, many of them badly wounded or dead. The initial wave of whitefaces swept past a trio of cook pots.

But as Doc approached that same position, he caught sight of three men cowering behind the large boiling caldrons. Evidence of what was stewing in the pots lay scattered all around. Piles of bloody long bones, skulls, discarded clothing, piles of entrails and half-dismembered, skinned-out, human carcasses. The three hiding in back of the pots were bloody-faced and bloody-handed; it wasn't their blood.

As soon as the death camp butchers and chefs realized they'd been spotted, they sprang forth and charged at Doc brandishing a meat cleaver and stir paddles, respectively. The old man stopped and, bracing himself from behind with a sword-point dug into the glass, raised the LeMat. He blew them off their feet, one by one, with single balls to center mass.

Amid the caustic gouts of smoke and glittering sparks of burning powder, the cooks crashed onto their backs.

Then the dogs, with a great scrabbling of claws on glass, raced past him, jostling and buffeting him as they went. The animals held back their bloodlust until they shot past the front of the whiteface charge, and then on cue, they attacked everyone in their path. Slaves, turncoats, she-hes, they were all the enemy.

And the enemy had to be torn into as small pieces as was possible.

In a frenzy, running thirty yards ahead of their masters, they launched themselves at the back of a retreating she-he. With their sheer weight, and coming at the prey from every conceivable angle, they negated the effect of the EM shield. Either that, Doc reasoned, or at a critical moment its power supply failed.

Again, it became less a question of deflecting incoming ordnance and more about keeping armored boot soles planted on the ground. Bowled over and onto her back, the cockroach had the jaws of hundred-pound dogs firmly attached to feet, legs, arms, hands and helmet. Shaking and twisting their heads, the animals tried to get purchase on the slick, segmented armor with the points of their fangs, to crack or penetrate it. They pulled in all directions at once, using their back legs, fighting one another. The she-he could get no traction, couldn't regain her feet. In the battlesuit, flat on her back, she was skidded around on the nukeglass like an overturned turtle.

Three fellow cockroaches rushed to her aid, firing their laser rifles from the hip as they bolted from the mine entrance. They weren't worried about hitting their downed comrade. The laser beams couldn't penetrate the battlesuit's EM shield.

For everyone and everything else, the sweep of their claw-footed, triple-muzzles created a whipsaw of destruction. To avoid it, Doc threw himself belly down on the glass. Before him, the very air burst into throbbing, green flame.

Six of the war dogs literally fell to pieces, their severed limbs and torsos dropping to the glass. Squealing, the dogs that still could—the half dogs—crawled away on their forelegs, the stumps of their bisected hindquarters smoking. The surviving animals scattered from their intended prey, clearing a path for the rescuing she-hes. When the dogs' weight came off her, the fallen cockroach jumped to her feet, joined the others, and they began a hasty retreat toward the mine.

If the leading edge of the warriors hadn't been so close to the four she-hes, Doc knew that Burning Man could have put his pipe bombs to good use. As it was, he had to hold fire or annihilate his own soldiers. As the she-hes backed away, they took full advantage of the situation.

The bloodlessly severed parts of men hit the ground, mixing with the severed parts of their dogs. Limbs. Torsos. Heads. Grievous wounds steaming in the cold night air.

As Doc pushed up from the massif, not ten yards away

Besup was caught by intersecting, vibrating lines of emerald green. The beams passed right through his body, like his flesh and bone was no more substantial than smoke, and without uttering a sound, he collapsed.

When both his knees impacted the ground, the result of the laser strike, the angled cut from the right side of his neck down to his right hip became evident. That part of his body simply slid off the rest of him and flopped down onto the glass. One look told Doc that Besup had lost the arm, his collarbone, ribs, one lung, probably a kidney, half his intestines and most of the right hip joint.

The wound should have been immediately fatal, but cruelly it wasn't because the laser weapon cauterized what it cut away.

Besup remained upright on his knees only for a few seconds. Before Doc could reach him, he collapsed onto his good side on the glass. He lay there, violently shivering, his eyes bugging out of his head, tears streaming down the side of his painted face, but he still had the power of speech.

And the power of will.

He called out to his brother whitefaces, shouting over the raging blasterfire and the clustered explosions, his voice cracking from the intensity of his pain as he screamed, "Chill me! Chill me now!"

But his brethren did nothing.

Those that had seen him fall were too shocked to move, too horrified by his wounds to act. Or they were caught up in following the dog pack, so they didn't even realize what had happened to their leader.

When none of the nearby warriors rushed forward to

Chapter Nineteen

With bullets skipping off the glass around him, Jak dropped to a knee beside Washaskie, turning sideways to the incoming, making himself as small a target as possible. The fallen warrior choked and sputtered blood from deep in his throat. It ran in crimson rivulets down his white-painted cheeks. He was drowning in his own gore, his body trembling with the final, frantic spasms of life.

The albino teen raised his Colt Python and returned fire on the water tower. The enemy perched there was no longer taking careful aim, but instead, spraying blasterfire, trying desperately to turn back the assault.

The hundred yards to the water tower was well beyond the accurate range of Jak's handblaster. And he couldn't even adjust for the trajectory because he couldn't see where his rounds were landing. Smoke from the pipe-bomb explosions drifted between him and his target, intermittently obscuring it from view. However, none of that stopped him from emptying his weapon at the enemy. Even a near miss could make the shooter hesitate and cease fire.

But the shooter didn't seem to notice the six .357 rounds Jak sent barreling his way. As Burning Man and the whitefaces advanced on the row of black huts, the hail of fire from the tower continued unabated.

Jak swung open the cylinder and dumped the smoking empties onto the glass, then reloaded.

As he snapped the cylinder closed and once again took aim, the incoming blasterfire stopped. Over the Python's sights he got a glimpse of a dark shadow tumbling from the platform. He watched the body take a hard landing on the ground beneath. It lay in a heap and didn't move.

Somebody had nailed the turncoat bastard good.

Whoever had made the shot, it had come far too late to help Washaskie. The whitefaced warrior had stopped breathing. His bloodshot eyes stared fixedly up at the night sky. Jak was fumbling amid the blood, trying to find a pulse in the man's neck when a shock wave slammed his back with numbing force.

Squinting into the swirling blast of hot wind and flying debris, he saw that two of the cockroach huts had been hit. They looked like broken black eggshells. Shattered arcs of plasteel fluttered down through the smoke, back to earth—and that wasn't all that fluttered down. The she-hes who had managed to bail out of the huts before the explosion had been lifted into the air by it. Tribarrels cartwheeling out of their grasp, they crashed onto their shiny black backs, their momentum sending them skidding across the nukeglass. When they stopped sliding, they were slow getting up, as if they had been stunned by the concussion or the impact with the ground, despite the high-tech armor.

So much for cockroach invincibility, Jak thought. Then he flinched as multiple explosions ripped into one of the surviving huts.

A she-he, late to the party, was trying to exit the hut

when the pipe bombs detonated. The blasts hurled the cockroach in a reverse somersault, and heels over head it disappeared into the smoke and the hut's wreckage.

Burning Man turned his ruined face to the sky and let out a blood-curdling yell. Then he pulled the protective goggles down over his eyes, and with a whoosh ignited the nozzle of his flamethrower.

When the baron broke ranks and charged the hut, Jak abandoned the warrior dead on the glass and ran after him.

But not too closely.

The pistol-grip nozzle of the igniter dribbled fuel, and left a trail of flaming puddles behind.

As Jak and Burning Man neared the dome, something stirred amid the boiling smoke. A figure in black rose to full height and stumbled over the ruptured wall with tribarrel laser rifle in hand.

The baron was fifty feet away. Still running full-tilt, he let fly with the flamethrower.

Not a weapon of precision, to be sure.

A plume of fire roared from the nozzle, shot a good forty feet and fell, splattering upon the she-he and the surrounding wreckage. Caught in a flaming waterfall, the cockroach swung up the laser rifle. A beam of brilliant green light blazed from the triple muzzles, but missed the target, cutting a bubbling, jagged gash in the nukeglass two yards to the baron's right.

Burning Man didn't let up for a second. The nozzle's trigger pinned, he continued the assault, following his target as it tried to juke clear of raining hell.

Unable to escape, a fireball on two legs, the cockroach dropped the tribarrel, staggered and collapsed.

Even after the she-he fell to the glass, flapping arms and flopping from side to side, the baron continued to roast it. The smoke that poured off the burning fuel was black and caustic.

Burning Man stood over the thrashing form, pouring on the flame, his disfigured face alight in its dancing glow.

"Cook them in their shells," the baron told Jak out of the functional side of his mouth, never taking his eyes off the target. "Turns out the battlesuit's EM shield doesn't stop the penetration of sustained high temperatures. Something we learned the hard way on my Earth trying to put down the Consumer Rebellion."

In a matter of seconds the heat of the burning fuel had melted the surface of the glass. And the supine she-he sank full length into the murky gray puddle that had been created. When the baron finally shut off the spray of pressurized gasoline, the pool of fire burned itself out, and molten glass quickly rehardened around the suit of armor, and its unmoving and apparently dead occupant.

Burning Man waved Jak and the other pipe bombers onward, after the retreating she-hes, toward the water tower.

The clatter of blasterfire from behind made the albino teen glance over his right shoulder. Besup's force had already covered half the distance to the mine, weapons blazing.

The turncoats at the mine entrance returned fire.

Caught in the middle were the slaves. The ones who panicked and left the relative protection of the sleeping pits were blown off their feet in short order, struck by bullets coming from both directions. Their bodies and blood littered the glass.

Jak didn't hear the signal for the release of the war dogs, but suddenly they were on the loose, racing through and past the mob of running whitefaces as if they were standing still. In a blur of snapping jaws and twisting bodies, they tore into slaves and turncoats alike.

And the sleeping pits were no protection from their fangs.

A huge animal held a man pinned to the glass on his back. While the unlucky bastard kicked and thrashed, the dog buried its maw in the front of his neck, shaking its head, its back muscles rippling.

The head popped up with a mouthful of throat and Adam's apple—a bloody rag sprouting long white stems of tendon clenched between its jaws. Then with a toss of that same bony head, the animal repositioned the awful gobbet in its maw and gulped it down.

Faces, necks, chests dripping with gore—and still unsated—the dogs attacked everything that wasn't whitefaced, everything that breathed. A handful of them, working in a pack, pulled down a she-he. Even though some of the dogs fell to the lasers of the cockroach's rescuers, it didn't break the spell that held them. The surviving dogs and their packmates circled around and attacked from different angles, hounding the she-hes in retreat.

Chill-crazed devils.

They weren't the only ones.

"Hit 'em, hit 'em!" Burning Man shouted at his warriors, pointing with his flamethrower nozzle at the quartet of rapidly backstepping cockroaches. "Blow 'em all to hell!"

The warriors looked at him in disbelief.

"Quick, before they're out of range!"

When they didn't move at once to obey the command, the baron thrust a hand deep into Jak's backpack, searching for a pipe bomb of his own to chuck. The albino youth twisted in the pack's straps, and with his left hand caught and held the NOMEX-gauntleted forearm. For a split second, in the middle of the battle's mayhem, it was a standoff, strength against main strength.

White Wolf wouldn't yield.

"Too close," Jak snarled up at him, his ruby-red eyes unblinking as he wrapped the fingers of his right hand around the free end of the capped length of pipe. "Blow to shit Besup, warriors and companions."

Burning Man jerked his hand free, leaving the bomb in Jak's grasp, but the fury in the mobile half of his face remained.

The baron turned his wrath on another target.

"Take down the fucking tower!" he shouted, waving his men after him with his flamethrower's dripping nozzle. "Do it, now!"

To get in throwing distance of the tower they had to run another twenty yards under fire from the mine entrance. When a warrior who had sprinted ahead of Burning Man buckled and dropped in a heap, the baron paused long enough to bend down and snatch the loaded backpack from his shoulders.

The spray of bullets took a heavy toll on the teams of lighters and throwers. By the time they were in range of the target, half the men had been lost, left sprawled behind on the glass.

One lighter with glowing cheroot did the job for three throwers.

Jak shoved the fuse end of his bomb down at the grinning whiteface. Three arms, three bombs. The kneeling warrior held the fuses together, and when the tip of his cheroot had them all sputtering, Jak and the others turned and heaved.

The pipe bombs landed short and skittered on the glass, rolling between the legs of the structure. A second passed, and then tremendous, nearly simultaneous explosions lit up and rocked the underside of the holding tank.

Two of its three legs were blown off. The third held for a moment more, the latticework of steel screaming as it slowly bent under a weight it wasn't designed to bear. The tower began to topple over, falling faster and faster. When the huge tank crashed to earth on its side, the top burst open. Its contents swooshed over the glass in a three-foot-high wave, washing the whitefaces, dogs and slaves closest to it off their feet.

By the time the rush of water reached the far side of the sleeping pits, it was stained pink with blood.

Chapter Twenty

The overweight man high-kicked for the darkness, his arms pumping, his chin up, his brimmed canvas hat smashed down onto the back of his head.

Although J.B. swung up his scattergun and dropped the safety, bringing the muzzle around to take a swinging lead on the target, he didn't press the trigger. That would have been a waste of a perfectly good round. Big Mike was already out of effective knock-down range of the short-barreled 12-gauge.

Ryan had likewise shouldered the Steyr, but he didn't fire, either. When J.B. checked back, he saw his friend wasn't looking through the scope, he was sighting around it. J.B. reckoned the light was way too dim for a scoped shot on a target moving away from Ground Zero. Apparently too dim for any shot, as Ryan lowered his weapon.

In another second, the man with no hands had disappeared into the blackness, heading back the way they'd just come, back for Slake City.

When J.B. started to pursue, Ryan caught hold of his shoulder. "No time for that," he said.

"We're going to just let the lying, murdering sack of shit get away?" J.B. said.

"Chances are, when we hike out tomorrow we'll find

him a couple miles from here, dead by the side of the road," Ryan said.

"Like to have blasted the bastard personally," J.B. said.

"You and me both, but we've got other, more pressing business."

The sounds of the fighting rolled over the ridge: the ringing booms of the pipe-bomb detonations, the strobe flashes of the explosions against the sky, the blaster-fire sawing back and forth, the shrill screams of the wounded. Towering pillars of smoke rose into the air above Ground Zero, underlit by the kliegs.

Ryan slung his longblaster, unholstered his SIG and said, "We'd better get on with it."

Without a word, the diminutive Armorer aimed his scattergun toward heaven, and followed his companion into the already raging battle. Something he had done many, many times before—too many to even count.

Only this time it felt different.

It felt…wrong.

Ever since they'd made the fateful detour off the highway and onto the hell-blasted volcanic plain, he could smell an impending disaster—like the pong of cigar, butt stank and vinegar in a single-wide trailer gaudy. A helpless, waking nightmare, waiting somewhere down the line to be played out in flesh, blood and bone.

Everybody died.

Everybody knew that.

And on the brink of eternity, everybody thought, not here, not now.

That's what J.B. was thinking as he walked through the gap in the ridge beside his oldest surviving friend, feeling the rumble of explosions through the soles of his boots and in the pit of his stomach.

Not here. Not now.

His instinct was telling him just the opposite; that this was it, that this was the one. This was where he got on the last train west.

He had been feeling the sense of doom for days now, but he couldn't explain it to the others. He couldn't put it into words that didn't sound two-week jolt-binge, scab-assed crazy. Inch by inch, even though he had tried to keep it from happening, he and his companions had been sucked deeper. Until it was too late.

Who was kidding who?

It was too late the second they stepped off the predark highway.

J.B. remembered all too well what the she-hes' laser rifles could do to a human being. And how useless plain old bullets were against their shiny black battle armor. The Bannock-Shoshone's whiteface, spiritual mumbo jumbo was going to get them all turned into ghosts for real.

But if dying in this wretched, awful place was his true and only fate, if it was what Destiny had in mind for him all along, J.B. knew he couldn't run from it. There was no escape.

So be it, he told himself as he screwed his hat down hard on his head. And fuck it.

When they rushed out onto the sloping verge of Ground Zero, J.B. immediately slung the M-4000 scattergun over his right shoulder. There was no one close enough to shoot at, and besides, the whitefaces were between them and the enemy. They had a lot of ground to cover to catch up to Besup's forces.

The two of them sprinted for the rear of the charging column. J.B. had difficulty keeping up with Ryan, who had longer legs and took longer strides.

As they ran, they jumped the pools of blood and the bodies of fallen warriors. Not just shot. Shot to shit. Chests, heads blown apart by stitchings of full-metal jackets. The footing was made even trickier by the litter of spent cartridge casings and bits of shrap from the pipe bombs.

Though he had to watch where he slapped down his boots, J.B. kept glancing downrange for the black-armored cockroaches. But none was in evidence. Not yet. His nose and throat burned from the smoke that overhung Ground Zero's shallow bowl. His lungs burned from the exertion of the sprint.

Then dazzling green beams shot from the row of milspec huts, sustained beams spearing into Besup's left flank. Two hundred yards ahead of them, men dropped as they ran, skidding on the glass. J.B. got his first glimpse of the real enemy, crouching to fire beside the domes.

Flashes, thunderclaps, multiple, overlaid explosions sent the cockroaches flying off their feet, and slamming to earth.

The sight of them blown sky-high made J.B.'s spirits leap. Maybe he'd been wrong. Maybe the she-hes weren't invincible. Maybe Burning Man wasn't a total whack-job, maybe really he knew how to fight and beat this enemy. Maybe this wasn't the end of the road after all.

He would have shouted for joy, but he couldn't spare the breath.

As they closed ground on the rear of Besup's forces, he saw the dogs released by the handlers, on cue. The front wave of the attack had already reached the edge of the sleeping pits.

His legs aching, J.B. struggled to keep up with Ryan, who was pulling away from him. Then, through the clouds of smoke he caught sight of a familiar figure. Tall, gaunt, scarecrowlike.

Doc stood over a fallen man, with the LeMat in hand. The man's face was painted white. Then Doc cocked back the hammer spur and took aim.

Nukin' hell, J.B. thought as he recognized the man down was Besup.

For a split second, everything seemed to stop. The clamor, the movement, the shouting. Everything and everyone went still as Doc blasted Besup point-blank.

The man's entire body jerked as the lead ball split open his skull.

Only when J.B. got closer could he see what the she-hes had done to the warrior. And understand why the old man had taken upon himself the onus of a mercy shot. Their tribarrels had left alive two-thirds of a man. Neck to hip was a char of flesh, bone and blood vessels laser-welded shut.

Ryan didn't pause to inspect the damage. He kept on running, through the sleeping pits, toward the point of the attack.

When J.B. reached Doc's side, a cluster of close concussions numbed the left side of his face and body. As hot shrap whistled overhead, he and the old man ducked and dropped to a knee on the glass.

J.B. turned in the direction of the explosions, and saw the water tower topple to the ground and break apart. The released wall of water roared across the flat ground, straight at them. He stood up, bracing himself to meet the surge. It slammed into his knees, sent him sliding and nearly bowled him over.

Far enough ahead to miss the main force of the flood, Ryan took command of the suddenly leaderless and hesitating whitefaces. Out of the forty-five who began the charge, more than half of them were wounded, dead, or dying. Shouting for the warriors to regroup, he led them onward in the final fifty-yard dash.

As J.B. and Doc took off after them, to the left, Burning Man and his bombers pressed the attack. From behind the ruins of the tower, they chucked explosives on the run at the cockroaches trying desperately to reach the protection of the mine entrance. Again, in flashes of light and ear-splitting detonations, the enemy was sent airborne. And they were slower to get up this time.

Still, all of the fleeing she-hes made it through the entrance.

No sooner had they vanished inside, than the war dogs shot through the breach after them, followed closely by Ryan and the whitefaces.

J.B. and Doc were running hard, and they were less than a hundred feet from the entrance when the air was ripped by a different sort of thundercrack. This one was in the ground under their boots. It was the roar of the massif splitting apart.

The cumulative effect of all the explosions sent a craze

of fresh crevices racing across Ground Zero. The ankle-deep standing water poured into them in torrents.

And the seams gaped wider and wider, blocking the path.

J.B. put on the brakes, stumbled and nearly fell into one headfirst.

Doc, on the other hand, vaulted the gap in an easy stride of scarecrow legs.

J.B. pushed up to his feet. Realizing he couldn't jump the crack from a standing start, he turned back to get a running jump on it. As he did so, Krysty and Mildred raced up to join him, along with the remainder of the baron's third reserve force.

"Where's Ryan?" Krysty said.

"Already in the mine," J.B. said.

From the entrance came muffled sounds of blasterfire and explosions.

"No time to waste," Mildred said.

"Come on, come on," Doc urged them from the far side of the crevice.

The three of them vaulted in unison.

Everyone was converging on the mine entrance, but Burning Man and his force had the clear lead. J.B. saw Jak running stride-for-stride beside the NOMEX-clad baron, who in addition to his flamethrower carried a heavily loaded backpack. When the baron suddenly stopped, thirty feet short of the opening, so did Jak, skidding.

Burning Man immediately bent over the pack and took out a pipe bomb. Using the sputtering nozzle of his flamethrower, Burning Man lit the fuse, then dropped the bomb back inside.

"Gaia, what's he doing?" Krysty cried.

Before Jak could stop him, the baron used the pack's straps to hammer-throw the entire payload through the mine entrance.

"Oh, fuck, no!" J.B. shouted.

To keep him from going after it, Doc had to tackle him and take him down from behind.

Then it was too late for anyone to do anything but hit the dirt.

The explosion jolted the ground so hard that it blurred J.B.'s vision. Nukeglass boulders shot like cannon balls out of the mine entrance, bouncing across the massif. The volley of flying rock was followed by a blinding, choking rush of smoke and glass dust. The klieg lights overhead faltered, going from white to yellow, threatening to wink out entirely, then brightened again.

When the debris stopped falling and the smoke and dust began to clear, it was obvious that combat was over for the moment. Through the haze, J.B. could see the entrance had collapsed in on itself. There was no way of telling how much of the shaft had come down with it.

The forces outside the mine were sealed off from the fight.

If there was any fight left.

"Could Ryan have survived?" Krysty cried, her prehensile hair drawn up into tight ringlets of alarm. "Could he have survived that?"

No one answered her.

No one wanted to say aloud what they were thinking.

Mildred draped a consoling arm over Krysty's shoulders. Tears were already streaming down the doctor's face.

J.B. struggled to sit up and draw breath. This was the worst of unexpected consequences. That the "doom" he had foreseen wasn't his to suffer after all. That he would live and Ryan would be the one to die.

Rising to his feet, J.B. marched across the smoking ruin of the battlefield. He stepped up to Burning Man, who stood half-grinning as he admired his own handiwork. Without preamble, the Armorer shoved the muzzle of his 12-gauge scattergun hard under the baron's chin. Then, finger on the trigger, hand on the forestock, he used it to raise the man's disfigured face, to stretch his neck for all to see.

Burning Man let the flamethrower nozzle fall from his grip. His protective goggles reflected the klieg lights.

"Keep smiling, baron," J.B. said, "you're about to buy it."

Chapter Twenty-One

The crushing waves of pain kept Auriel doubled over and on her knees in front of the row of cells. While Dr. Huth looked on helplessly, scanner in hand, the specters slid back and forth inside her, dragging, rasping their substance across the surface of her heart, lungs and stomach, shifting position so they could apply maximum pressure against the walls of her torso as they expanded volume. The combined outward force grew more and more intense with every throb. She could feel her soft tissue beginning to tear and knew the bones would soon start to split.

Then her battlesuit com link opened and a voice roared in her head. "Commander, we are under attack!"

It was Saffa, one of the sisters off duty aboveground.

Through the helmet speaker's static, Auriel could make out the unmistakable rattle of gunfire and the rumble of explosions.

"Who are they?" she wheezed.

"Adversaries unknown. They are using crude but powerful explosives. We can't hold ground against them. Have to—"

The transmission was broken by a piercing squawk, the microphone overloaded by the proximity of the explosion.

"Who are they?" Auriel demanded, gritting her teeth as she used the cave wall to get to her feet, and the stock and barrels of her laser rifle as a third leg to keep her upright. "How many of the enemy are there? How did they get past the sentries? Identify the attackers! Come in, Saffa!"

After seemingly interminable seconds of hissing static, the she-he came back online. She was out of breath and whimpering in pain.

"Have you been wounded?" Auriel asked. "Is your battlesuit environment compromised?"

Saffa responded, but her voice had suddenly become so faint that her words were unintelligible.

"Say again," Auriel prompted.

"My armor is intact," came the strained reply. "Have full oxygen pressure. EM shield operational, all systems appear functional. Something's not right, though. Something *inside* me isn't right. I'm feeling something…oh… it's moving…oh…oh, it hurts. Others, too. Can't fight. We have to fall back. Everyone fall back!"

"No, do not fall back!" Auriel shouted. "You must defend the jump zone!"

The squawk of another close proximity blast cut off the transmission.

Who would dare cross the massif in the dead of night to attack them? Auriel asked herself. Not hardscrabble dirt farmers trying to rescue their loved ones. Not a pack of thieving murderers out for booty. When she glanced up at Dr. Huth, he looked dazed and paralyzed. When she really needed his whitecoat training and ingenuity, he was worse than useless.

He was deadweight.

"Who are they?" Auriel roared into her microphone.

The helmet speakers' only answer was a steady, vacant hiss.

With an effort, Auriel moved visor-to-visor with the whitecoat and seized hold of his plated arm. "Are the others all infected?" she asked.

Unable to back away, Dr. Huth opened and closed his mouth, struggling to come up with an answer that would placate her. "It's possible that all of the sisters are infected," he said at last. "There is no way of telling how far it has spread. I am not feeling any symptoms of infection myself."

Before she could press him further, there came an ominous rumbling from above—explosions muffled by the depth of the glacier—then a screech and shudder as enormous masses of glass slipped along their fracture planes.

If the sisters couldn't defend themselves, Auriel told herself, if they couldn't secure the jump zone, they had no good options left.

It was time to take a bad one.

"Retreat into the mines!" she yelled through the com link, this to anyone still able to hear her voice and obey. And even as she issued the fall-back order, she knew that was probably exactly what this enemy wanted. To trap them inside the shaft.

But the sisters needed to buy whatever time they could. Even if it turned out that all the effort was for nothing, it was her duty as commander to play the hand they had been dealt to the final card.

"Help me," she growled at the whitecoat. "We have

to climb out of here and join the others in the main tunnel."

From above them, the massif shifted again, a grinding squeal of hundreds of thousands of tons of glass on glass.

As they began to move out of the dank corridor, toward the foot of the spiral passageway, Auriel's pain crescendoed, and both her legs stopped working. She had to lock her knees and clutch at Dr. Huth's arm to keep from collapsing on the spot. No longer was the tearing sensation focused on a single point within her; the entire circumference of her rib cage felt like it was cracking apart and she couldn't draw breath. Only when the specters shrank back in volume could she take in air and move her feet.

As she shuffled forward, she saw the look in the whitecoat's eyes. And she knew he wanted to leave her behind. He was trying to figure out a way to pull it off, to bail on her and the others, and save himself. That was how he was applying his highly trained scientific mind to the problem at hand. But Auriel still held the tribarrel in her gauntleted fist. And that kept the toothless piece of shit meekly by her side.

When they had passed under the explosive-packed ceiling and reached the bottom of the spiral, there was an even more powerful quake overhead, a much louder explosion, and as chunks of the roof started falling on their EM shields, everything went black.

Stone, impenetrable black.

Auriel realized at once that the explosion had cut the mine's main power supply.

"Detonate the ceiling!" she commanded Dr. Huth.

She would have done it herself, but she couldn't move quickly enough. "Seal off the corridor!"

In the darkness she felt the whitecoat slip away. But there was no immediate, massive explosion, no thundering fall of tons of ceiling. When she switched her visor to infrared mode, she saw that the coward hadn't budged more than a couple of feet from her side. Bringing down the ceiling would have killed them both.

Then the emergency power generator kicked in and the corridor's lights came back on, albeit dimly.

Looking down the narrow passage Auriel knew that it was already too late.

It didn't matter that the systems were back online. The momentary loss of power had to have caused the force fields to drop.

The field at the far end of the corridor containing the wild stickies.

And worse, the one keeping the specters in check.

No longer held back, the stickies rushed into the corridor, making their awful kissing sounds, waving their spindly arms, sucker adhesive dripping in strands like mucous from their palms and fingertips. In infrared mode, they were a lemon-yellow wave, filling the hallway from wall to wall with their hate and blood lust.

Their intended targets were Auriel and Dr. Huth, the blacksuited tormentors of their brethren, and they had no idea what was in store for them. They couldn't see or hear the specters zipping over their heads like fluorescent green javelins. Some of them seemed to sense the alien presence in the air above them. They swung their arms and swatted the empty space to no effect.

Their mouths gaping wide, their needle teeth bared, they looked around in confusion.

As Auriel watched, the specters stretched themselves out into fine filaments and then slithered into the open mouths and down the unprotected nostril holes of the mutants in the middle of the pack. First one thin ribbon entered a living body, then another, and another after that, sinuous bands of lime green following the predecessor's trail, flowing into and flooding the stickies' bodies with...themselves.

Did it feel cold to be thus violated?

Did it feel hot?

Auriel didn't know; that wasn't the way they entered her.

It certainly had to have felt like *something* because the mutants stopped in their tracks, halting the rampage halfway down the corridor, clutching at their skinny necks and then at their bellies.

In this final stage of the specters' existence there was no delay, no gestation period before they gained the power to destroy. Before Auriel's eyes, the stickies' naked torsos began expanding, swelling like inflating balloons. And like the skins of balloons, the more they expanded the more translucent their outer surface became.

Then came the snapping of bones.

Rhythmic snapping, in time to the coordinated pulsations of the invaders.

The bones of stickies were mostly cartilage. Soft. Pliable. Even their skulls, an adaptation that allowed them to squeeze through impossibly small spaces.

Under the internal pressure, their heads expanded

as well. Visibly expanded. Their brains short-circuited, their spinal cord nerves pinched off. They dropped to the floor, one by one. Their expressionless black eyes bugged out, shrank back, bugged out again, then popped from the sockets, held to their skulls by a thin twine of tissue. Blood sprayed in jets from ears, nose and mouth.

Maybe they were already dead, Auriel thought.

That would have been a mercy, deserved or not.

The skin of their bloated bellies stretched so tight that it was transparent. She could see the fat, green oblongs moving inside them.

Then, at random along the pile of the fallen, here and there the stickies' torsos began to burst with explosive force, splattering the passage's walls and ceiling with gobbets of yellow flesh and flying green gore.

This broke the spell that had the rest of the mutants paralyzed. They panicked. Some of them turned and ran back into the bowels of the massif; the rest charged straight for her. Once again freed, the specters formed a mad cyclone overhead, then joyously began chasing down fresh victims.

Auriel turned to Dr. Huth for help and found him gone.

Chapter Twenty-Two

When Ryan saw Doc cocking his ancient blaster in Besup's face, he realized what had to have happened. Before he could take two more strides, the weapon discharged almost straight down, flame and black powder smoke enveloping the warrior's head. Besup's legs gave one violent kick and then he was still.

Doc looked up as Ryan bore down on him, his long face contorted by anguish. Besup lay in two parts on the nukeglass; the massive wounds were still steaming. Wounds that should have killed, but hadn't.

A mercy shot. No doubt about it.

How long could a man live with an injury like that? Ryan thought as he ran past. For a warrior, any time was too long.

A terrific explosion from behind and to his left staggered him in midstep and he nearly fell face-first, flat out onto the glass. Breaking his fall with an outthrust hand, he glanced over his shoulder and saw the tower come down. Pushing up at once, he outran the wave of water that swept forth, hissing over the massif and flooding the sleeping pits.

Ahead of him, the front of the whiteface assault was starting to falter. Some of the warriors had slowed, others had stopped altogether. They were staring back at the fallen tower and the field littered with their dead.

But most of all, they were looking back for Besup. The black hole of the mine entrance loomed before them—a meat-grinder maw. Without hesitation, without backup, their war dogs raced through it. Ryan knew that someone had to step in and lead the warriors or the attack was going to fail. They had to keep charging the entrance; they had to take it before the she-hes regrouped.

The companions were only seconds behind him. He figured they would catch up with him inside.

Ryan sprinted through the whitefaces, shouting for them to follow. He was running too hard to put up effective covering fire with the SIG. And he didn't slow down until he neared the opening. As he ducked under the overhang, he saw four bodies in gleaming black armor, all of them facedown on the ground, and clearly not about to get up anytime soon, if ever. Farther down the shaft he heard people screaming and the dogs snarling and baying. He brought up his SIG-Sauer and advanced. The surviving whitefaces, about twenty of them, entered behind him.

Over the sights of the blaster, down a long, dimly lit straightaway, he saw packed bodies. Seventy or eighty people jammed the corridor. Dirty-faced, skeletal, clad in rags. They were mine slaves. The war dogs tore into them, pulling victims down at random, cutting a path of mayhem through their ranks.

At first Ryan didn't understand what the slaves were doing there, why they hadn't made a break for freedom.

Then the reason became all too clear.

They were being held at laser-point.

Crisscrossing emerald-green beams lanced from the

darkness on the far side of the crowd, deeper in the mine. The beams sliced through the packed bodies like they were made of nothing. Slaves, living and dead, hit the floor. War dogs, sliced and diced, hit the floor. Ryan felt a blast of impossible heat on his face, and the wall over his head began to melt. Blasterfire clattered, and slugs smacked into the bubbling ooze.

Again, the conventional-shooting turncoats were using the laser beams as targeting tools.

"Bombs!" he shouted, firing back over the throng of prostrated bodies with his blasterpistol. He couldn't make out the detail of the enemy position, but they appeared to be firing from behind a floor-to-ceiling obstacle that jutted into the passage.

The whiteface behind him produced a sputtering explosive and offered it to him. Ryan switched the SIG to his weak hand, grabbed the length of pipe and chucked it hard and high down the shaft. Hard and high enough to clear the mass of bodies that covered the ground.

There was a brilliant flash; a simultaneous explosion rocked the tunnel.

The laser barrage stopped, but only for a few seconds. Through the clouds of dust and smoke, the green beams flash-cooked the air. The suspended particles exploded in showers of sparks.

Ryan called back for another bomb, but before it could be lit, they were slammed by a concussion wave from the entrance behind them.

The force was so great that it knocked him unconscious—instant blackout—and sent his limp form flying down the tunnel. When he came to, it was pitch-dark. He was laying on top of something warm, soft and wet, and his legs were pinned by a heavy weight. The familiar shape of the Steyr lay under his arm; the SIG was lost. He had no recollection of how he got there. The dust was so thick that it choked him.

Some of the lights along the ceiling came back on, but weaker because of the dust. And flickering.

When Ryan looked down, he realized the something warm and soft was also something freshly dead, something human, but the weight of the nukeglass block on his legs kept him pinned. It took a few minutes for him to shake off the disorientation and mental confusion of the concussion.

Though his ears were ringing, he could hear the sounds of moaning all around him. As the dust slowly cleared, the moaning turned to screaming. All around him he saw slaves crushed by blocks of the fallen ceiling, impaled by shafts of nukeglass. Others were trapped as he was, or wounded by flying shards.

The incoming fire had ceased.

Carefully, he began shifting the weight of his lower body, inching his legs to the side so the downward pressure of the slab fell upon the body beneath him. When the corpse was taking most of the weight, he pulled himself forward, hand over hand, until he was free. The SIG lay on top of the rubble a few feet away. He picked it up and checked the action. The weapon seemed undamaged.

When he turned and looked at the entrance, his stomach tightened. All he saw was a solid wall. The explosion had completely blocked the tunnel with massive boulders. And probably for fifty or sixty feet.

There was no way out.

Ryan caught movement under the rubble. He helped one of the whitefaces to his feet. Then the two of them started turning over rocks, looking for more survivors. They found four warriors alive—the rest were lost under the boulder fall. One of the four died in front of their eyes. Once the pressure of the blocks that pinned him was released, he bled out from dozens of deep cuts.

"What are we going to do, now?" the first man he'd rescued asked him.

"We fight," Ryan said. "We still have a couple of satchels of pipe bombs left, and we have ammo. We push them as deep down the shaft as we can, then we seal them in."

"What happens to us, afterward?" another of the warriors said. "We're still trapped in here."

"If we live that long," Ryan told him, "we'll work it out. Keep some pipe bombs ready."

He waved the warriors onward. They didn't stop to help the wounded. There were too many them, and most were too far gone. They stepped over them, moving along the tunnel wall.

Beyond the bodies, Ryan split up his diminished force, and they approached the passage's obstacle from two sides. Up close, it was clearly a blaster position, and built of laser-cut blocks of nukeglass that were stacked, fitted and remelted together. It had firing ports and a single, narrow entrance and exit. The pipe bomb he had thrown had blown the front off the emplacement. It had also blown away the light directly overhead.

They cautiously probed the interior. On the ground lay a jumble of bodies, two of them in cockroach suits.

When nothing moved, Ryan holstered his SIG and

grabbed one of the she-hes by the boot. A whiteface helped him drag the body out into the light.

Ryan kneeled and looked at the visor, the inside of which was painted solid crimson. He couldn't see the enemy's face for the wash of blood. Then he thought he saw something move behind the curtain of red. Like a shudder passing through it. Nothing else moved—arms, legs, nothing—so he figured it was either a muscle firing, postmortem, or he had imagined it.

"Dead?" the warrior asked, giving the side of the helmet a kick.

"Yeah, dead," Ryan said.

The other she-he was likewise permanently out of commission—face plate awash in gore.

"I want to see the bastards' faces," one of the warriors said. "Let's take the helmets off."

"Hell with that," another whiteface said. He picked up a ten-pound hunk of nukeglass and smashed it down against the visor. The EM shield deflected the rock off the target with such force that it flew out of his hand.

"You didn't even scratch it," the first man said.

"We've got no time for this," Ryan said. "Take my word for it, they look just like you and me."

The mournful baying of the few dogs who had gotten past the blaster emplacement drifted up from deeper in the mine. There were human screams as well.

"Come on," Ryan told the warriors, "we have work to do."

They leapfrogged one another, alternating cover and advance, until they reached the tunnel's dogleg right, then Ryan signaled for a pause. When he peered low around the corner, he saw slaves and ore carts. They were packed along the sides of the tunnel; the center of the shaft was clear. The slaves were doing all the screaming. They were fighting to cram themselves into the vertical crevices that lined the passage, side shafts in the mine—this to escape the pair of dogs that were doing their damnedest to pull them out and tear them into pieces.

On the far side of the slaves and their attackers was another blaster emplacement. It was identical to the first: floor-to-ceiling glass blocks that stuck out into and narrowed the corridor, funneling the traffic into a tight, easily controllable kill zone. The distance to the hardened site was about 120 feet. Ryan couldn't see movement behind the blasterports, couldn't tell if it was occupied.

There was only one way to find out.

He waved two of the whitefaces to the opposite side of the shaft, both of them ready to throw pipe bombs. Then he and the other two warriors broke from cover and started zigzagging down the tunnel, moving from ore cart to crevice to ore cart, bypassing the slaves and the dogs.

There was no incoming.

When they reached the emplacement, the reason became obvious. It was manned by three more downed cockroaches.

Permanently downed.

"Let's have a look," Ryan said. They pulled all the bodies out. The visors were coated red, from the inside.

"We didn't do this," one of the whitefaces said. "So, what's killing them?"

"What killed them?" a whiteface repeated.

"Your guess is as good as mine," Ryan replied.

"Do you think they're all dead?"

"Have we won?"

"They could be hiding in the side shafts," one of the warriors said.

"There's only one way to find out," Ryan said. "We need to recce the entire mine. First thing, though, go retrieve those damned dogs, harness them up, whatever you need to do to get them under control. We'll take them with us to sniff out trouble."

When the four whitefaces returned holding the panting, bloody-faced dogs tethered with short lengths of rope, they weren't alone. About forty of the slaves were right behind them. They had come to look at the dead she-hes.

A shirtless man, about six foot three in height, with an enormous tattooed blue dragon wrapped over his shoulder and back, and a little woman with short red hair seemed to be their leaders.

"They really are dead?" the man said. "Just like that?"

"Seems too quick, too easy," the woman said, "after the living hell they put us through."

The man with the tattoo extended a hand to Ryan, the fingers and palm roughened by countless scabbed glass cuts and said, "My name is Ronbo. Ronbo Myles. And this is my friend, Ti."

The diminutive woman looked up at him and nodded.

"I'm…" Ryan began.

"Cawdor, One-Eyed Cawdor, I know," Ronbo said. "I've heard stories about you."

"We both have," Ti said.

"Never thought you were flesh-and-blood real," Ronbo told him.

"We've got to find all the cockroaches and the turncoats, and make triple-sure they're dead," Ryan said. "There's only the five of us to do the job. Could use some help sweeping the shafts. You folks willing to take the risk?"

"You betcha," Ronbo said. "Just keep those wild dogs off our butts." Then he turned to the other miners and shouted, "Search the bodies of the slave masters. Pick up any weapons you can find. We're going cockroach hunting!"

This announcement was met with raised fists and pickaxes, and cries for vengeance.

For a couple of frantic minutes the slaves foraged more axes and shovels, and a few tribarrels and turncoat AKs. Ti had picked up one of the Kalashnikovs, and as Ryan watched, she quickly checked the chamber for a live round. Finding none, with the ease that only comes from practice, she dropped the 30-shot magazine, looked at the round-counter and then slapped it back in place. With a flick of the wrist, she worked the actuator, chambering the first cartridge.

The tattooed man appeared to have some familiarity with the tribarrel—not hands-on experience, but from watching the she-hes saw his fellow slaves in two. Ronbo armed the short, stout, black weapon system.

"Everyone with a blaster come up front with me,"

Ryan said to the crowd. "Everyone else, don't bunch up behind us. Spread out."

One of the warriors took point with a leashed war dog and they began their descent. The dog sniffed at the side passages that had been laser-cut into the massif, first one side of the tunnel, then the other. When it found nothing of interest, they continued along the passage.

Farther down, they came upon a cell that looked like a makeshift whitecoat laboratory. Ryan's quick glance revealed no signs of life. The cluttered space contained an assortment of electronic gear, whose function he couldn't begin to guess. All the gear seemed to be powered up and running. He did recognize the computer vidscreen, and the remote view it offered of Ground Zero and what had been the mine entrance. As the camera panned across the landscape, he saw his companions—Krysty, J.B., Doc and Jak—all alive, apparently uninjured. Behind them, the battlefield was decorated with corpses.

"Nothing here," Ronbo said.

They moved on, down the corridor, until they reached the third turn, a bend in the road Ryan didn't remember from years ago. And when he rounded the corner, he realized that the straight hallway had become a spiral, angling downward.

Immediately, the scout dog started whimpering in excitement, pulling on the lead, trying to break free.

"Caught a scent," Ti said.

The dog suddenly became more agitated, snarling and snapping its jaws and rearing up on its back legs.

"Let it go," Ryan told the warrior.

When he released the lead, the animal shot away, vanishing around the next turn.

Shortly thereafter they heard the now-familiar sounds of canine attack, the growling, the grunting—the shrill cries of a captured prey.

Ryan hoped it wasn't another unlucky slave.

When they rounded the bend, weapons up, he saw the dog had a young stickie pinned to the ground, jaws buried in its face. The pale sucker hands had already pulled off clumps of its fur and bleeding divots of its flesh, but the dog would not relent. Flexing the powerful muscles of its neck and back, it shook its head and ripped off half the mutie's face, from eye socket to chin, then sank its fangs into the unprotected throat. Big dog, little mutie—it was over in a blink, with one more whipcrack of the head, like killing a rat.

Then the dog was off on the hunt again before anybody could grab it.

They circled around the spiral, a complete 360 in space. As they did, Ryan noted freshly opened cracks in the walls. Cracks wide enough and tall enough for a small person to slip through.

Somewhere not far below them, the loose dog snarled, then yelped in pain. Faintly at first, but rapidly growing louder came the muffled sounds of bare feet slapping against the nukeglass.

The tramp of lots of feet, coming up fast.

"Shit!" Ryan cried, swinging up his blaster. "Get clear firing lanes!"

There was hardly time to do anything of the sort. A mass of stickies raced around the bend, filling the corridor wall-to-wall with their bodies. Leaping and waving spindly arms, they charged right into the muzzles of the waiting blasters.

Ryan, Ti and the warriors opened fire in the tight space, chopping down some but not nearly all of the muties. There were too many, they were too fast, and they were already too close for blasterwork. The muties who weren't struck down by the initial salvo didn't respond with the maniacal attack typical of their species; instead they brushed past and dashed around easy victims, and kept on running. Ryan and the others turned and reaimed their weapons, but had to hold fire because the stickies plowed headlong into the press of miners who were bringing up the rear.

At that moment Ryan realized that bloodlust wasn't driving the stickies. This was panic. Blind panic.

Even though the miners bludgeoned with shovels and pickaxes, and Ronbo applied the butt of his tribarrel, the muties didn't attack them. They threw themselves at the shoulder-to-shoulder slaves blocking their escape from the spiral, and in a desperate frenzy actually tried to climb over them.

Ryan could see nothing close behind, nothing pursuing them up the passageway. What were they running from? he asked himself. And why were they pissing themselves to get away?

One of the stickies stopped by the packed slaves reversed course and charged right at him. As it ran its mouth opened wide and it let out a piercing screech of agony. For the first time he got a good look at the thing's belly. It was huge. About to give birth. To quintuplets, at least.

It was also very obviously male, which was a considerable puzzlement.

It didn't seem to notice or care about the four blasters

aimed at its head. Before Ryan, Ti and the four warriors could fire, the stickie exploded.

Literally, under their noses.

Its torso blew apart with a resounding, hollow *whump!* And hot gore splattered the walls and ceiling, and sprayed across Ryan and his newfound friends.

The other stickies, the ones trapped by the miners, started screeching and bleating, and then their legs gave way and they collapsed onto the floor. Ryan saw that they, too, had horribly bloated bellies. Looking closer, their heads appeared swollen much larger than normal. Then one by one they exploded—in exactly the same way as the first, like they had all swallowed frag grens.

Only afterward it didn't smell anything like burned RDX.

It was over, start to finish, in less than fifteen seconds. Blood and bowel contents dripped from the ceiling, and from the faces and chests of the stunned spectators.

Backhanding the sewage from his cheek and chin, Ronbo exclaimed, "Nukin' hell, what is going on!"

His mouth was still hanging open when he jolted violently head to foot, as if something large had just leapt down his throat.

Then again, and again, and again, the tall man jerked, backstepping, dropping the tribarrel to the floor.

"Ronbo!" Ti cried. "What is it? What's wrong?"

His eyes bugging out, he clamped both his hands around his throat as if trying to squeeze it shut, or strangle himself. Choking himself blue, he turned, his long legs quivering.

Suddenly he wasn't doing the rictus dance solo.

Others in the crowd were choking, gagging, reeling, convulsing. Miners and whitefaces, alike.

The affliction appeared to be completely random. The slaves who weren't stricken tried to back away from those who were.

Under the light of the corridor, Ryan could see the tattoo on Ronbo's back, and his rib cage violently expanding. Not from an inhaled breath; more like it was being pumped full of something. His torso kept on growing outward, stretching the skin until the dragon's detail was completely lost, until it looked like an enormous pale blue birthmark. When Ronbo turned toward them again, his bare stomach had become a huge, weighty protuberance, the skin stretched to translucence, and both his eyes had popped from their sockets.

"Ronbo!" Ti screamed.

As she started to rush to his side, Ryan seized her by the shoulder. He didn't understand what was happening, but he knew getting too close wasn't a good idea. It looked like something very deadly was passing rapidly from one person to the next.

"There's nothing you can do for him," he said, holding her fast in his grip.

And as if to prove this point, the tattooed man blew apart in a ballooning red mist, shreds of his flesh and shards of bone peppering them.

"We have to get out of here," he told her. "We have to go *now*."

Then the others started exploding.

"Run, damn you!" Ryan said, pushing the little woman ahead of him down the spiral. "Run!"

Together they sprinted down the helix, around the

winding turns, past more holes in the walls created by the massif's shifting plates. Above them, there was screaming and sporadic gunfire.

"He's dead, he's dead," she muttered through her tears.

Even as Ryan ran, he was trying to connect what had just happened to the dead she-hes. Did whatever it was make them explode inside their battlesuits? Did that explain the gore that coated their visors?

"We've got to fight back!" Ti said. "They chilled Ronbo…"

"Fight what?" Ryan said. "Fight who?"

Ti glared up at him, but kept on running. Evidently she didn't have an answer, either.

The bottom of the spiral opened into a narrow, low hallway, lit by widely spaced bulbs. Ryan's attention wasn't focused down the dank corridor; he was staring up at the wires that festooned the ceiling.

"Tell me that isn't what it looks like," Ti said.

"They've mined the ceiling with explosives," he said.

"I'm not going under there," she told him. "If those charges blow, we will be squashed flat."

"We don't have a choice," Ryan said. "We can't hide from whatever it is in this hallway."

When she refused to move, he said, "Look down the passage, in front of the cells. What do you think that wet gunk is on the floor and on the walls? Whatever killed Ronbo, it's already been here. Which means it could come back at any time."

Ti squinted down the corridor into the weak light, at

the litter scattered on the floor. "Were they stickies or people?"

"Doesn't matter. Come on, let's move it. And triple-time. Keep your weapon up and ready to fire."

They started past the row of niches that had been laser-hacked into the nukeglass, leapfrogging each other from one side of the hall to the other. The first crude cells were empty, save for the bracketed cylinders along the walls and the heaps of ashes and bits of charred bone on the floor.

When Ti looked into a cell about halfway down the line, she froze with her AK shouldered and aimed inside. Poised to fire the autorifle, every muscle tensed, she exclaimed, "I've got one! I've got one!"

Ryan brought his SIG to bear on a figure standing slumped against the interior wall. A figure clad head to foot in shiny black battle armor.

A gasping, amplified voice said, "You don't want to do that...."

Chapter Twenty-Three

Ryan sensed that Ti was about to cut loose on the un-armed cockroach, at point-blank range.

"It won't do any good," he told her. "You open fire and that thing's EM shield will just deflect the bullets. All you'll accomplish is getting us both caught in the spray of ricochets."

The little woman lowered the Kalashnikov's muzzle, swung the weapon around and tried to bash the she-he in the head. The steel-shod butt never got within two feet of its target. The rifle bounced back, apparently off thin air, and with a force that sent her arms flying backward.

"There's a force field blocking the entrance to the cell," the cockroach said slowly and with considerable effort.

It was nearly as tall as he was.

Ryan felt the creature's eyes on him, burning into him, but he couldn't see them—or the face—through the opaqued helmet visor.

"At least for the time being," the she-he said, "this space is free of them."

"'Them'?" Ryan said.

"The specters. If they have a name for themselves, we have never discovered it." The she-he paused for breath before continuing. "The force field is what's keeping them out of this cell. It's the only safe place for you on this level of the glacier."

Again, a pause for breath, and when the she-he resumed speaking, her voice was tight and full of pain. "I'll lower the field, so you can come inside, but you have to move quickly. I can't risk leaving it down for more than a second."

Ryan glanced down at Ti and she nodded. As grim and dead-ended as it was, it looked like their only hope.

The cockroach slowly raised a gauntleted hand. "On the count of three—one, two, three…"

The air in front of the cell shimmered, and Ryan and Ti stepped through it. It was like walking under a warm waterfall. Then they were inside, in the dank, cramped space, ankle-deep in ashes.

Whatever the she-he did unseen, inside the glove, she undid the same way, with an extended, armored index finger. The air at the entrance stopped shimmering.

"What are these 'specters'?" Ryan said. "We can't see them. Where are they from? What do they want?"

"They're invisible in full spectrum light," the she-he said. "They attached themselves to us during a reality jump. We've jumped replica Earths four times since then, and haven't been able to shake them."

Amplified breath sounds filled the cell, gasping sounds.

"Don't believe her, Ryan," Ti said. "It's some kind of trick…"

When the she-he reached for a compact electronic device attached to the waist of the battlesuit, Ti shouldered her weapon again, cheek to buttstock, her finger on the trigger.

Ryan caught the barrel behind the sights and firmly pushed it aside and down. "No good," he repeated.

The cockroach offered the device to him. "Here, have a look through this. All you have to do is hold it up to the entrance and look at the screen."

Ryan angled the gizmo so they both could see the LCD.

Lights.

Fluorescent green.

Brilliant oblongs, like flying snakes, shot back and forth down the hallway. They moved so fast and so erratically that they blurred in Ryan's vision.

When he looked above the little device's screen, the hall was empty; when he looked at it again, the lights had gathered in the hall in front of the cell, a mass that swarmed in midair like a nest of levitating eels.

"Nukin' hell, what are they?" Ti said.

"We don't know," the she-he replied. "Now that they've targeted you, they won't leave, not until you're blown apart."

"But you brought them here?" Ryan said.

"Yes."

"Why did you bother to save us?" he asked. "You could have just let us die."

"There's no point in my fighting on. All the battlesuit life-sign transponders are transmitting flatlines. I'm the only sister left. The last of my kind. And there's another, even better reason…"

The she-he reached up and touched buttons on either side of the armor's raised collar; there was a whoosh of depressurization, then she began to unscrew the helmet.

Lifting it off her head, she said, "Hello, Ryan Cawdor…"

The shock of seeing his own features in her face—the same long black hair, icy blue eyes, even the set of his chin—rocked him to the core.

"No," he said. "No, it can't be."

"But it is," she said. "You can't look at me and deny it. I am Auriel. Auriel Otis Trask."

Ti looked back and forth between them. "Are you brother and sister?" she asked. "How is that possible?!"

"Not brother and sister," Auriel said, grimacing, biting out the words.

"Too long a story to explain now," Ryan said.

"Never thought I'd meet you face-to-face," Auriel told him. "Never imagined that if it ever did happen it would be like this." Then she whimpered, struggling to breathe, hanging on to the wall with a claw of a gauntleted hand. Her eyes were racked with incredible pain, but she shed no tears.

Seeing her so twisted up in agony sent a sympathetic pang shooting right through him. If he had any doubts that she was the flesh of his flesh, in that moment they were erased. "What's wrong with you?" Ryan said. "Are you wounded?"

It took more than a minute for her to recover enough to answer him. "There's one more reason I let you through the force field," she said. "The things in the hall are inside of me. They're about to burst out. After they do, you will be trapped in here with them, and they will surely kill you, too."

"I don't understand," Ryan said.

"The only way to keep them from bursting out is for you to kill me first. They will die along with me, and you'll be safe behind the force field. You have to do this, Father, before they blow me apart. I watched my mother, Dredda, die that way. I don't want to go like that."

Ryan's fingers tightened on the grip of his blaster, but he didn't raise it from his side. It suddenly felt like it weighed ten thousand pounds. Shooting one's own child, even a child who was a stranger, was like committing suicide.

"Then give me your gun," Auriel said, holding out her hand to him, "and I'll do it myself."

Ryan didn't move.

"You've seen what they will do to you," Auriel said. "They'll do the same thing to every living creature on your world. You've got to end this. End my suffering and save your own lives. Save your glorious Earth."

And still he hesitated, her eyes pleading him to do the last thing he ever wanted to do. This was the beautiful, brave daughter he would never know.

An ear-splitting bang rocked the cell. Auriel's head jerked back and the rear of her skull exploded, spraying brains and bone over the back of the cell. When her lifeless body hit the floor, it raised a cloud of fine ash.

"I didn't think you were going to do it," Ti said as she lowered the AK.

Chapter Twenty-Four

As J.B. prepared to send fragments of Burning Man's skull seventy feet in the air, he heard Mildred's voice behind him.

"Look around, J.B.," she said urgently. "Before you pull the trigger, look around…"

Raising the muzzle higher, making the baron stand almost on tiptoes, he glanced over his shoulder. Mildred stood with her back to him, her Czech wheelgun raised in both hands. She was aiming at the whitefaces who were sighting in on her. The other companions all had the same problem: outnumbered three to one, weapons ready to fire, they stared down the barrels of their former allies.

Even Jak, the whiteface scout, was under the gun.

"We're not going to win this one, J.B.," she said. "There's too many of them and they already believe they're the walking dead. Look at them—they're smiling at us. They don't give a shit."

Then, from across the nukeglass, Krysty yelled to him, "Ryan could still be alive. We have to find him. Every second counts…"

J.B. eased off the pressure, letting Burning Man come down off his toes. When he removed the M-4000's muzzle from under the baron's chin, it left a 12-gauge-diameter ring indent in his flesh.

Burning Man flipped his goggles up onto his forehead.

"You made the mess," J.B. said. "How do we clean it up? We can't dig them out with our bare hands."

The light in the man's eyes made J.B.'s skin crawl. It wasn't the look of a man who'd just nearly had his head blown off. It was the look of a man on the verge of completing his life's holy mission.

"Scrounge up the dropped tribarrels," Burning Man said. "Use them to cut through the cave-in. Have to be careful and go slow, or you'll saw up the survivors, or burn 'em to death with melting glass."

"Everybody!" Mildred shouted. "Weapons down! Right now! Let's find some laser rifles and get to work."

As the companions holstered their blasters, the white-faces lowered their blasters, too. Standoff over.

"You can help us look for the cutting tools," J.B. told the baron.

"There's something else that has to be done first," Burning Man replied. He pointed behind them, at the other side of the ore processer. "The jump zone," he said. "That needs to be destroyed immediately. It's the she-hes only way out of here. We can't let any of them escape. And we can't leave any of their technology intact."

"Go ahead, we'll start without you," Mildred said

"Let's do it, then," J.B. told the baron. "And let's be triple-quick about it…"

Burning Man took a satchel of pipe bombs from one of his warriors and broke into a run. J.B. followed him to a crude circle etched into the nukeglass. At the circle's center was a squat bank of electronic machinery, a single black cabinet the size of a small wag, with its own set of batteries.

The steady hum of the system was audible. "It's running," J.B. said.

"They're keeping the apparatus ready, so they can jump at a moment's notice," the baron said. "Better stand well clear. This will only take me a second."

J.B. backed away as Burning Man stepped inside the circle.

Crossing the empty space at a trot, the baron knelt on the glass beside the machinery, opened the loaded satchel and took out a single pipe bomb. J.B. saw him light the fuse. When he had it sputtering, he dropped the bomb into the open bag, alongside the rest of the explosives. Then he shoved the pack hard up against the black cabinet, positioning it to do the most damage.

As J.B. turned to put even more safe distance between himself and the ensuing bang, he glanced back at the baron, who was sprinting away from his handiwork, full-out. He got only as far as the perimeter of the jump zone, the crudely etched circle. When he reached it, his head lowered, arms and legs pumping, he slammed into an invisible wall and bounced back into the circle like a NOMEX-clad rag doll.

As a thin haze of residual, mixed smoke and dust swept across the jump zone, J.B. glimpsed the domed outline of a force field. Somehow the baron had managed to accidently enable it.

J.B. watched spellbound as Burning Man scrambled to his feet and raced back to the satchel. He had the bag open, and was frantically searching around inside, when the whole package blew up.

With a muffled, baritone boom, the inside of the force field dome bloomed white-hot, and the nukeglass shuddered underfoot. In the overturned bowl, white turned to orange as the air itself ignited.

The force field held its shape for five or six seconds, then it dissolved before J.B.'s astonished eyes. When it did, black smoke boiled upward and a shower of crimson spatters fell onto the ring of charred nukeglass.

It was all that was left of Burning Man.

And at the same instant, the power to the kliegs surged, their brilliance momentarily blinding.

As if in final salute.

Chapter Twenty-Five

Ryan swept the hall beyond the cell's entrance with the scanner for the tenth time in as many minutes. "They're gone," he announced.

"Are you sure?" Ti said.

"See for yourself."

The little auburn-haired beauty took the device and had a look. As she lowered the unit she said, "Just because they're not right out in front, doesn't mean they aren't waiting for us somewhere around the corner."

"Auriel said they wouldn't leave before they'd infected us and blown us apart like the others," Ryan said. "Something had to have made them move from their station out there. For all we know it even chilled them."

Ti gave him a scowl.

"We can't stay down here forever," he told her. "There is no food and no water. The power is going to run out eventually, and when that happens we'll be trapped here in the dark. We'll never escape."

"Okay, I get that, and you're right. But what about the force field? We're stuck in here."

"The off-switch has to be inside the battlesuit glove," he said. He bent over Auriel's body, and after some gentle fumbling, found the release button for her right gauntlet.

When he pulled it onto his own hand it was still warm

inside from Auriel's body heat. The sensation filled him with a crushing wave of sadness. Ryan shook off the unsettling upwelling of emotion, pointed the index finger at the force field and waited.

Like magic, the field fell.

"What now?" Ti asked as they warily stepped out into the corridor.

He dropped the glove to the floor. He couldn't blame her for shooting Auriel. She had done the right thing, the only thing, for all concerned. "We're going to look for survivors," he said. "And then find a way out."

They cautiously but steadily climbed up the spiral passage, until they reached the clot of exploded miners and whitefaces. The remains were so pureed that they were unidentifiable even as human.

Ryan picked up a tribarrel from the floor, where it lay against the base of the wall. Probably the one Ronbo had been carrying, he thought. One side of the weapon, barrels to buttstock, was slick with red fluid and textured with flecks of bone. He wiped it off with his palm, sweeping the residue to the ground.

He and Ti continued upward. When they reached the laboratory, they had another look inside. It was still unoccupied.

Ryan waved the woman over to the lab's computer screen. The remote cameras at the mine's entrance showed the companions and whitefaces cutting their way into the shaft with captured tribarrels.

"Help is coming," he said. "We're going to get out of here."

As they advanced up the main passage, both of them began shouting for people to come out of hiding, telling them that the immediate danger was past, and that they had to work together to get out while they still had operational lights.

Slowly, pale faces began to appear at the entrances to the mine's side passages ahead of them. Then the slaves who had lived through the specters' attack staggered out into the shaft.

Ryan counted just fourteen survivors; none of them were whitefaces.

"We need to gather up all the tribarrel rifles the cockroaches dropped," he told them. "We're going to use them to burn our way out of here."

As they moved toward the entrance, full of high spirits and new purpose, the miners went through each of the blaster emplacements, turned over bodies and looted the laser weapons.

When they got to the floor-to-ceiling barrier, Ryan sensed the wind going out of their sails. Great slabs of glass were mixed with the boulders and rubble—all of it razor-sharp, and some of it teetering on the verge of avalanche.

He called the miners with weapons forward, and ordered the rest of the people to stand well back and against the tunnel's side walls.

"Rescuers are coming toward us from the other side," he said. "They're using lasers to melt through the glass. With any luck, we'll meet them in the middle. If you don't know how to power up these weapons, this is the button here that does the trick…"

He hit the tribarrel's power button and armed the weapon system.

When the three slaves had their tribarrels humming,

he said, "We'll start at a single point, focus all our beams on it, and work out from there. We're going to have to cut a fairly large hole, otherwise the glass melt is going to fall on us while we work." He turned to the people along the walls. "Make sure you stay back from the center of the floor," he warned them, "because the molten glass is going to flow out of the hole we're cutting and there's going to be a lot of it."

Ti appeared by his side, holding up a strip of rag. She said, "Better cover your nose and mouth with this. You don't want to breathe in the smoke that comes off the melting nukeglass."

After tying the mask in place, he braced the tribarrel against his hip and pressed the trigger. A fine green beam shot from the muzzle and stuck the barrier. The glass immediately began to smoke, then drip like hot, green-gray candlewax. The others fired their weapons at his impact point, and the drip suddenly became a splashing fountain.

Boring through the collapse was sweaty, dirty work and not just because of the caustic black smoke. Even after the glass had solidified, it radiated sweltering heat. Ryan and the other men carved out a roughly rectangular tunnel, foot by foot, yard by yard. The laser beams fused together the loose material, so the five-foot-wide walls and ceiling didn't fall in on them.

The laser weapons' power was just starting to give out when Ryan caught sight of a shifting green light on the other side of the blockage.

The light was growing brighter.

Ryan waved for the miners to get back. "The other side is going to be breaking through any second," he told them. "We have to get out of the way or those beams are going to cut us, too."

After they'd cleared the entrance to the passage they'd made, he shouted through it to the companions, "You've got about four more feet to go!"

Moments later, blinding green beams sliced through the last of the barrier, stabbing deep down the shaft for hundreds of yards.

"Everybody stay put!" Ryan shouted when the tribarrels ceased fire. "The hole has to cool off."

Waiting was hard. The slaves were champing at the bit to put the depths of hell behind them forever.

Ryan let everyone else go first. He came out of the hole after Ti, under the blazing kliegs and the dark night sky, into the open air and endless space, and found himself locked in the passionate embrace of a lovely, long-legged woman.

Ryan and Krysty held each other for a long moment. When she relaxed her grip, he noticed that she was staring fixedly at the little auburn-haired former slave, who was staring right back.

"That's Ti," Ryan said. "She was a prisoner here. She was a big help in getting us all out. Ti, this is Krysty."

The two women acknowledged each other with nods of the head, but didn't exchange words of greeting.

The other companions surrounded Ryan, slapping him on the back and smiling from ear to ear.

"Where's Burning Man?" he asked.

J.B. pointed toward the former jump zone. "The baron's that big wet spot over there, on the other side of the processer," he said. "Whitefaces might want to scrape it up and put it in a jar to take home."

"He was the last of the invaders," Doc said. "The last of the conquistadores."

"Good riddance to 'em all," J.B. spit.

Ryan took in the carnage scattered across the width and breadth of Ground Zero. At what cost? he thought. Bodies and parts of bodies were strewed everywhere. "Buzzards are going to have quite a picnic come sunup," he said.

"No picnic," Mildred said. She gestured back toward the mine entrance. "It was already decided. There's going to be a mass burial."

Ryan saw whitefaces and ex-slaves pushing emptied ore carts out of the mine and onto the massif. Tenderly, they lifted their dead into the cargo boxes, and then they ferried them back across the glass into the depths of the mine.

It took a long time to collect all the bodies and move them belowground. When that was done, the companions chucked the drained tribarrels into the shaft. Then the whitefaces used the last of their homemade explosives to demolish the ore processor and reseal the mine entrance.

As the smoke and dust of the final explosions blew past the banks of lights, across the desolate wasteland, Krysty said, "This place was never meant for humans to see."

"No human will ever have a reason to see it again," Mildred said.

"A place forever cursed, forever avoided," Doc agreed. "There will always be evil lurking in this spot. Terrible evil and terrible sorrow."

"More than you ever know," Jak remarked cryptically.

"Jak, do you know something that we don't?" Mildred asked. "What do you mean?"

"Mean nothing," the albino youth said. He turned his back to all of them and stared across the ruin. He didn't say another word.

BECAUSE THEY HAD to wait until daybreak to start the long walk out of Ground Zero, the companions and the other survivors searched the pits for dry places to sleep.

In an open hole, under the glare of the klieg lights, Ryan and Krysty huddled together, face-to-face, locked in each other's arms to stay warm. She kissed him softly on the mouth, and as she did, the tips of her prehensile hair clung to and stroked the sides of his neck.

"When the entrance blew up," she said, her lips a half inch from his, "I didn't think anybody could have survived."

"The rest of the whitefaces didn't," he said.

"I thought I'd lost you."

"Not a chance."

"Should I be jealous of that little cutie with the AK? You know you have a thing for redheads."

"For one redhead in particular," he said.

Her emerald eyes flashed with pleasure. "When are you going to tell me what really happened down there?" she said.

Ryan said nothing.

"It was something triple-bad, wasn't it?" she went

on. "I can see it in your face. You can't hide something like that from me, lover. I know you too well."

Ryan still said nothing.

"You have to tell me what happened."

"The cockroaches got themselves contaminated again," he said. "Only with something much worse than what they picked up in Deathlands the last time they dropped in. They brought the contamination with them to Deathlands when they jumped here. I can't really even describe it to you, except that down in the mine it killed all of the she-hes and a lot of innocent people, too. Whatever it was, it's gone now.

"Krysty, some things just aren't meant to be. No matter how much we want them to happen, no matter how hard we fight or how much we pray, we aren't in control of events. The she-hes thought they were in charge, and they learned the hard way that they weren't. Turns out the only thing we can control is our own thoughts. And honestly, I don't want to think about this, now."

He paused for a long moment, then said, "You know, I really miss my boy…"

"I know, lover. I miss Dean, too."

She squeezed him so tight he thought his heart would break. And then he told her about Auriel.

Epilogue

Big Mike acted like he was invisible. Something impossible, even ridiculous, for a man of his size and bulk had the whiteface warriors' attention not been focused elsewhere. As his captors charged through the gap in the ridge, heading for the bright lights of Ground Zero, he simply moved slower than they did. While he pretended to keep up, he actually slipped farther and farther back in the mob.

When there was no one else behind him, he turned and ran in the opposite direction, toward the darkness, hoofing it hard down the road to Slake City. Getting away was so easy, he had to stifle the urge to laugh.

The blasterfire and explosions had already started by the time he reached the limit of the kliegs' illumination. When he entered the shadows he knew that he'd made it to safety. Because he couldn't see more than a few feet of the road ahead, because he wasn't in good physical shape, he had to drop his pace to a walk. He didn't stop, though. He wanted to put a lot more distance between himself and Ground Zero—just in case the cockroaches decided to send out a hunting party before dawn.

The battle at his back grew more and more intense. The booms of explosives overlapped, and the clatter of blasterfire was constant. Big Mike did a happy little turn in the middle of the road, a dance-move pirouette on the toes of his boots. Pleased as punch, he was. A consummate actor, at least in his own mind, he had played dumb and defeated. He had waited for his main chance and when it appeared, he had seized it. In a matter of minutes, all the whitefaces and Ryan and friends would be laying in chunks on the glass of Ground Zero. This while Big Mike lived to enjoy another Deathlands sunrise.

As he continued walking, taking careful, deliberate steps, he began to visualize a brilliant new career, a new future for himself. He had no hands, but he still could talk. And he had the gift of gab. He saw himself as a Firetalker, perhaps installed as a featured part of the live entertainment in an upscale gaudy house. A mug perpetually clutched in his prosthetic fingers, and perpetually topped off with premium joy juice. Free rides on the ponies whenever business was slow. And oh, the stories he had to tell, all with the same central theme—how much more clever he was than everyone else.

How Big Mike had outplayed hundreds of whitefaces.

How Big Mike had escaped the deadly alien menace.

The sounds of battle continued to rage behind him, a counterpoint to his lurid imaginings.

And then he just couldn't hold back his exuberance any longer. Braying with laughter, he closed his eyes, and holding his pancaked hat down on his head with his prosthesis, cut a series of wild dance turns. And as he did, he tripped and inadvertently blundered off the shoulder of the road.

When he opened his eyes, he stopped himself short. He knew he hadn't veered far off course, but he couldn't see anything, and he didn't know which direction he'd come from, so he couldn't retrace his steps.

"Oh, shit," he moaned.

Big Mike stood frozen in place, trying to figure out which way to go. The terrain around him was treacherous beyond belief, a veritable minefield of very nasty ways to die. He looked up at the stars and realized that if he had bothered to check them before he got lost they might have given him his bearings. Now they were useless.

It was amazing how quickly someone remarkably clever could turn into a triple-stupe droolie.

One thing was for sure, he couldn't stay where he was until daybreak; he had to be much farther away from Ground Zero by sunup. Like a tightrope walker, arms outstretched to keep his balance, he began to shuffle his boots and move forward on the glass, a foot or so at a time.

The surface he traversed offered precarious footing— knobs of melted glass, knives and sawteeth blocked his path. With his toes he felt for cracks in the surface. Between the roar of explosions in the distance, he could hear the massif moving, creaking, sighing, snapping around him. Using the stars as a guide, he tried to at least maintain a straight course over the broken ground. The idea of circling endlessly over this landscape terrified him.

Then, as Big Mike looked up to check his position against the carpet of stars, he saw a towering, shadow shape to his left. He remembered walking past a ruined, glass-encased building on the trek in. It stood within a hundred feet of the edge of the road. Awash with relief, he began shuffling doggedly in that direction.

When the ground gave way beneath him, it did so

without warning. With a shriek of splitting glass, a crevasse suddenly yawned underfoot, far too broad to jump. As he started to drop he somehow managed to twist his body and throw his arms over the edge of the break. This slowed but didn't stop his fall.

If he'd still had hands, he might have pulled himself out. But he couldn't hold on. He slipped backward on the down-tilted plate, then dropped from its edge, bouncing off the sides of the chasm as he plummeted downward.

Big Mike crashed in a heap, the air knocked out of him. He had no idea how far he'd fallen. And it was so dark he couldn't see his artificial hand in front of his face. There was an awful pain in his lower stomach. When he reached down and touched it with his bare stump, it was wet, and there was some kind of stuff hanging out.

Coils of stuff.

"Oh, crap," he wailed.

He frantically tried to push his guts back in with the prosthetic hand and stump of a wrist. They wouldn't stay inside; they kept flopping back out.

Finally, he just gave up. He was so tired, more tired than he had ever been, and growing so very cold. He couldn't feel his feet or his legs. Even the excruciating pain in his stomach was fading away. Wedged in at the bottom of the crevasse, in the blackest of black pits, he sensed a gradually building glow around him, and dim shapes moving at its verge.

Hopeful to the last, Big Mike said, "Mommy? Mommy, is that you?"

DR. HUTH WAITED, hidden in a side crevice of the helix until he was fairly sure the killing around him was over. The screams and the dull whumps of exploding bodies had long faded away. His helmet visor's infrared mode showed an absence of specters passing in front of the vertical opening, a turn of events that he found remarkable. Something clearly had happened, something unexpected.

Levering himself out of the narrow crack, he climbed the spiral, making for his lab. He paused a few times en route to listen for footsteps or voices, and hearing nothing he hurried on.

When he reached the cell, he headed straight for the computer monitor. Adjusting the view of the remote cameras with a few deft keystrokes, he took in the entirety of Ground Zero. He was astonished to discover that some of the Deathlanders had actually survived the battle. Then he saw the jump machinery was gone. Obliterated.

And suddenly everything fell into place.

The connection that had so eluded him had been there in plain sight all along. Dredda, then Auriel, had kept the jump machinery in suboperational mode ever since the first encounter with the specters. That meant the corridor between universes was never one hundred percent closed. It was the idling jump machinery that had provided a link, an open portal to the Null through which they had passed. Without it, the specters couldn't have reached into this or any other universe.

A simple, elegant solution.

Now that he had figured it out, he found it rather amusing and droll. They'd left the jump machinery running so they could get away from the specters at the drop of a hat, but leaving the machinery on is what had allowed them in.

To end the threat, all they had to do was shut down the system and break the link to the Null.

Dr. Huth had allowed himself to be blinded by the paradigms of his own science, forcing the facts, the observations to fit erroneous assumptions and faulty theories. It struck him that probably he'd been wrong elsewhere as well. Perhaps the specters weren't individual entities, after all. Perhaps they had no intelligence, no instincts of their own.

They didn't need instincts—or DNA or RNA if their division wasn't actually reproduction—if they were all part of the same macroorganism, like the fingers on a hand, or the tendrils of an anemone.

Tendrils that reached out through the reality corridor to harvest those who had been targeted. Severing the connection to the source would make the specters vanish or die, like the amputations of ghostly limbs.

Dr. Huth couldn't actually confirm any of these conclusions. And even if they were correct, there remained lingering, tantalizing mysteries. He still didn't know what the macroentity was, how it lived, why it killed, or what it harvested from those it slaughtered. Questions that could never be answered because the jump machinery couldn't be repaired or replaced.

It was a realization that he found disappointing, but only marginally so. If a lifetime of whitecoat training had taught him anything, it was that tantalizing mysteries were a dime a dozen.

He watched on the monitor as the whitefaces and

slaves gathered and carted their dead back into the mine. When the one-eyed man and his short friend with the fedora carried all the tribarrels into the entrance and returned empty-handed, Dr. Huth grinned toothlessly.

Cackling to himself, he unfastened and removed his battlesuit helmet. There was no longer any need for the damn thing, now. He breathed deeply and felt the humid air against his sweating face.

The cameras showed the whitefaces busily mining the entrance, about to blow it closed.

"A lot of good that will do," Dr. Huth said aloud.

Repowering the depleted weapons with the mine's generators was a piece of cake. And once that was done, he could laser his way out in no time. With the tech gear that remained in his lab, he could rekindle his own personal dream of conquest through science. Deathlands and it inhabitants would become his playthings.

The blast of the explosion at the entrance shook the floor of the lab and rained sparkling glass dust from the ceiling.

As the echoes dwindled, Dr. Huth heard a distinct noise behind him, from the cell's doorless opening, a soft kissing sound that made his blood run cold. He had assumed that all the wild stickies were dead, that the specters had hunted them down and killed them. If one was alive, then…

From behind came a chorus of soft kisses.

Before he could recover his battlesuit helmet, the muties had him by the face and neck and they were dragging him, kicking and screaming into the darkness.

* * * * *

The Don Pendleton's
Executioner®
RAW FURY

A Malaysian school becomes a deadly battleground....

When rebels take the students of a Malaysian private school hostage, tensions in the region threaten to explode. In a country filled with unrest and on the verge of civil war, peaceful negotiation is not an option. It's up to Mack Bolan to find a way to free the hostages...even if he must make the ultimate sacrifice while taking down any who attempt to stop him!

Available October wherever books are sold.

GOLD EAGLE®

www.readgoldeagle.blogspot.com

GEX383

TAKE 'EM FREE

2 action-packed novels plus a mystery bonus

NO RISK

NO OBLIGATION TO BUY

SPECIAL LIMITED-TIME OFFER
Mail to: Gold Eagle Reader Service

IN U.S.A.: P.O. Box 1867, Buffalo, NY 14240-1867
IN CANADA: P.O. Box 609, Fort Erie, Ontario L2A 5X3

YEAH! Rush me 2 FREE Gold Eagle® novels and my FREE mystery bonus (bonus is worth about $5). If I don't cancel, I will receive 6 hot-off-the-press novels every other month. Bill me at the low price of just $33.44 for each shipment.* That's a savings of over 15% off the combined cover prices and there is NO extra charge for shipping and handling! There is no minimum number of books I must buy. I can always cancel at any time simply by returning a shipment at your cost or by returning any shipping statement marked "cancel." Even if I never buy another book from Gold Eagle, the 2 free books and mystery bonus are mine to keep forever.

166/366 ADN E7RP

Name   (PLEASE PRINT)

Address   Apt. #

City   State/Prov.   Zip/Postal Code

Signature (if under 18, parent or guardian must sign)

Not valid to current subscribers of Gold Eagle books.
Want to try two free books from another series? Call 1-800-873-8635.

* Terms and prices subject to change without notice. Prices do not include applicable taxes. Sales tax applicable in N.Y. Canadian residents will be charged applicable provincial taxes and GST. Offer not valid in Quebec. This offer is limited to one order per household. All orders subject to approval. Credit or debit balances in a customer's account(s) may be offset by any other outstanding balance owed by or to the customer. Please allow 4 to 6 weeks for delivery. Offer available while quantities last.

Your Privacy: Worldwide Library is committed to protecting your privacy. Our Privacy Policy is available online at www.eHarlequin.com or upon request from the Reader Service. From time to time we make our lists of customers available to reputable third parties who may have a product or service of interest to you. If you would prefer we not share your name and address, please check here. ☐

Help us get it right—We strive for accurate, respectful and relevant communications. To clarify or modify your communication preferences, visit us at www.ReaderService.com/consumerschoice.

GE10

AleX Archer
PHANTOM PROSPECT

A sunken treasure yields unfathomable terror....

Intrepid treasure hunters believe they have discovered the final resting place of *Fantome,* a legendary warship that wrecked off Nova Scotia almost two hundred years ago. When Annja is asked to help with the research, she must brave the cold, deep waters—as well as the menacing shark known as the megaladon—in order to uncover the truth.

Available November wherever books are sold.

www.readgoldeagle.blogspot.com

GRA27